Praise for the novels of
USA TODAY bestselling author
Victoria Dahl

"Hits the emotional high notes. Rising romance star
Dahl delivers with this sizzling contemporary romance."
—*Kirkus Reviews* on *Close Enough to Touch*

"A delightful romance between two people
who struggle to discover their own self-worth."
—*RT Book Reviews* on *Bad Boys Do*

"This is one hot romance."
—*RT Book Reviews* on *Good Girls Don't*

"A hot and funny story
about a woman many of us can relate to."
—*Salon.com* on *Crazy for Love*

"[A] hands-down winner, a sensual story
filled with memorable characters."
—*Booklist* on *Start Me Up*

"Dahl smartly wraps up a winning tale
full of endearing oddballs, light mystery
and plenty of innuendo and passion."
—*Publishers Weekly* on *Talk Me Down*

"Sassy and smokingly sexy,
Talk Me Down is one delicious joyride of a book."
—*New York Times* bestselling author Connie Brockway

"Sparkling, special and oh so sexy—
Victoria Dahl is a special treat!"
—*New York Times* bestselling author Carly Phillips
on *Talk Me Down*

VICTORIA DAHL

Too Hot to Handle

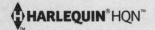
HARLEQUIN® HQN™

Recycling programs
for this product may
not exist in your area.

ISBN-13: 978-0-373-77746-4

TOO HOT TO HANDLE

Copyright © 2013 by Victoria Dahl

All rights reserved. Except for use in any review, the reproduction or
utilization of this work in whole or in part in any form by any electronic,
mechanical or other means, now known or hereafter invented, including
xerography, photocopying and recording, or in any information storage
or retrieval system, is forbidden without the written permission of the
publisher, Harlequin HQN, 225 Duncan Mill Road, Don Mills, Ontario
M3B 3K9, Canada.

This is a work of fiction. Names, characters, places and incidents are
either the product of the author's imagination or are used fictitiously,
and any resemblance to actual persons, living or dead, business
establishments, events or locales is entirely coincidental.

This edition published by arrangement with Harlequin Books S.A.

For questions and comments about the quality of this book,
please contact us at CustomerService@Harlequin.com.

® and TM are trademarks of Harlequin Enterprises Limited or its
corporate affiliates. Trademarks indicated with ® are registered in the
United States Patent and Trademark Office, the Canadian Trade Marks
Office and in other countries.

Printed in U.S.A.

This book is for my girlfriends.
Jif, Jodi, Jami and Jess, to name a few. Thank you.

Too Hot to Handle

CHAPTER ONE

THE NOW FAMILIAR sound of the toaster popping up woke Merry from a dead sleep. She opened her eyes and immediately flinched from the brutal sunlight spearing between a gap in the curtains of the living room window.

"Are you sick of me yet?" she groaned, her voice muffled by the pillow. It was the same question she asked every morning. At some point the answer would be yes. But not today, thank God.

"Are you kidding?" Grace called from the kitchen. "If I kick you out, I lose more than half of the furniture in this place."

"And one very intrusive sofa bed."

"Not to mention my best friend." Grace appeared next to the fold-out couch and held out a mug. "Coffee?"

"God, I love you," Merry groaned.

"You're using me for my coffee."

"And your apartment."

"Would you drop that?" Grace complained. "Anyway, you're supposed to say you're using me for my hot bod. It makes me feel beautiful."

Merry sat up and dared a sip from the steaming mug before she shook her head. "No way. I don't take sloppy seconds. And from what I can tell, Cole's been using you up."

Grace snorted. "Maybe. Or maybe I've been using him up."

"Here I thought that limp of his was still left over from surgery."

Grace had turned to walk away, but she spun back and leaned down to kiss Merry's head. "All kidding aside, I'm glad you're here. I mean that. I've missed you. Stay as long as you want. Six months. A year. It doesn't matter."

"Yeah, I want to sleep in your living room for a year," Merry scoffed. But it was just a front. She'd happily sleep on the floor, just to have her friend back. They'd lived fifteen hundred miles apart for three years, and Merry had missed having her near. The living room was fine by her. She had no need for a big bed and a locking door. There were no men hanging around waiting for a shot at her. Hell, she'd given up masturbating half a year ago. Even her imagination had gone celibate, completely defeated by the unending dry spell. So she'd given in with a sigh and moved on to solving crossword puzzles on her phone.

"I'll make breakfast," she volunteered once she'd gotten a few more sips of coffee in her.

"I've got it already. Hand-toasted bagels. My specialty."

Half an hour later, they were out the door. Merry dropped Grace off at the photography studio where she worked setting up location shoots and scouting for film companies. Then Merry drove out of Jackson and into the valley beyond.

She'd been here a week now, but the mountains still surprised her. No, *surprised* wasn't the word. They *overwhelmed* her. Awed her. They made her feel tiny, and she liked that. Though she wasn't model tall at five-seven, she felt too noticeable all the time. She wished she were little like Grace. Wished she could hide in a crowd instead of feeling big and awkward all the time. Mostly awkward. Her body was fine, but she didn't know anything about clothes. She didn't wear heels. Didn't know what to do with makeup unless Grace was there to help. She was just the girl in jeans and a funny T-shirt who was hyperaware of the easy cuteness of the other women around her.

But none of that mattered anymore. This wasn't Texas, where girls were born with perfectly coiffed hair and polished nails and the ability to walk in heels before they could crawl. This was Wyoming. And she worked in a ghost town.

Smiling, she turned her old sedan onto a ranch road and gravel pinged against the undercarriage. She couldn't wear anything *but* jeans and T-shirts out here. Maybe that would change when she got the actual museum up and running, but for now her workplace was a ghost town. Literally. Her personal collection of broken-down, graying wood houses, waiting for her like an adventure every day.

Okay, the town didn't belong to her, per se, but she still grinned when she briefly spotted the peak of the church steeple rising above a hill far ahead. The car dipped down into a valley again and the steeple disappeared.

The town didn't belong to her, and she'd only been working there for a week, but she already loved it like mad. It was lonely. Some people might even call it sad.

Just a scattered little group of eighteen buildings, half of them collapsing in on themselves, but Merry breathed a sigh of relief as she rounded the final curve and the town came into sight.

Providence, it had been called. And it was that and more for Merry.

It was providence that she'd found this job, here in this part of Wyoming when her best friend had moved here not nine months before. And it was amazing luck that she'd been hired after only a year of experience working in a small-town museum. She was a newbie, but the Providence Historical Trust had believed in her, and Merry was going to make them proud. She was going to make *herself* proud.

She pulled into one of the patches of bare, hardened ground at the edge of the narrow dirt road and stepped out of her car. The sound of her car door closing echoed across the meadow that stretched behind her. In front of her stood Providence, the buildings spaced along either side of a wide road that had been overtaken by grass and the occasional clump of sagebrush. Beyond the town, the hills rose up into patches of rustling green aspen.

Merry took a deep breath, inhaling air that was cleaner than any she'd ever breathed before. This was a good place to make a life for herself. She couldn't fail here. She knew it. This tiny little dot of land in the middle of Wyoming was the most beautiful spot she'd ever seen. How could it be anything but good?

She shifted the bag she'd slung over her shoulder and started along the trail that cut through the grass.

Regardless of how much she loved Providence, failure wasn't an option at this point, anyway. She was thirty years old. She'd been floating through life like a bit of dandelion fluff on the wind. Oh, she'd touched down occasionally. Held jobs for a year or two. Bank teller, sales support, blackjack dealer, dog walker. She'd even gone to school to learn to do hair, but the only thing good that had come out of that had been her friendship with Grace.

She was a jack of all trades, and while she hadn't mastered anything, she was a hard worker. She wasn't lazy. She wasn't dumb. Even if her cousins had given her the nickname The Merry Slacker a few years before. Even if, when her mom had bought a new condo, she'd cautiously explained to Merry that it only had one bedroom, so she wouldn't be able to take Merry in again.

That had hurt. Merry had moved in with her mom for a few months once, but that had been four years before. "What are you talking about?" she'd huffed, trying to hide her injury with irritation. "Why would you even say that?"

"I just thought you should know, sweetie. I won't be much of a safety net anymore." A safety net. As if Merry were a circus performer with a terrible track record.

Okay, maybe she'd also moved home a few times after college, but those had been short stays. And yes, she lived life one day at a time, unlike her cousins who were both attractive, driven and financially successful. Family gatherings were a little painful, but Merry could deal with it. What she couldn't deal with was her newly hatched self-doubt. Hell, her mom had always been a free spirit, and now it seemed even she was expressing concern.

Squinting against the bright morning sun, Merry stepped over a tall purple wildflower she could never bring herself to step on, despite that it was smack in the middle of the trail.

Over the past year, what had started as a niggling worry had steadily grown into an irritation. A grain of sand beneath her skin. Slowly the minerals of anxiety and fear had begun to accumulate around it, just above her breastbone. Pressing. Displacing. Now it was like a stone she could feel every time she swallowed.

She'd always been happy. And she'd always assumed that someday she'd stumble onto that one good thing. The job that made work into a passion. The love that transformed her single life into something bursting with joy.

It hadn't happened. Because things like that didn't *happen*. She'd decided that attitude would only buy her more years of floating over life, mindless and untethered, tossed about, content to be lost.

Not anymore. Not this time. Not in Providence.

Merry walked confidently up the wooden steps that led to the surprisingly sturdy porch of the first little house. She opened the door and pretended she wasn't doing a quick scan of the doorway for spiders before she stepped in.

Providence might look like eighteen dying buildings surrounded by weeds and harsh mountains, but she was going to make it into a destination. A fascinating tourist stop. A quaint little museum. She would do that. This town would be her triumph.

THIS TOWN WAS going to be her Waterloo.

Another week had passed, and Merry was losing her mind. The board of the Providence Historical Trust was made up of five lovely people who all happened to be over sixty years old. And two of them had been married to the benefactor of the trust, Gideon Bishop. Not at the same time, of course. One woman had been married to him for forty years, though there was a first wife before her somewhere. The third wife had only spent five years with him, but she'd been his wife when he'd died, which seemed to give her pride of place at the table. At least in her mind. The other three were men who each claimed to have been Gideon's best friend at some point.

It could have been like a lovely family reunion when they met every other week. Instead it was like an episode of Passive Aggressive Theater. None of them could agree on anything, or even seem to remember the same event the same way.

"Please," Merry begged for the third time that day. "I need to do *something*. Anything."

Ex-Wife Jeanine nodded. "Well, there are those files."

"Yes, I finished organizing them a week ago."

"Ah," Harry said, "You know what could be helpful? The Jackson Historical Society. I bet they'd have all sorts of pictures and stories and—"

"Yes," Merry ground out, feeling guilty for cutting the old man off even before he finished his sentence. "I mean, of course. You pointed me in that direction last week. I already spent hours there, but it seems Gideon had finished up there. I couldn't find anything new."

"The library?" Third Wife Kristen suggested.

"That, too." Merry tried to smile. "I'm working through all the books I could find on the history of the area, but—"

Levi Cannon slapped his hand down on the table so hard that Merry squeaked. "I've got it! Teton County Historical Society!"

Merry felt a little twinge of excitement. That was one place she hadn't visited. But the excitement died like an ember swept up into the cool sky. "I'll check it out. But…you brought me here to start a museum. To draw people to Providence. That's what Gideon wanted, right? And that's what I want, too. I can make copies of pictures and gather more information about the founders of the town and the flood that led to its destruction, but that's not going to get people out there. I need to get the buildings restored. Grade the road. Build a parking area. We need to come up with plans. Hire workers. Do *something*."

Third Wife Kristen cleared her throat and shot a look at Harry who looked at Levi.

"Well…" Levi said, then paused to pull a handkerchief from his pocket to swipe over his nape. "You see, there's a bit of a problem."

"Problem?" Merry felt a quick crawl of anxiety over her skin. It slipped down her arms and made her fingers tingle with the guilty suspicion that she wasn't good enough. "What problem?" she asked. "Is it my résumé? I know I've only got two years of experience, but I promise you won't find anyone more dedicated. I already love Providence like it was my own. If—"

"No, no," Jeanine interrupted. "You were quite the bargain. We couldn't possibly have afforded someone with more experience, what with the— Ouch!" Jeanine jumped and glared at Third Wife Kristen. "Did you *kick* me?"

"You're being rude!"

But Merry didn't mind. She was a bargain. Or a cheap knockoff of someone who really knew what they were doing. But she was too damn happy about being here to care.

"It was Levi's idea!" Jeanine said on a rush.

"What was?" Merry asked as the others tried to shush the woman.

But Levi just sighed and scrubbed at his neck again before tucking the handkerchief away. "There's a bit of a lawsuit."

"A *bit* of one?"

"Well." He folded his hands on the table. "Aside from the Providence town plot, Gideon left all the land to his grandson. The boy doesn't want the town, but he's fighting the trust, so the money is a little…tied up for a time."

"How long of a time?" she asked, narrowing her eyes.

They all shifted in their seats and traded looks again. "We're not exactly sure," Jeanine finally admitted.

"But I don't understand! You brought me out here to work!"

"Well, yes…" Jeanine offered a sympathetic smile. "Of course, but… We decided to hire you as more of a strategic move."

Kristen snorted. "*You* decided!"

Jeanine glared at her. "The judge freed up a small amount of the trust for administrative costs. *We* decided our best move would be to go forward with Gideon's plans, or at least give the appearance of doing so. It gives us a position of power. Possession is nine-tenths of the law and all that."

"The appearance," Merry murmured, too shocked to say more. The appearance. They hadn't wanted her at all. This wasn't her big chance to succeed. This was just a move in a legal battle.

Marvin, who up to this point hadn't said a word to Merry, sat forward and cleared his throat. "None of this nonsense is your concern. You're being paid. Let these idiots spin their wheels and you keep your head down and do what you can."

"With what?" she snapped. "Tumbleweeds?"

"You're the idiot, Marvin Black!" Kristen screeched. "You're the one who planted this whole damn nonsense in Gideon's head in the first place. All your big ideas about history and heritage!"

"Bah! If you can't live on what he left you, then you're nothing but a spendthrift floozy, anyway. Gideon wanted to build a legacy."

"A legacy," she scoffed. "More like a fool's errand."

"Well, if that's the way you feel about it, what are you even doing here?"

Merry listened to them snipe at each other, but she didn't really hear them. She was reeling. "What am I supposed to do?" she asked no one.

Levi answered. "We'll try to get more funds released for you next month. In the meantime, you should definitely visit the county historical society. See what you find." He patted her hand in dismissal, and Merry let herself be dismissed.

She stood and wandered out onto the front porch of the home where Gideon Bishop had lived his whole life. He'd died here, in Kristen's loving arms, according to her, and he'd left behind a legacy that nobody much cared about. Gideon had only had one child. A son from his first marriage who had run off decades before. And then two grandsons he hadn't spoken to in years. Gideon had ended up with more money than any one person could need, and he'd sunk everything into a stupid ghost town. Just like Merry.

But she'd misunderstood. She'd thought the trust had brought her here because they'd believed in her. She'd been surprised at the call. Overwhelmed, actually. And overjoyed. But in that moment she'd known that her passion had shown through and eclipsed the wild inconsistencies in her résumé. The letter she'd written had moved them, and they'd chosen her to bring Providence to life.

Or...they'd chosen her because she was the cheapest clearance item they could get away with passing off as legitimate in court. They hadn't believed in her at all. She was a placeholder. And this would be another failure in her life.

Merry raced down the steps of the wide front porch and jumped into her car, wanting to escape before the tears fell. She almost made it, but the first fat drops slipped off her cheeks before she'd slammed the car door.

They hadn't meant for her to succeed here. They hadn't meant for her to do *anything.* "Those shitty old... *coots.*" God, she couldn't even bring herself to call them something they really deserved. She wasn't tough that way. She wasn't hard enough. She was dandelion fluff, floating in the wind.

Angry at her own self-assessment, Merry threw the car into Reverse and hit the gas pedal. This was a good place to get her emotions out with a wild ride. After all, she was out in the middle of nowhere at the end of the dirt road. There was nothing out here except sagebrush and—

A hard clunk interrupted her daring thoughts and sent her stomach tumbling. She slammed on the brakes as her mind raced through all the possibilities. That hadn't been sagebrush, but it had been solid. Not a sweet sheepdog or a barn cat or… She pulled forward a few feet and then scrambled out, her eyes flying over the dried-out grass at the edge of the yard.

The mailbox. The *mailbox*. Oh, shit. It was a white wooden number with the name Bishop spelled out in custom black letters across the top of the box. And now it was lying on the ground like the victim of an assassination.

Oh, God. She glanced toward the house. She couldn't just leave it there. It would look as if she'd done it deliberately because they'd insulted her. And she couldn't go back in and confess, because she'd left in a huff and their only apparent attachment to her was her cheap price tag.

"Oh, God!" The tears flowed freely now, inspired by panic and anger and the awful knowledge that she could feel as humiliated as she wanted but she couldn't lose this job. She couldn't.

Merry looked helplessly down at the mailbox, feeling as if she'd murdered some precious icon. The thick white post wasn't broken. Maybe she could just stick it back in the ground. A glance at the house confirmed that no one else had left yet. They were probably still bickering over whether it had been dishonest to hire her for a job that didn't exist.

A job that didn't exist. The perfect job for a bit of fluff like her.

Rage pushed her past her guilt over the mailbox, and Merry bent down and wrapped her arms around the box, lifting it with a grunt of impatience. She slid it a few inches and fit the tip of the post into the hole. It dropped right in.

"Thank God." After pressing down a little, she let it go…and watched the mailbox tilt toward the left. Crap. Merry wrapped her arms around it and straightened it again, then pulled down as hard as she could. She lifted her feet and let her body weight hang for just a second. This time, when she stepped back, it only tipped a tiny bit. Like the erection of a man just registering that you'd made a *Star Wars* joke in the middle of foreplay.

Not that that had ever happened to her.

Merry took a few more steps back, hands raised as if she could catch the mailbox if it fell. But it held steady, and with one last look at the house, she darted to her car and drove away.

But as she drove down the gravel road, watching dust billow behind her like a plume of guilt, Merry set her jaw and steeled her heart.

It didn't matter why they'd hired her. It didn't matter who they thought she was. She'd come here to make a place for herself, and that was what she was going to do.

SHANE HARCOURT WAS so damn tired he wasn't sure he could make it up the front steps of the Stud Farm. Two weeks of carpentry work on a ranch in Lander, followed up by a week of fencing on the high plateau outside Big Piney, and he was dead on his feet and nearly weaving side to side as he opened the door and headed for his apartment.

Not for the first time, he thanked God that Cole had finally gotten back on his feet and out of Shane's ground floor place. Shane couldn't have trudged up to the second floor today. Not in this state. He watched his key disappear into the lock like he was watching the perfect porn movie. A beer. A hot shower. Bed. Then he planned to sleep for two days straight. Sheer pleasure.

He turned the key.

"Shane!"

Shane blinked at the idea of his neighbor Grace greeting him with such unbridled excitement. Frowning, he slowly turned around, hand still hopefully clasped to the doorknob.

"Hi!" a woman who was definitely not Grace said.

He took in the tall brunette in the Oscar the Grouch T-shirt and automatically touched the brim of his hat in greeting. "Morning," he said.

"It's afternoon now," she answered.

"Is it?" He realized he was just standing there staring while she grinned at him. Her long dark hair framed a harmless round face and an open smile. "Do I know you?"

"Seriously? Wow. I'm kind of insulted."

Shane's brain scanned quickly through the past few sexual encounters he'd had, just in case. But there weren't that many, and he was almost immediately sure he hadn't slept with this girl. "Sorry?"

"Shane, I'm Merry."

Mary? He stared.

"Merry Kade. Grace's friend?"

"Oh," he said. Then "Oh! Merry. Right. Hi."

Her wide smile had faltered at some point, so Shane tried again. "It's good to see you. Are you visiting?"

"No, I moved here. I'm living with Grace for a little while."

"Oh, that's nice. Good." His eyes nearly crossed with exhaustion.

"Anyway, I'm glad you're finally back. You're a carpenter cowboy, right?"

"I'm just a carpenter, not a cowboy."

"Sure you are." She waved a hand up and down his body. "Look at those boots. And the hat."

"Being a cowboy is a job. It's got nothing to do with the boots."

She looked pointedly at his Stetson.

"Or the hat," he said wearily.

"Okay, but you *are* a carpenter." When he nodded, her smile returned, lighting up her fresh face. "You're just what I need!"

Too tired to bother with a sly reply, Shane just nodded. "Need some help with a bookshelf or something?"

She laughed so loudly that her voice rang through the entry. "Sure, something like that."

He forced a smile. "Okay, I'll come by later. Right now—" He held up a hand to stop the words forming on her lips. "Listen, I've been working twelve-hour days for two weeks. I would normally come over straightaway and assemble your shelf, but I'm swaying on my feet and my eyes can't focus. All I can even consider is a microwave burrito, a quick shower and then ten hours of sleep. Actually scratch the shower. That'll wait."

Her eyes flickered down before she blinked a few times. "Sure. It's no problem. The shelf can wait. You sleep. And eat. And shower."

"Thanks, um…Merry. I'll come over later." He pushed through the door and nearly stumbled over a thick envelope that must have been slipped through the old mail slot that no one used anymore. When he spotted his lawyer's name printed across the top, Shane picked it up and set it on a table to open later. He didn't need to think about that bullshit right now. The only thing worse would be trying to navigate a conversation with his mother. He couldn't think coherently about even the simplest thing, such as being polite to an acquaintance.

He turned, meaning to apologize to Merry before he closed the door, but she was gone, the only evidence she'd been there the sound of Grace's door clicking shut.

"Shit." He'd go over to Grace's as soon as he'd showered tonight. But first… He locked the door, shucked off his boots, forgot about lunch and headed for bed to collapse.

CHAPTER TWO

GRACE FROZE IN THE ACT of sliding a perfect smudge of black liner across her lash line and aimed a hot glare in Merry's direction. "What do you mean Shane's coming over?"

Merry stared in wonder. "How do you do that?" she asked for the hundredth time since she'd met her best friend. "I don't get it. When I put eyeliner on, I look like a five-year-old playing dress up. Or an eighty-year-old alcoholic trying to recapture her glory days."

"Close your eyes." Grace scooted Merry around and swiped the pencil quickly over her lids. "There. I've shown you a million times. Now tell me why Shane's coming over."

When she opened her eyes, Merry sighed at the sight that greeted her. Her plain brown irises now looked large and whiskey-colored. At least she was living with Grace right now. She could use her friend like a personal makeup artist whenever she wanted. Of course, that didn't change the fact that Merry's liner would be smudged and smeared within an hour. Her body rejected any transplants of prettiness.

"I need a carpenter," she said as she fluttered her lashes at herself. Then she looked from Grace's hair—gorgeous, choppy and recently brightened with chunks of Crayola red color—to her own. Plain brown and slightly dented from the ponytail she'd worn that morning. God.

"So?" Grace asked.

"Shane's a carpenter. I'm hoping he'll give me the Stud Farm discount."

"The Stud Farm discount," Grace muttered. "I don't like the sound of that at all. I think I should hang around."

"Thanks, Mom, but I promise not to get into your vodka stash."

"I'll call Cole and tell him to pick me up later."

"You will not. First of all, Cole's going to die when he sees that red in your hair. And by die, I mean he's going to jump on you like a cowboy riding a stubborn bronco."

"Nice."

"Secondly, what's your problem with Shane?"

Grace shrugged and leaned forward to finish her makeup. "I don't know. He's slick. Too removed. I can't read him."

"I think he's nice."

"Yeah, that's why I'm hanging around. You think everyone is nice."

"I do not," Merry denied. "And even if I did, you have nothing to worry about. He didn't even remember who I was. I doubt he's currently concocting a plan to seduce me and steal my virginity as a trophy."

Grace snorted. "What virginity?"

"The one I regrew after two years of celibacy."

"A good sex toy should take care of that."

"I don't want to talk about it," Merry groaned. "I'm pitiful."

"No, you're not. You're safe and picky which is exactly how I want you to be."

"I'm not picky. I'm just not on the radar. *Anyone's* radar. I'm the government's top-secret stealth snatch project."

Grace burst into an uncharacteristically hearty laugh. Merry just stuck her tongue out and flounced out of the bathroom.

"I'm serious about Shane," Grace said, following her to the living room. She pulled on a pair of black boots that would have looked clunky and mannish on Merry, but somehow looked both tough and adorable on Grace. "Watch out for him. He can be charming." She drew the word out like it was a smear. "And take off that eyeliner. You look too cute."

"You can scrub this liner off my cold, dead body. Actually that won't be necessary, because it'll melt off within the hour."

"Use that primer I gave you."

"Sure," Merry said, instead of telling her friend that she'd tried the primer and somehow she couldn't get it blended right and ended up looking like she was wearing sparkly white goggles.

"Don't get charmed," Grace warned, pointing a finger at Merry's chest. "I'm serious. I don't want to have to murder my boyfriend's best friend. Okay?"

A knock interrupted their conversation. Merry went out to say hello to Cole, but for a moment he was overwhelmingly distracted by Grace's hair.

"Hi, Merry," he said, his gaze locked on his girl-friend with an intensity no man had ever had for Merry.

"Hi, Cole. Grace's hair looks great, huh?"

"Hell, yeah, it does." Grace kicked him, and for a moment his gaze only got more intense. Then he blinked and visibly shook it off. His easy smile appeared and he turned to Merry. "How's the ghost town, darlin'?" he asked, leaning in to kiss her cheek. "I still don't like you out there on your own."

"I studied all the wildlife guides you gave me. If a rattlesnake comes near, I can identify it in less than two seconds, I swear."

He winked. "Good."

"You know, you two are actually worse than having parents. My mom was never this overprotective."

Cole patted her arm. "I've never had a little sister."

"I'm not your sister! Jeez. Now go show your girl-friend how much you like the new red hair. I'll see you later."

Cole dragged his woman out the door, but Grace leaned back in for one last warning. "Watch out for that guy."

"I promise it won't be a problem!" she huffed.

It never was. Men were always disappointingly re-spectful of her. She locked the door behind Grace and then wandered back to the bathroom to put on some lip gloss and brush out her hair. Thanks to Grace's profes-sional skills with the eye makeup, Merry looked almost nice. And the Oscar the Grouch T-shirt really set off her complexion.

Just as she was thinking of changing, there was an-other knock on the door, which helpfully saved her from the decision of which Darth Vader T-shirt she was going to choose.

She opened the door with a wide smile that she felt freeze on her face when she saw Shane Harcourt.

He'd definitely taken that shower. The thick stubble that had shadowed his face had been shaved off to reveal his hard jaw, and his dark hair was still pressed to his nape in damp strands.

"Hi, Merry," he said, and she had the distinct feeling he was proving that he remembered her name this time. Not very flattering. When she'd visited Jackson last fall, they'd spent three hours together at Grace's birthday party. Not enough time to make an impression on him, apparently.

"You look like you're feeling a lot better," she said, waving him in.

"I am, thanks. And sorry about earlier." He flashed that charming smile she'd heard about. "I was dead on my feet."

"Yeah, you looked like a cattle rustler who'd been on the run for weeks."

His smile wavered. She had a way of doing that to men. "So where's the bookshelf?"

"Ha. There is no bookshelf."

"What?" He turned in a slow circle, looking over the apartment. "You said you wanted help with a bookshelf."

She let her eyes wander down to his ass while he wasn't looking. Cowboys were so sweet, the way they never wore those awful baggy jeans. And Shane was especially sweet, generously showing off his tight, muscular ass in a dark pair of Levi's.

She cleared her throat. "No, *you* said I wanted help with a bookshelf."

"All right. So what's going on?" He sounded suspicious, probably worried she was going to try to make a move. It was so uncomfortable when you had to fight off the girl next door.

"Why don't we sit down?"

Still looking wary, he took a seat on the couch. He'd look even warier if he knew he was sitting on her bed. Merry smothered a grin as she sat next to him. "I need a carpenter for a bigger job than a few shelves."

"Yeah? You might want to rethink any remodeling. I doubt Rayleen would approve. She's a pretty strict landlord."

"I wouldn't dare cross Rayleen," Merry answered, shuddering a little at the idea of pissing off Grace's crazy great-aunt. "I actually do need you to remodel something, but it's not an apartment. It's a ghost town."

"A ghost town?" Shane sat straight and blinked several times. "Excuse me?"

She couldn't help but laugh at the disbelief on his face. "I know it sounds crazy. But it really is a ghost town. It's called Providence. Have you heard of it?"

"I…I think so."

"It's north of the Gros Ventre. I was hired to get it ready to be a public exhibit."

"You?"

Was the whole town conspiring to destroy her confidence? "Yes, me. Listen, it's going to be spectacular! Really. It may sound strange to say a ghost town is exciting, but I'm so excited!"

"Yeah, I see that."

Merry realized she'd clasped her hands together and leaned closer to him. "It's an amazing place. Truly. The most beautiful place you've ever seen. If you take the job, you'll see—"

"Take what job?"

"I want to hire you to start the restoration."

Shane sat back. He stared at her for a long moment before he let his head fall to rest on the couch. His gaze bore into the ceiling. "You want to hire *me*."

"Well, I don't know a lot of carpenters in Jackson." Or anywhere else. "And!" She rushed on, not wanting to offend him, "You're Cole's best friend, so that's all the recommendation I need."

"Merry…" His eyes squeezed shut for a moment, and she wondered if he was still too tired to think. "I'm sorry, but I'm a little lost here. What exactly are you doing here and why are you working in Providence?"

"Oh! Right. You missed the first few weeks of this. Well, I've been keeping an eye on jobs in Jackson for a while now. I loved it when I came out to visit Grace, and I wanted to be closer to her, of course." *And my mom bought a one-bedroom condo and hung out a Do Not Disturb sign.* "Unfortunately I don't ski. Or know anything about skiing. Or even know enough to pretend to know something about skiing. So that career route was closed."

"Okay. Got it."

"But when I saw this job pop up… It was serendipity. I'd been working at a local historical museum for a year, remember?" Of course he didn't remember, but he made an affirmative sound. "So I applied and…" She didn't want to finish the story this time. It no longer made her happy. Her pulse still sped, but it wasn't with excitement and pride. It was anger fueling her now. And embarrassment. And just a tiny pinch of desperation. She hoped he couldn't hear that part of it. "Here I am!" she finished with a bright smile.

"Here you are. And you want me to help get your ghost town ready for display."

He didn't sound excited. In fact, he looked downright weary. His eyes were closed again, and she was sure she could already see stubble forming beneath the skin of his jaw. "Are you okay, Shane?" She reached out to put her palm to his forehead, only registering that she might be invading his personal space when he jumped and looked at her with wide eyes.

"Sorry. You just seem out of sorts."

"I'm fine," he said in a clipped voice that made her wonder about this slick charm Grace was worried about. Apparently Merry didn't merit charm. Or slickness. But that wasn't what she needed. What she needed was a man with a hammer.

"So will you do it?"

He shook his head. "You have no idea what you're asking." Before she could figure out what he meant, he cleared his throat and leaned forward, hands clasped between his knees. "Summer is my busy season. I only have a few months to get all the outdoor work in, and there's a lot of it."

"Oh. Right. I didn't think of that." Her heart sank. She'd had a very clever idea to pay a carpenter out of her own salary, only it suddenly didn't seem quite so clever. Shane was booked up for the summer. That was why he'd looked like he'd been riding the trail for a month.

Everybody else was probably overworked, too. Which meant they'd have no reason to go for her half now/half later payment proposal. "Shit," she whispered, falling back to collapse into the fat cushions of the couch.

"Plus, I don't know anything about restoration. That sounds like a specialty job."

"This part is pretty straightforward," she murmured. "I need the porch on the saloon fixed. It's not safe right now, and it's my favorite building. I think it'll be a real draw. There weren't a lot of saloons around here back then, since a lot of the settlers were Mormon. I've read some great stories about that place."

"You've got a saloon right next door," he said, waving his hand toward the Crooked R, where old Rayleen reigned like a not-quite-benevolent queen.

She shrugged. "It's not the same."

"Look, you just started. It's the busy season for everyone in construction. You're going to have to be content with taking your time. Nothing is going to happen this year. My advice is to sit tight and plan for next year."

Oh, God. The idea of spending months like this... She'd run out of things to do during the winter. She could start building a website, maybe, but that wouldn't take more than a month, and she couldn't even make it live, because Providence was currently too dangerous to have curious visitors poking around.

Maybe she could design the signs that would eventually be posted on each building. Yes, that would be fun. Then she could put them in storage for two years until the first of the buildings was restored. Maybe in five years they could have a ribbon cutting ceremony, assuming the whole thing hadn't been shut down due to a lawsuit.

No, she had to make this work, starting right now. She had to make this a success before the board realized their ploy wasn't having an effect on the lawsuit and they let her go. Or until the lawsuit was dropped and they decided to bring a real curator in.

"I have to move forward," she said. "Do you know anyone who could help, even if it's just for a few hours a week? Please?"

"What exactly are your plans? Just to nail a few boards up and start charging tourists?"

"No! It's not like that. There won't even be a charge, just a donation box. I just need…" *Affirmation. Progress. Proof that I'm not a loser.* "It's a wonderful place and people don't even know it's there. I want to start sharing it with the community." Well, that was true, too. It had been even more true yesterday. "It's an important part of the history of this place," she finished feebly.

She glanced over, hoping to see sympathy on his handsome face. What she found instead was frustration. Or anger. But no, it had to be frustration. He was just a little…intimidating. And still not the least bit charming about it. Cole was so damn laid-back she couldn't imagine him being close with Shane, but maybe that was what drew them together.

Shane hadn't been quite so gruff at Grace's birthday party, though. She'd thought he was cute then. Really cute. Oh, hell, he was still really cute; he just made her nervous as hell. Same as every other cute guy.

"Maybe I could stop by on a few evenings," he finally said, pronouncing each word slowly, carefully.

"Really?" Merry squealed. When he nodded, she threw her arms around his neck and hugged him. He seemed too startled to hug her back. "Thank you! Thank you! Do you want to check it out? We can go right now."

"Right *now?*"

"Sure. We've still got two hours of daylight left. Let's scoot out there so you know what you're working with."

His gaze drifted toward the right as if he were looking through the wall toward the Crooked R and its cold pitchers of beer.

"I'll buy you a beer when we get back," she offered in her most flirtatiously tempting voice.

"I'm fine," he said flatly. "Let's just get this over with."

Her triumph tasted strangely like burnt pride, but she just smiled wider. "Great. I'll grab my keys."

HE'D INSISTED ON FOLLOWING Merry in his own truck. Or rather, she thought he was following, but he knew exactly where the Providence ghost town was. His dad had brought him out here dozens of times when Shane had been a kid. They'd spent whole days in the area, and sometimes nights in a tent next to the narrow creek that snuck through the piles of boulders at the mouth of the canyon.

As a kid, he'd thought of Providence as desolate and a little spooky. A place that people had abandoned. Walked away from. But that desolation had lent it a bit of reverence in his mind. To a kid, it had felt sacred and deliciously forgotten. Not a place to be turned into another tourist playground. Jesus, weren't there enough of those around here?

Now, as the town came into view, with its familiar graying roof peaks and crumbling walls, he didn't feel reverence. He felt…nothing. Nothing except irritation that it was causing him inconvenience.

He watched Merry glance in her rearview mirror as he followed her around the last curve of the dirt road. She'd looked into her mirror a lot on the drive, as if making sure he hadn't ditched her.

Shit. He'd been gruff. He knew that. But she'd blind-sided him with her news. Merry was just the out-of-town friend of Grace. She was a nice girl who smiled too much and wore goofy T-shirts and didn't seem to fit with her wild, tough friend from L.A. How had she suddenly become a next-door neighbor who was asking him to help her ruin his childhood haunt?

When she stopped, he pulled in behind her on a wide patch of dirt and got out. She was nearly bouncing on her toes when he joined her. "Isn't it amazing?" she squealed.

"It looks like a bunch of falling down shacks."

"That's because you don't know the history! What people went through to build this place, the lives they dug out from the dirt, the tragedies that drove them away. This place is alive, Shane. It's just…sleeping."

"More like mummifying," he muttered, but she ignored him and grabbed his arm.

"Come on. I'll show you the saloon. It's really in pretty good shape, aside from the porch."

Shane let her pull him along and tried to ignore a sense of déjà vu as he got closer to the first buildings. Her excitement was contagious, in the sense that it dispersed through the air like an infection that coated his skin, contaminating him with the phantom touch of the excitement he used to feel here. The mystery of the place. The snakes and lizards that would dart out from underneath foundations. The wonder of who'd walked here before, lawmen and outlaws and all sorts of people who'd never actually set foot in Providence. Of course, he'd been a child. He wasn't sure what Merry's excuse was, but he didn't like the feel of it, and he rolled his shoulders to shake it off.

"Here it is," she said. Her words weren't necessary. Even if he hadn't known it was the saloon, there was an ancient sign propped on the porch.

"So this is pretty good shape?" he asked.

"Yeah. Look at the mercantile next door."

He moved closer to the porch and shook his head. "I can't just fix it with new wood, Merry. This is a big deal. You'll want to use old wood. Wood that's been reclaimed and—"

"I know all that! I'm not a complete amateur. I can take care of everything. I just need your help."

Shane turned and looked at her. Really looked at her for the first time since she'd asked him for help. He looked past the smile, past the sweet round face and slightly tanned cheeks flushed with pink. Her brown eyes were unremarkable…except that if you took the time to look, they showed everything she was feeling. And right now, she was feeling worried.

"What's going on here, Merry?"

"What do you mean? I'm hiring a carpenter. You. I'm doing my job."

"So you own this place? You can do whatever you

want?" He knew damn well that wasn't the situation, but he needed to find out her angle.

Instead of answering his question, Merry shifted, then crossed her arms and walked farther down the road. Interesting. Shane followed. When she stopped and turned around, all traces of worry were gone and she looked cool as a cucumber.

"I think we should approach this in tiers. First, I need to know if the building is safe. The floors. The ceilings. If it's not safe, I need to know how much it would cost to make it safe. That's step one. Second, I'd like to see the most obvious repairs made. The sagging porch. Holes in the ceiling. That sort of thing. Lastly, I need to know how much a restoration would cost."

"A restoration? Merry, I don't have time for—"

"I get that. But we're not talking a full restoration. It would still need to be ghost-towny. No one wants to come to a ghost town and see a shiny saloon."

"Ghost-towny," he repeated wearily. "That an official term?"

"It is now. There's a shed at the east end of the town that's full of wood already reclaimed from collapsed buildings. No new wood, right? Just watch out for spiders." She shivered. "I try not to go into the shed. It's pretty chock full of spiders. It's like…a spider anthill."

"A…?" Realizing he was only going to be drawn deeper into her strange mind if he said any more, Shane shook his head and dropped the subject. "Okay. I guess you have thought this through."

"Yes. It's my job." Her chin rose a little, as if daring him to dispute it. She wasn't smiling now. Strangely her mouth looked wider in repose. More full and mysterious.

Shane rocked back on his heels, put his hands in his pockets, taking a little time to look over the ragged buildings around him. "When are you planning on opening this place, Merry?"

"Next year," she answered, her chin edging higher.

Next year. Shane couldn't let that happen. He had to stop this. "All right, then," he offered with a smile. "I'll do what I can."

All her false bravado disappeared and she was hopping up and down like a kid again. "You will? Really?"

"Yes."

"Thank you, Shane!" She threw herself at his chest, and Shane automatically put his arms around her. He also automatically registered how nice and feminine she smelled, a stark change from the men he'd worked with on his two weeks of ranch work. Then he very carefully set her back.

"I'm going to take a look at that spare wood. Do you want to walk over with me?"

"No! The spider anthill, remember?"

"Right." God, she was a piece of work. But she had information he needed, so Shane touched his hat brim and nodded. "I'll deal with the spiders on my own. And then I'll take a look at your saloon."

"Thank you!" she squealed, and he tried not to feel guilty as he walked away. Merry had stepped into something that she couldn't understand, and that wasn't Shane's fault. He set his jaw and walked on.

CHAPTER THREE

"WHERE WERE you last night?"

Merry sat up from a dead sleep, throwing her arms out to defend against the snarling monster crouched above her. The monster jumped back, quick as a hell-beast, its flame-tipped mane framing a...pale and pretty face?

"Oh! Grace. You scared me." Merry flopped back down onto the mattress, wincing when a spring poked her back. "What are you growling about?"

"Where were you last night? I called eight times! I tried to make Cole get up and drive me home."

"Yeah? What did he say?"

"He...distracted me."

Merry snorted and pulled the covers over her head, but Grace yanked them back.

"Merry! What did you do? Did you sleep with Shane? I mean...it's okay. You can tell me. I won't be mad."

The not-quite-suppressed violence beneath Grace's words sounded like static in her voice. Merry grinned at her. "You promise you won't be mad?"

"Yes," she said past clenched teeth and a painfully pleasant smile.

"Oh, my God." Merry laughed. "You're the worst liar ever. No, I did not use my super-sexy wiles to lure

Shane onto my fold-out sofa bed for a night of uncomfortable passion."

"I wasn't worried about *you* doing the luring!"

"Okay. No, Shane did not butter me up with *Star Wars* trivia and then 'accidentally' fall on me with his penis out."

"Merry, be serious! Where were you?"

Finally accepting that she wasn't going to get any more sleep, Merry crawled out of bed and headed to the kitchen to start coffee. "I went out to Providence. My phone must have been searching for a signal for an hour or two and it ran out of power. Sometimes I get four bars out there, and sometimes I get zero. I'm not sure how that works. Is it the wind? The clouds? What—"

"Okay, what about later?"

"Grace, what is your deal? First of all, why do you hate Shane so much? Second...I haven't had sex in two years. *Two years*. If I miraculously talked a man into wanting to have sex, wouldn't you be thrilled for me? I have needs, you know."

Actually she didn't. Not anymore. Those needs had finally dried up and died six months ago, at the exact moment that her cheap, knock-off vibrator had buzzed into a slow death. She'd replaced it with an even cheaper knock-off model but hadn't even bought batteries for that one. She'd just put it away, still in its tacky packaging, and never thought about it again.

Grace seemed to have deflated to her normal petite size. She always seemed four inches taller when she was pissed, but apparently she'd gotten past it, because she sighed and opened a cupboard door to take out coffee mugs. "Why haven't you been having sex?"

"You know why."

"I don't want to hear it, Merry. You've got an amazing body, you're funny as hell and you're cute."

"I'm not like you, Grace."

"What? Slutty?"

"You know that's not what I mean! I just…I don't know what to do with men. I get nervous. I make too many jokes. I act like a kid sister instead of their fantasy sex machine."

"Come on, Merry. Men don't want a fantasy. They want something real."

Merry frowned but tried to hide it by turning back to the coffeepot, which was trickling out that last little bit of caffeine. That was easy for Grace to say. Grace, in all her reality, *was* a fantasy. She was edgy and strong and striking. She intimidated men in a way that turned them on.

Merry, on the other hand, was a *friend*. A perpetual friend. The girl who always had a good joke and a smile.

She didn't know how to be sexy. And it didn't seem to be something she could learn, damn it.

"Whatever," she finally said. "It doesn't matter. My point is you don't have to worry about Shane. Shit, I wish you did."

"Okay, I'll drop it. I'm sorry, I just… You came here because of me. I feel like I need to watch out for you."

"Bullshit, Grace. You always say the same thing."

Grace shrugged and pushed the mugs forward for coffee. "None of those guys have been good enough for you. You know that's true."

"Good Lord, I'm not the Virgin Mary. If he's got a

job and a penis, he's already halfway up my scale. And I don't really care about the job."

Grace choked on laughter. "Shut up. That's not true. It'd better not be true or you're grounded, young lady."

Merry just shook her head. "You're the one who let me move into a place called the Stud Farm."

Grace rolled her eyes, but Merry laughed as hard as she ever did at the joke.

The apartment building was really the two-story house of the old Studd farmstead, converted into four identical apartments, two on the ground floor, and two upstairs. She didn't know if it had an official name, but everyone called it the Stud Farm after Aunt Rayleen's tendency to fill it with single young men. Young compared to her, anyway.

When Grace had blown into town last year, even Rayleen hadn't had the heart to send her away. She'd let Grace stay for a few weeks, and even though the old battlcax tried to hide it, Merry could tell the woman loved her niece. She'd let Grace keep the apartment, and she'd let Merry move in, too, but the Stud Farm name would probably never go away.

Merry elbowed Grace. "Go take a shower while I fold up the bed. You're probably filthy from last night. Which really pisses me off. I'm leaving in an hour, whether you're ready or not."

SHANE WALKED DOWN the hard-packed dirt road that ran through the center of Providence. Merry was sitting on the porch of one of the few buildings that still looked relatively safe. The porch beams weren't canting off toward the east. The stairs were still intact. He hoped she'd chosen well. He'd hate for her to fall through the floorboards into the spider nests that undoubtedly filled the space beneath. He'd better check out that porch just to be sure.

She didn't seem to have noticed him yet, so Shane took the chance to study her while she was so untypically still. Her dark hair looked black but he knew it was lighter than that. A deep brown like stained walnut. He'd never really had a preference in women's looks, as far as blond versus brunette, but he couldn't help noticing how striking she looked sitting there. Her tan skin looked pale in contrast to the curve of hair that fell over her cheek as she read, and her wide mouth was rosy-pink and tipped up in a small smile even in solitude. Merry was the perfect name for this strange girl.

At least she was smart enough to stay out of the sun. Even with her coloring, at this altitude she'd burn like hell, and her shoulders were totally exposed in the pink tank top she was wearing. So Merry was smart enough to stay out of the sun, but not smart enough to pay any attention to her surroundings. She had earbuds in her ears. Like every city person he'd ever met, she put more value on her electronics than the beauty that surrounded her.

He glanced toward the looming peaks of the Tetons, then back to Merry, her head bent over some sort of device. She couldn't hear the crunch of his boots against the patches of gravel and dried grass, but he could hear the tinny echo of the music that leaked from her ears.

Shane sighed as he drew within five feet of the porch. She didn't react. He stopped two feet from her and cleared his throat.

When she didn't notice, he coughed.

Still nothing. Was she this vulnerable every day? Did she think there weren't creeps and rapists in Wyoming? Hell, in addition to the residents, some of whom were pretty damn rough and mysterious, the place was crawling with strangers from all over the world.

Irritated by his own concern, Shane stepped forward and knocked on the porch rail. "Hello?"

Merry finally glanced up, and her whole body jerked in shock. "Ah!" she screeched, an iPad flying from her hands as if it were a bird startled into flight.

Her wide eyes left him to watch the thing tumble through the air and right over the railing. "Ah!" she screamed again.

She surged to her feet to stare in dismay at the cloud of dust rising up around her iPad. "Oh, my God! Oh, no!"

"Sorry. I tried to let you know I was here."

The cord of her earbuds dangled impotently against the railing. "What?" she breathed.

"I didn't mean to startle you. I thought I'd come out this morning and get a head start on—"

She leaped into motion so quickly that he bit back his words in shock as she took the three porch steps in one quick leap and swooped up the dropped iPad.

"Sorry," she breathed. "It's the only thing keeping me sane out here." When she cradled it like an injured baby, Shane doubted her claim of sanity. "I think it's okay," she breathed as she swiped one finger over the screen. "I think it's okay."

"Great," he said dryly.

"Yes, it is great, isn't it?" She finally looked directly

at him and a wide smile spread over her face. "Hey, Shane! I didn't expect to see you here this early!"

"So I gathered."

She hugged her iPad tighter, and Shane tried not to notice the way her breasts pressed up, revealing a beautiful amount of cleavage above the thin cotton of her tank. He *tried* not to notice, but he failed miserably. He was a man, and there were breasts *right there*. Her skin wasn't quite so tan where the shirt dipped down. It was pale and soft and gently rising, like—

"You're all cowboyed up again," she said.

He frowned a little at the delight in her voice. Did she think this was Disneyland, where people played dress-up and tried on a drawl?

"The hat," she clarified.

"The hat is for shade. I'm not a cowboy."

"Yeah, yeah," she said, waving a hand as her earbud cord bounced.

"What are we going to do today?"

"What are *we* going to do? This is so exciting!"

Oh, God. Fine. Shane took a deep breath and tried to let his grumpiness go as he followed Merry toward the saloon. He couldn't put a finger on when it had sunk so deeply into his flesh. He used to be able to let a bad mood go. He used to be able to forget his family and the years of betrayals and stress. He could work to forget. Or hang out with friends. And if that didn't work, there were always women. But the past year had made forgetting damned difficult.

"You should get some spurs!" she said, walking backward now. "A little jingling would really liven this place up."

He opened his mouth to respond, then realized he had no idea what to say to that. "Right," he finally said in defeat before closing his mouth again.

She nodded solemnly. "Yeah."

Shane suddenly had to consider that Providence might be a ghost town in an old episode of the *Twilight Zone*. It had to be. There was no other explanation for this odd woman plunked down in the middle of the dustiest part of Jackson Hole. There was no way to explain why she'd stumbled into his problems this way.

"I brought the estimates," he said, then jumped forward to grab Merry as she tripped over her own feet and almost went down on her ass. "Hey. You okay?"

"Sure!" Her laugh tripped over itself like a broken toy.

Shane frowned, sensing there was something more there, but if her reaction was simple embarrassment at her clumsiness, he didn't want to press further. When the warmth of her waist soaked into his fingers, Shane realized he was still holding her and stood back with an awkward pat of her ribs. "So…"

He slipped the envelope from his back pocket and handed it over. "There's the estimate. Why don't you take a look at that while I sort through the spare wood, then we'll make a plan."

Even as he spoke, Merry tore open the envelope and unfolded the papers. True fear twisted her brow into lines of tension.

Why? It wasn't her money. Hell, he'd expect that spending the money of a trust would be damn fun, especially when you were irritatingly excited about the project in the first place. "Not what you expected?" he asked. He was experienced, and not cheap, but he didn't think his hourly wage was exorbitant.

"Oh," she breathed, her eyes darting over the page before she flipped to the next. "No, of course not. It's… just…"

He kept his mouth shut, waiting for a clue as to what was going on. As he expected, Merry couldn't bear the silence, and she jumped to fill it.

"It's just… We'd better start with the first one. Just the porch. Then hopefully…"

Shane cocked his head.

"The thing is, can I pay you half now and half next month? I'm sorry. I don't know how you normally do it, but I'm having a little trouble getting funds, uh, released."

Whoa. Very interesting. So interesting that Shane finally found the strength to shove down his grumpiness and turn on the charm. This was exactly the kind of information he needed, and he needed it before Merry turned in an invoice. Shane would be fired quicker than he could say *legal espionage*.

So he smiled. And shifted a little closer. And turned on the Western charm that had worked before on cute tourist girls. "What's wrong, darlin'?"

"Nothing! I can pay you! It's not that. It's just…" The envelope slipped from her fingers, and Shane knelt to pick it up.

When he rose, he let his eyes drag over her body. There was nothing wrong with her body, after all. She wasn't stick-thin like the rich women who rolled through town with skis and fur boots. She was strong and tall and curvy. As his gaze dragged over the curve of her hip, he was struck with the sudden thought of what she might look like naked, and got lost in that for a moment before he remembered his charm and turned his smile up.

"It's just what?" he pressed.

Merry was watching him with slightly parted lips, as if she'd sensed his thoughts. "It's just... The board members are..."

He tipped his head a little closer, holding her gaze as he slid the envelope back into her grasp. His fingers brushed over hers. He let them rest there, just beneath the angle of her knuckles.

And then there was her mouth. Those slightly parted lips. A little too wide for beauty, maybe, but suddenly so soft. And inviting. And...

Merry edged back, her eyes narrowing. "It's nothing," she said firmly, the words wedging distance between them.

Shane found himself standing there alone, blinking in surprise. "Huh?"

"It's nothing. If you're okay with half now and half later, you've got a deal."

"Okay," he said. "Sure."

Merry smiled. "Perfect. Then get to work. What are you waiting for?"

Shane, charming smile still in place, found himself treated to the sight of Merry's ass as she walked away from him. Her hips swung. Her ass tipped side to side. He watched. By the time she disappeared around the corner of the little house she'd claimed, Shane found himself shaking his head and wondering what had just happened.

CHAPTER FOUR

"Ms. Kade, this is Levi Cannon. We have a bit of a situation."

Merry stood so quickly that her hair blew back. Phone clenched in a suddenly sweaty fist, she looked toward the makeshift parking area of Providence, then toward the saloon. How could they have found out so quickly? Maybe she could—

"Ms. Kade?"

"Yes. Hi, Mr. Cannon. What seems to be the problem?" The distant sound of boards being dropped filled up Merry's ears. She ducked inside the little house she used as a base, so panicked she didn't even look for spiderwebs first. One of them clung to her arm. She shook it like mad, swallowing her panicked cries.

"Mrs. Bishop—Kristen Bishop—came outside this morning to find that her mailbox had been destroyed."

Merry sucked in air so quickly that she choked on it and started coughing. The mailbox must've tipped over in last night's wind.

"Oh, don't worry. *Destroyed* was her word. A little further investigation revealed that it had only been pulled from the ground and left in the dirt. Not exactly mayhem."

"Right. I… That is…Mr. Cannon, I—"

"Kristen thinks it's an act of retaliation."

Merry snapped her mouth shut. Retaliation? She hadn't been *that* mad. And she'd tried not to convey any anger at all to the arguing seniors.

"Personally I think a drunk cowboy ran into it, but the Bishop house is damned isolated, so she might have a point. She thinks it's a warning."

Merry's throat finally unlocked. They didn't know it was her.

She drew in a deep breath. "I can't imagine that," she managed to say. "Maybe it was bored teenagers. Mailboxes. Baseball bats. It happens."

"It's a ways out of town for joyriding. And nothing like this ever happened before we hired you. I can't discount her suspicions."

Right. Nothing like that had happened before they hired Merry. That was for damn sure. She cringed and chewed her thumbnail. "But why retaliation? I'm sure it's nothing. I started two weeks ago, so the timing—"

"Oh, we just filed a new motion with the judge, letting her know that Providence is now actively being managed as a historic site. That was about a week ago, but it's possible the other side just found out about it. You can't think of anything else, can you? Maybe your work put you on their radar."

Merry cleared her throat and darted a look at Shane's truck. Had he told someone he was working for her? Just how pissed would the board be if she admitted that—? Wait a minute. She was buying into the conspiracy theory about mailbox destruction *she'd* committed.

"I can't think of anything. But listen, Mr. Cannon, if hiring me improves the visuals of this case, wouldn't moving forward with some of the renovations be even better?"

"Well… Yes, in theory. But we really hadn't planned for you to…um." His words, which had started out awkward and hesitant, died into pregnant silence. Her skin crawled with humiliation, but she forced herself to ignore that.

"I understand now that you may have hired me as more of a figurehead than a curator. I'm not saying I'm okay with that, and we'll have to have a different conversation about it later, but I *can* do this, Mr. Cannon. I may have only been at my previous position for a year, but I was a workhorse, and my superior was…" *As old as you.* "She was easing into retirement, so I carried a lot of responsibility." She took a breath.

"I've already sorted through the wood we have on hand here. I'm not going to go wild and head out to a lumber store for new pine and woodscrews. We'll use the original wood, and I even found a bucket of handmade nails. They're rusty, but I'll be sure that Sh— um…any contractor is up-to-date with tetanus shots, and I'm sure they use gloves, anyway, right? And when we run out of those nails, I found a place online that forges them."

When she finally stopped to catch her breath, Mr. Cannon sighed. "Merry, listen. I can tell how much you want to work, and I admire that, especially in someone your age, but we—"

"I just want a chance. *Please.* I need a chance. We could get this place up and running faster than you think. The house I use as a base of operations is totally safe. And the saloon only needs a little work. And the church! The church is beautiful. I'm brainstorming a brochure now and—"

"Work on the brochure," he interrupted, latching onto that idea with a sigh of relief. "Work on that, and I'll…I'll talk to the others about freeing up a little money. A *little*."

"Oh, my God. Thank you. Thank you!"

"I'm not promising anything! You just sit tight, okay?"

"Sure," she said, her face flushing with guilt.

"And work on a brochure. Holding something like that in their hands could help the board loosen up the purse strings a little."

"Thank you, Mr. Cannon. I'll get right on it."

Merry dragged her chair inside and sat at the beat-up old table Mr. Bishop must have moved in at some point. She'd found little clues like that all over the house, proof that Gideon Bishop had been using the house as an office, gathering up ideas for the ghost town. She'd only poked around gingerly before, too afraid of spiders to settle in, but the sunlight was too bright to do this kind of work outside, so Merry set her iPad on its stand, fired up her portable keyboard and got to work.

She worked so hard she nearly forgot entirely about Shane. She noticed when he stopped in that night to say he was leaving. And she vaguely noticed the next day when he came by around 5:00 p.m. to do a couple of hours of work. She even wandered out once or twice to be sure he was doing only the work they'd agreed on.

But she didn't go out to watch him hammer, or to marvel at the wide stretch of cloth across his shoulders or the tight wonder of his jeans. She didn't notice the way hair glinted on his strong forearms when he moved. She didn't notice any of that until he stopped by on the second night and delivered a moment of grace that hit her like a wave of lust.

"Don't worry about paying me for this now, all right? Catch me next month."

"What?" she asked, visions of the brochure fading from her eyes like a clearing fog. She repeated, "What?" in a breathless voice.

"It's okay. You seemed stressed out, and I don't want my bill to add to your stress."

"Oh, I can pay it. You don't have to—"

"Really, Merry. It's no problem."

Well, that was embarrassing. Just the sound of his mouth forming her name gave her goose bumps. Or maybe it was the effect of looking up at him as he stood so close to her. Those shoulders loomed above her. Those forearms flexed as he slipped off his hat and ran a hand through his hair. And this late in the day, his jaw was rough with stubble again. As he moved, she could actually smell him. The laundry detergent on his clothes, and another more intriguing scent: his skin, hot from the sun, a touch of sweat.

Shane cocked his head in question, and she realized she'd been staring up at him as if he was a work of art she wanted to study.

"You're really sweet, Shane."

"Ah. Not so much." His cheekbones flushed a little as his eyes shifted past her. "Is that for Providence?"

"Yes! But don't look yet." She covered the screen with her hand. "I'll finish the layout tonight and then I'll show you. Okay?"

He smiled. "Sure. Are you going to be here long? I hate to leave you out here alone this late."

Merry looked out the window to see startlingly long shadows stretching across the sagebrush.

"I'd feel better if you let me walk you out."

Now Merry was the one flushing. "Thank you, Shane. And thanks for coming out here at all. I know you already put in a full day. It means a lot that you're doing this for me."

He picked up the computer stuff as she turned it off. "It's nothing. No need to thank me."

God, he was so cute. No matter what he said about not being a real cowboy, he had that modest chivalry she associated with movie cowboys. And that steadiness. That self-possessed silence.

She snuck a look at him as they walked toward her car, noting how much taller he was than her. Four or five inches, maybe. She'd never been with a guy as tall as Shane was, but, then again, she'd never been with most types of guys. Two men did not make a control group.

Regardless, she was intrigued by him. His height and strength, the scarred hands and blunt fingers. What would it feel like to be held by him, to be taken? What would it feel like to be up against a wall with this man's body pressed against her? With those rough, strong hands sliding up her shirt? Would he—?

When he glanced at her, Merry almost melted in sheer embarrassment. They were friends. Maybe just acquaintances. If he knew she was having those kinds of thoughts about him, he'd likely recoil in horror and find a way to never be alone with her again.

"Everything all right?" he asked.

"Sure!" she chirped. "I'm excited." Excited. Right. "I mean…I can't wait to finish the brochure layout tonight!"

"Well, I can't wait to see it."

"Great!"

She was excited about the brochure. But she was also excited about something very different. Something she hadn't felt in a very long time. Hopefully the layout wouldn't be her best work of the night.

CHAPTER FIVE

"Oh, God, yes!" she gasped, holding the vibrator up in triumph.

She'd decided she needed it thirty minutes ago. Those thoughts of Shane hadn't gone away on the drive home. They hadn't even gone away when she'd tried to work on the brochure. She'd finally decided she needed to indulge her rediscovered lust and go for it while she was still in the mood.

So she'd texted Grace to be sure she was gone for the night. Then Merry had taken a quick shower. Poured a glass of wine. Gulped the wine down and poured herself another. The last step had been finding the vibrator. Three boxes later, and she had that little sucker in her hand.

"Thank God." She sighed before heading to the kitchen to dig for batteries. And finally, she was ready.

Amazingly she felt almost nervous. Had it really been that long since she'd touched herself? So long that she felt fucking *nervous?*

Well, now she was determined.

Merry unfolded her sofa bed, piled on the covers and slid beneath crisp sheets.

Shane was right next door. She'd heard his shower earlier, so Merry imagined him there, naked and wet,

God, he must be beautiful. Long and lean and hard. Hard *everywhere*. She'd love to touch him. Run her hands down his slick back. Dig her nail into his naked, taut ass. Press herself into him and stretch like a cat in heat while he—

Merry started and shook her head. No, even if the man were naked and in her shower right now, she could never just climb in there and start manhandling him. Not even in a fantasy. Because what she'd really do is screw up the courage to slip into the shower naked, and then she'd stand there awkwardly while he soaped himself. She'd probably crack a joke. Then make an excuse about how crowded it was and just slip away.

"Stop it," she muttered to herself, then slid deeper under the covers and shifted the fantasy around.

He'd been in the shower, yes. All soapy and wet and hard for her. But now he was out and drying off, and when he heard her knock, he slipped on a pair of jeans and answered the door in nothing but half-buttoned Levi's.

"I was just thinking about you," he said, giving her that dark, unreadable look he did so well.

Merry's heart sped just as it would have if her fantasy were real. She slipped her hands over her breasts and down her body, feeling nerves shiver to life as she imagined Shane pulling her into his apartment and pressing her to the wall. He put his mouth to her neck and whispered how much he'd been wanting her, how often he'd thought of her. His impatient hands slid beneath her clothes, inspiring nervous gasps that he took as agreement. His skin felt so good that she let herself fall into it. She let him touch her, kiss her, but when he started to push her shirt up and off her body, Merry hesitated.

"Shane, wait. I hardly know you. How can—"

"Please," he rasped. "I need this. I need you. Just once. Please, Merry. You've been driving me mad. I need to taste you."

Merry turned on the vibrator and gave herself up to the story, just as she gave herself up to his hands in her mind. His hands and mouth and fingers. Oh, God. Yes. His fingers teasing her, then slipping inside her. Driving her crazy until she felt just as mad as he did. Until she was murmuring *yes, yes* when he unbuttoned his jeans and freed his erection. He eased a hand beneath her knee and pulled her leg high as he positioned himself between her thighs.

"Please," Merry whispered into the empty room. "Please." She wanted that. Needed it. She slipped the toy farther along her body, sending delicious shivers racing to branches of nerves that hadn't stirred in so long. Oh, God, yes. This was going to feel so good, a need she'd ignored so long it had seemed extinct. But it was back now, and her hips strained forward as she eased the vibrator inside her body with a whimper of relief.

And then her world came crashing down. Or at the very least, her door sounded like it was about to crash in. Not that the knock was especially loud, but her senses were a little heightened. And the door was only three feet from her head. And she was lying there with her legs spread and a vibrator buzzing.

Merry froze, eyes wide in panic, hoping that if she didn't move, the wolf wouldn't spot her through the tall grass.

When the knock came again, she eased her finger over to turn off the vibrator, alarmed by how loud the silence was afterward. Had that buzzing sound filled the whole room? Had it been audible from the hallway? What if it had been—

"Merry, it's Shane. Are you home?"

Shane?

No. "Yes!" she yelped in complete panic, trying to bite back the word even as her body volunteered it. Her eyes slid over the blankets, noting the shape of her body beneath the covers, knees parted wide, arm disappearing beneath the cozy bedspread at a suspicious angle. Then her gaze moved to the door.

Oh, God.

"I was hoping to see the brochure. Can I come in?"

"Uh…" Merry finally forced her body to let go of its frozen panic and *move*. She pulled the vibrator out of herself with a wince of shock, snapped her legs closed and sat straight. "Uh, sure. Just give me a second." Why had she spoken? Why hadn't she just kept her mouth shut and let him leave?

Stupid blind panic. Merry shoved the vibrator under the covers and leaped out of bed to race to the bathroom where she'd left her clothes. "Idiot," she cursed herself at another misstep. She should have just said no. *No, I'm not dressed, I'll see you tomorrow.* Except not being dressed had been way too close to the truth: *I'm not dressed and I'm frigging myself three feet away from you. Sorry!*

She frantically pulled on her jeans and the yellow Doctor Who T-shirt she'd been wearing earlier, then raced back to the living room to yank the covers tight across the bed.

She took a deep breath, pasted a smile on her face and unlocked the door. "Hey!" she chirped as she opened it just enough to wedge herself between him and the room. "What's going on?"

"Hey." His answering smile tipped down a little at the edges. "Are you okay?"

"Sure! Yes. Absolutely. Why?"

"You just… Were you working out?"

"Yes, I was working out!" It was the perfect answer for the sweat prickling her hairline and her rapid breathing. But then his eyes traveled down her body to the jeans and bare feet. "Anyway!" She waved a hand.

"Well…I was thinking about you."

Merry flashed back to her fantasy so quickly that she felt dizzy. Was he about to grab her? Ravish her? Push her against the wall and slip off her shirt? Would she let him? "Me?" she finally breathed.

"All this work you're doing for Providence. I'll admit, it seemed silly at first. I can't say I understand it or even approve. But now that I'm working out there with you, I'm curious. May I…?"

He gestured toward the door, and Merry automatically opened it, cursing her natural Texas friendliness for digging her even deeper. She watched his gaze focus on the unfolded bed.

"Early night?"

Guilty embarrassment leached from wherever it was the body stored it— spleen? Appendix?—and suffused every cell in her body. "I like to work in bed." She ignored the fact that her pile of work stuff was still on the

kitchen table and grabbed the end of the fold-out bed to
flip it back into a couch.

Shane reached out to help, but she gave a mighty
heave and it folded with a wretched groan of springs...
followed immediately by an ominous rubbery thunk
when she tipped the bed up for its last fold.

Oh, shit. Oh, no. She glanced into the shadowy hol-
low of the couch and saw her pink vibrator lying there
on the hardwood like a giant finger of accusation pointing at her. *You were jerking off to naked thoughts of an
innocent friend. You secretly violated your nice neighbor!*

A noise of horror squeaked through her throat, and
she shoved the mattress down with so much force that
the couch slid two inches. Even though the mattress
obediently folded up, it wouldn't quite close all the way.
She remembered the blankets she'd piled on and gave
another desperate shove.

"I think it's stuck," Shane volunteered as she put all
her weight on it. "Here, let's pull it out again and—"

"No!" Why the hell had she picked out a fluorescent
pink toy? Why hadn't she gone with a nice tasteful...
beige? Or translucent! A vibrator that could blend into
its wild surroundings no matter where she was!

"It's fine," she grunted, bouncing her weight up on
her toes.

Shane's gaze went to her breasts and then away.

"This always happens," she finally said, and grabbed
one of the couch cushions. Shane grabbed the other,
then eyed the crooked hill they'd made with suspicion
as she picked up her iPad and plopped into an uncomfortable seat.

Luckily Shane's old-fashioned chivalry must have kicked in, because he just offered a puzzled smile and took a seat next to her, probably thinking that she was one of those stereotypically unhandy women. Fine. She'd perpetuate that prejudice, as long as he didn't realize just how handy she'd been a minute ago.

Her hands froze over the iPad screen just as he leaned closer to watch. The brochure bloomed to life in full color beneath her fingers, but all she could do was stare at her hands. Her guilty hands. The glowing screen drew Shane's attention like a spotlight to every digit that had acted out her dirtiest thoughts about *him*.

"Would you like a beer?" she squeaked, jumping up and dropping the iPad to the couch where it slid down the slope of the cushion before getting caught in the corner.

She didn't hear his answer; her heart was pounding too hard as she rushed to the sink and turned on the hot water. She tried to imagine how she'd feel if she went to a near stranger's house and found out he'd just been masturbating to dirty thoughts of her. Shuddering, Merry scrubbed her hands and regretted even considering getting her groove back.

This was the last straw. It was going to be the nunnery for her. Maybe she could find one in commuting distance.

SHANE KNEW THAT Merry was acting strangely. She was up to something, maybe something underhanded concerning Providence. He knew that, but he kept getting distracted by her breasts.

She'd always had breasts, obviously, but this time she

wasn't wearing a bra under her T-shirt, and unfettered breasts were an entirely different distraction.

They looked fucking perfect. So perfect he had the urge to blurt it out to her, just because it needed to be said. Her yellow T-shirt was so pale he thought he could see the faint darkness of her nipples beneath the fabric, but he was left wondering because the picture of a weird telephone booth on it interfered with the play of shadow and light. It teased him with the possibility. He kept watching in hopes of being more sure.

When she brought a bottle of beer he downed half of it quickly and told himself to stop being a creep. Not that that was possible. After all, he'd come over here with the sole intent of gathering information about the ghost town. That ridiculous ghost town. He felt bad that she was so damn enthusiastic about it, but what business was it of hers? She'd come here from Texas. The town was a lark for her. For him, it was a bad memory and now a serious nuisance. His grandfather had left him the burden of the Bishop land and none of the damned money. How was he supposed to pay tens of thousands of dollars of property tax every year? Shit, he could charge grazing fees to neighboring ranches, but the federal land higher up was a hell of a deal compared to what he'd need to charge.

All he really wanted to do was build a house on the land that had been passed to him. And he wanted to preserve that land. Not in a way that brought tourists *to* it, but in a way that kept them out.

Jesus, his ancestors hadn't founded Providence to attract strangers. They'd built a town in the middle of nowhere because they'd wanted it to be their own.

Not that he gave a damn about that. It was just another reminder that the men of his family ran. First, they'd run to Wyoming Territory, leaving behind whatever complications they hadn't wanted to deal with in Missouri. Then, after a little trouble with water, they'd left Providence behind, too, and moved on to greener pastures.

The habit hadn't died with the early twentieth century. His grandfather had been married three times. And Shane's father had taken running to a new level. One day, when Shane had been ten, his dad had kissed his wife goodbye, bought a trailer and disappeared with his girlfriend. Neither of them had ever been seen again, though the rumor was that they'd gone to Mexico to live on a beach. Shane suspected his dad had probably started a cattle ranch. He couldn't picture his dad on the beach, and ranch land had been cheap in those days.

Shane's younger brother had followed the pattern on the day he'd turned eighteen. He hadn't gone to Mexico, though. He'd gone east somewhere, though he hadn't been specific about his destination. He'd just…disappeared. After that betrayal, Shane had never bothered looking for him. If Alex wanted to be gone, he could stay gone.

Shane had stayed, but it had felt like a fragile truce with his life, even before all this.

When Merry said, "Okay," under her breath, he looked over to see that she'd drained half her beer, too. Her shoulders rose on a deep breath, and then she smiled at him and grabbed the iPad. "The brochure! You have to be honest, all right?"

"I'll be happy to be honest, but I don't know anything about this kind of stuff."

The front of the brochure appeared on the screen, the background a black-and-white shot of the long street, buildings marching down on either side of it. *The Town of Providence,* the title read. *Established 1884. Abandoned 1901.*

Even to him, the words were powerful, promising angst and drama, but it was nothing romantic to him.

Still, it was nicely done, and he told her so.

The next page was titled The History of Providence. He skimmed it, not needing to know more than he already did. On the third page was a picture of the saloon.

"Obviously I'll take a new picture when you're done with the work. It's going to be amazing, Shane. That building is so perfect. People love a saloon! Look how popular the Crooked R is."

"To be fair, that saloon still serves liquor."

"I know, but it's the possibility. The strangers that came through. The adventurers and outlaws."

Shane smiled, remembering his own childhood imaginings.

"And people are fascinated that their great-great-great-grandparents hung out in bars. They drank beer and whiskey. Maybe there were even prostitutes!"

He looked at the small, inset photograph of the saloon that was taken at the turn of the century. A man in an apron stood on the porch, a towel clutched in his hand. "I don't think my… I don't think the women of Providence were the prostitute type."

"I don't know." She stared at the far wall. "I'd bet there might have been a lonely widow or two who got tired of sleeping alone. Women have needs, too. And there were all those lonely cowboys."

"We still talking about Providence, Merry?" he asked.

She choked on laughter and smacked his arm. He tried not to look at the bounce of her breasts under the T-shirt. She wasn't that kind of girl. She was goofy friend Merry Kade, who didn't even realize that the press of her hard nipples against cotton could drive a man to distraction or she'd go put on a damn sweater.

"So you started this job when I wasn't in Jackson. When did they bring you in?"

"I'd been watching job listings for the area. I've missed being near Grace and it's so beautiful here. It just felt right when I visited, you know?"

He'd heard so many compliments about Jackson Hole over the years that he just nodded absently. It was beautiful, yes, but beneath the surface, it was no different than any other place, as far as he could tell.

"When I found this ad, I thought it was perfect. I had a little experience, and I thought I could really make a difference. I thought…"

"You thought what?"

Her brow tightened. "I thought I'd truly be needed."

"But you are, aren't you?"

"I don't know, Shane. I mean, I feel like I'm needed. But it turns out…"

Shane leaned forward, his eyes never leaving her face, even though she didn't look at him. "What is it?"

"I don't want to tell you."

"Come on. What is it?"

She finished her beer and set it so carefully on the

table next to her that it didn't make even the tiniest clink against the stone coaster. "Apparently there's some sort of probate fight. Something to do with Gideon Bishop's heir. I think they only brought me in as a symbol. Something to help fight the case. They don't actually want me doing the work."

Shane didn't say a word. He didn't even dare to breathe. On one hand, this was crucial information. Important news he could take to his attorney. Merry was only being used to weaken Shane's case.

On the other hand, she looked devastated, and he wasn't a monster. She blinked hard, as if she were holding back tears. "Hey," he whispered. "It's okay. I'm sure that's not true."

"I'm pretty sure it is."

"But…" He couldn't think of anything to comfort her. There certainly weren't any honest words he could give. After all, his future lay in the promise that Providence *wouldn't* happen. That it would continue to be nothing more than dead wood and tumbleweeds. But Merry had something to prove now.

Shit.

"I'm sorry they brought you here under false circumstances, but you're doing a good job, regardless. The brochure looks great."

"Right. And I was smart enough to hire you."

The watery smile she aimed in his direction was like a twisting knife in his gut. Hiring him could, in fact, get her fired. But only if the board found out.

"Look, I admire your enthusiasm for this. And whatever is going on with the board isn't your fault. Why don't you consider my work on the saloon a gift."

"No! I didn't tell you that to make you feel sorry for me. You deserve to be paid. I'll win them over."

Not by tossing his name around, she wouldn't. "I'll call it pro bono work. Giving something back to the community." Or just helping himself.

"I can't ask you to do that."

"You didn't ask."

Now there were definitely tears in her eyes. "I can't…"

"Come on, Merry. We're neighbors. It's no big deal."

But apparently it was a big deal to her. She threw her arms around his neck and hugged him tight. Shane felt schizophrenic; half of his brain registering the soft, warm press of her breasts to his chest, the other half telling him he was a selfish, lying asshole and she was going to regret any kind feelings she had for him.

But when he settled his hands on her back, the more noble thoughts disappeared, because damn, she was warm and nice under his touch. The cotton was a smooth expanse of heat, reinforcing his knowledge that she was naked beneath this thin fabric. And fuck, she smelled delicious. Like fresh soap and some spicy, feminine scent that made him feel a little dizzy. Dizzy and…hard.

Damn.

He pulled back and cleared his throat, hoping like hell she wouldn't notice the uncomfortable tightness of his jeans.

"Thank you, Shane," she said, sniffing back tears while he tried to keep his eyes off her breasts.

"You're welcome."

"Want another beer?"

He said yes in the hopes that his dick would give up its vigil by the time she came back, but he took the beer happily enough when she returned with it.

"Did you grow up here?" she asked as she plopped back into her crooked seat. He forced his eyes to stay on her face.

"I did. Did you grow up in Texas?" he asked, changing the focus. He never liked talking about his family, but especially in this case, it was a topic best left alone.

"Kind of. My mom is a bit of a hippie. She was raised in a tiny town in Northern California. I was born there, and we lived in a few different places while I was growing up. But I spent the last ten years of my childhood in Texas."

"And your dad?"

"Never met him," she said cheerfully. "It was just me and my mom."

"I'm sorry."

"Oh, no big deal. I think I was better off than my friends who had asshole fathers, you know? I was scared of dads when I was young. They always seemed to be yelling about something."

Shane considered her theory. His dad had been pretty decent, though obviously flawed, but maybe he and Alex would've been better off if their father had never even been around. Maybe it would've been better than thinking your dad loved you until you woke up one day to realize he didn't give a shit after all. At least Merry could tell herself her dad's disappearance had nothing to do with her. But Shane had been left to wonder.

"So your mom was a hippie. That's how you got the name Merry?"

"Of course. When I was born, she looked into my eyes and said she could tell I was a happy soul."

"You are."

"I suppose I am," she said so cheerfully that Shane chuckled. "It would've been so awkward if I wasn't."

Shane thought of Grace and the way she fought hard against her moniker, but he didn't point that out to Merry. "So you had a happy life."

"Oh, you know. You make the best of things."

"What things?"

She waved her beer dismissively. "Tough times. Bad neighborhoods. But you learn to make friends with everyone, and any place can be a home. My mom is great, though. She worked so hard to make our life better."

Suddenly Shane had a completely different take on this girl. She seemed carefree and goofy and sheltered. But now he couldn't help but read between the lines. No dad around. A single mom who probably had to work one or two jobs at a time to put food on the table. And Merry trying to find her way.

"I've never lived anywhere but here," he said. "I can't imagine."

"It's different, living in a big city. I can't deny that. But people are all the same, really. There's good and bad everywhere. But considering that people are all the same, I have to say that the scenery is pretty damn awesome here. There's really no reason for you to go anywhere else."

"That's a relief. I can't say I'm inclined to."

"How did you become a carpenter? Was your dad a carpenter?"

"No, my uncle was. I started working with him when

I was twelve." His dad had been a horse trainer and rancher, but Shane left that off.

"Hey, I got my first job at twelve, too! A taco joint."

"You can work in a restaurant at twelve?"

"You can if you've just hit a growth spurt and they pay you cash under the table. I was so excited to have spending money, I don't even think I kept track of how much they paid me. Three dollars an hour, probably. One of the perks of hiring child laborers."

"Well, you were smarter than I was. My uncle figured I was earning an education. I didn't get paid anything. But that's typical for rural kids. You work the farm or ranch for the privilege of learning the life."

"That's so cool."

Shane smiled. "It's pretty damn boring, actually. Hanging around leathery old men all day. It can be torturous when you're a teenager and there are never any girls around. The ones that are nearby are all mooning for the guys on the junior rodeo circuit."

Merry gasped. "You did that, didn't you?"

"Did what?"

She pointed a finger at his chest. "You did rodeo stuff. You saw all the girls paying attention to those boys and you joined the rodeo, didn't you?"

Shane laughed. Hard. "First off, you don't join the rodeo like you join the circus. But…yes, I may have tried a little calf roping in my day."

"See, you are a cowboy!" She poked him, then her gaze drifted down to his chest, and she poked him one more time as if she were testing his give. She drew her hand back slowly.

"You wouldn't say that if you saw how badly I lost to

the real cowhands. And I discovered that it wasn't just being a rodeo cowboy that got you attention from girls, but actually doing well at it. Rodeo losers are no different than other losers. Although...if you get injured, there are some girls who like playing nurse."

"Oh, my God! Dirty!"

Something about her saying the word *dirty* was sexy as all hell. It didn't help that his brain had flashed through a quick and happy dance down memory lane of his first kisses and teenage groping. Now he imagined making out with her, right here on her uncomfortable couch. Daring to move closer. Hoping she wouldn't stop him.

He was staring at her, tempted as all hell to taste her, when he heard the faint trill of his phone ringing across the hall. He knew immediately who it was: his mother. Only one person called there. Everyone else called on his cell, but Shane had refused to give her that number. When she got a bug up her ass, she'd call incessantly, and she must have one now, because this was the third call since this afternoon.

Merry was watching him. He liked her eyes, always slightly turned up at the edges in a smile. And her mouth, wide and pink and tempting even when he shouldn't be tempted.

He leaned back into the sofa and finished his beer.

He didn't want to go home. He didn't want to leave. But he shouldn't want to kiss her, regardless. Merry was a nice girl. And he was a man no one needed to be around. Not for longer than a night. He'd learned that lesson. He knew who he was.

Merry Kade was not the kind of girl he could sleep

with and then make a polite and permanent exit from her life. First of all, because she very obviously wasn't the one-night-stand type. In fact, she seemed inclined to make friends with anyone who came within earshot, as far as he could tell. Second, because Grace would likely castrate him if he used her friend for sex, and Cole might happily hold him down to help his girlfriend out. Third, and perhaps most important, was the fact that she lived next door. Not exactly a comfortable situation even with the most open-minded of women. He'd had long-term "friends" who were happy with nothing more than casual sex, but neither he nor they had ever flaunted other lovers in each other's faces. Not cool.

Close proximity had never come up as a problem in the past, since no women had lived in the building. He was going to have to add it to his off-limit list.

"So are you saying you never did anything stupid to get attention from boys?" he finally asked.

Merry yelped with laughter. "Me? Boys never noticed me! I was tall and awkward and into *Star Wars* and video games."

"But boys love *Star Wars.*"

"Strangely, that love isn't transferrable. Unless you're the kind of girl who likes to dress up as the Jabba the Hut slave version of Princess Leia."

Oh, yeah. He'd never been that into *Star Wars,* but he sure remembered that scene.

"So…just to be clear…you never dressed up like that?"

"Shane!"

"Maybe just once? For a Halloween party when you were eighteen? Work with me here."

"Good God, it even infected cowboys in the wilds of Wyoming."

"Hey, we had satellite dishes and VCRs. And active fantasy lives."

Merry groaned. "No, I only dressed up as Princess Leia once, and that was the kick-ass rebel fighter Leia."

"I have no idea what you're talking about."

"Figures," she sighed, then shook her head in disgust. "Wait a minute. Have you ever seen *Firefly?*"

"No. Is that a *Star Trek* thing?"

"Star Wars," she muttered. "And no. It's a completely awesome sci-fi series that's like an epic space Western. You have to watch it. Have to!"

"Okay."

"Seriously. We'll rent the first episode one night, okay? Please?"

Shane found himself grinning wildly at her, but told himself it was probably just the beer. "Let's do that."

He liked this girl. Really liked her, which settled the issue. He couldn't touch her. And he definitely couldn't sleep with her. Not unless he wanted to live with the sure chance that at some point in the future she'd hate his guts. Even without the complication of the lawsuit, it always ended the same for him.

He couldn't commit. Women tried to accept that, but eventually they left and made clear that he was an asshole and an immature prick. He was. There was no denying his genes.

Shane dropped his head. "Next time, let's do that."

Reluctantly he stood and set his empty beer bottle down. "I'd better go. I've got an early start tomorrow, but I'll try to get to Providence in the evening."

"Don't wear yourself out. I feel guilty enough as it is."

"It's not a problem," he said. And the strange thing was…it wasn't. His goal was to make sure that Providence was never anything more than its current state: a forgotten ghost town remembered only by a few old-timers. But somehow being out there with Merry was the most relaxing thing he did all day. Knowing she was close by, even when he couldn't see her…he liked that. He'd like it even more if she came by and bothered him as much as he'd expected her to.

"I'll see you tomorrow, Merry."

"Night, Shane."

He closed the door behind him and waited to hear her lock it. Somehow the world was heavier out here, and the weight only got worse as he walked the few steps to his door.

Hearing the beep from his answering machine as soon as he stepped in, Shane grabbed the phone in resignation and called his mother.

"Mom, it's late," he said without greeting her. "I have to get up early tomorrow."

"I know, hon, but it's important."

"Is everything okay?"

"Well, you know. As okay as it ever gets. But listen to this new story I found."

"Just—" he interrupted, then paused to take a deep breath so he wouldn't lose his temper with her. "Mom, please. It's the internet. I've explained before that—"

"Yes, yes. You can't believe everything you read on the internet. But that doesn't mean some of it's not true."

He couldn't argue with that, unfortunately. He couldn't, but he'd tried plenty of times.

"Listen! 'A sixty-five-year-old man whom locals in Guyana call The Gringo is rumored to be an American man who appeared without any identification in 1998, claiming to have no memory of who he was or where he'd come from. The man—'"

"Dad left years before that."

"I know! But what if he'd just been wandering? What if—?"

"Mom!" he snapped. "Dad left and he didn't want to be found, end of story. I'm not having this conversation with you anymore."

"But, honey, he would never have done that. Never. Not to you boys and not to me."

Shane ground his teeth together because he didn't want to say the cruel things that were piling up in his throat. *Dad was having an affair. He had a girlfriend. He bought a trailer and hooked it to his truck and he left with her. He didn't love you or give a shit about any of us. He wanted a place where we didn't exist.*

But he choked it down and swallowed hard. "No one ever found his truck or the trailer. If he'd been hurt or suffering from amnesia—of all the ridiculous things I've ever heard—someone would've reported an abandoned truck to the police."

"Or they might have seen a free truck sitting next to the road and stolen it!"

Shane couldn't count the number of times they'd had this exact conversation. "It would've turned up at some point, Mom." He sighed. "Someone somewhere would've run the VIN at some point, and we would've heard. He ran off, he disappeared, he made a new life. And at some point he died, or he's dead enough according to the state of Wyoming." He'd been declared dead ten years ago and good riddance to all the ridiculous problems the man had caused with paperwork and taxes and every other damn thing he'd walked away from.

"But, Shane, just listen to the rest of the—"

"I've got to get up early. Take care." He hung up, not feeling even a twinge of guilt. He'd done it too many times to feel that anymore.

When he'd been a kid, his mom's wild imaginings and excuses and explanations had kept him hoping. He'd believed her and she'd strung him along for years. At the drop of a hat, she'd pull him and his brother out of school and pack them into the car to drive hundreds of miles because of some rumor.

Alex had been pissed off from the start, raging that he never wanted to see their dad again even if they did find him. But Shane… He'd held on to his love for too many years and had only opened his eyes on the day Alex himself had skipped town, leaving nothing but a terse note. Alex had been right the whole time. Dad wasn't coming back. The man had walked away and ruined his family without even a second thought.

At nineteen, Shane had legally changed his name to his mother's maiden name. He'd cut off his dad's family entirely, which hadn't exactly been difficult. The only one left was his grandfather and stepgrandmother, neither of whom had ever been warm or supportive. Hell, the old man had even screwed Shane over in the end.

Shit.

Shane hadn't planned the lawsuit. Hadn't even

wanted it at first. But the provisions for the creation of
the Providence Historical Trust had been a last minute
addition before Gideon Bishop's death, and Shane's lawyer had said he'd be a fool not to demand the money that
should've gone with the land. He knew Gideon Bishop
had created the trust out of spite. The man had told
Shane as much when he'd refused to change his name
back to Bishop. But when Shane had realized that the
trust involved creating a tourist trap on his land, and
what a fucking waste that would be, Shane had gone all
in. Screw it. Everything had been meant to go to his father, the last living descendant of that generation. And
from there to Shane and Alex.

He was fighting his grandfather's will. He was getting what was rightfully his. And he couldn't let it matter to him whether he liked Merry or not.

CHAPTER SIX

"No," MERRY BREATHED, eyes wide and heart pounding. She stared at a spider poised on the ceiling of the small room, but the horror of the spider didn't come close to the words her mother had just spoken. In fact, Merry didn't even run from the room. The spider crawled toward a fly caught in its web, and Merry just stood there and listened to her mother chatter in her ear.

"Mom. Wait. Please tell me you didn't say what you just said."

"What do you mean, sweetheart?"

"Crystal," she whispered, hoping her mom would laugh and ask where in the world she'd gotten that. But that's not what happened.

"She'll be there tonight! Not to stay with you, of course."

Of course. Crystal didn't stay with relatives when she traveled. She stayed in avant-garde hotels with espresso machines in the rooms and turndown service.

"She doesn't want to see me, does she?" Merry asked past clenched teeth.

"Of course she does! Honey, it'll be fine."

Merry took a deep breath and closed her eyes. Maybe it would be fine. As far as Crystal was concerned, Merry had a good job and she was living in a beautiful place. She didn't know that it was all a lie. "She's not so bad," her mom said in a familiar, admonishing tone. "And we don't have enough family that you can pick and choose."

God, Merry had been hearing that since she was a kid. But her mom was right. Crystal wasn't so bad. Her perfect glow just put all of Merry's shortcomings in a spotlight…that she went to the trouble of aiming into Merry's eyes whenever she got the chance.

"How's it going there, sweetie?"

"Great!" she said too brightly. She opened her eyes to find she'd lost track of the spider and now she couldn't see it. Merry backed slowly out onto the porch. "It's great, Mom. Really busy but fun."

"The pictures you send are so pretty. And they make me miss you so much. And how's Grace doing?"

"Well, let's see, she's got a super hot cowboy boyfriend who carries her off to his ranch house nearly every night. She seems pretty good."

"I'm going to have to come out there just to see that."

"You should, Mom. I miss you." She swallowed her sudden tears and changed the subject. "How are you, Mom?"

"Great!"

"Are you seeing anyone yet?" This was an old conversation between them. Her mom had rarely dated when Merry was growing up and nothing seemed to have changed since then. Merry sighed at the silence. "Come on, Mom. You have to try."

"Oh, I don't know."

"I feel like you gave up dating for my sake, and I want you to meet someone. There's probably someone in your life right now if you'd just open your eyes. You have so many friends. Everyone likes you. I thought your new neighbor seemed interested."

"Who, Charles?" She laughed. "Oh, my gosh, no."

"Then who?"

Her mom stayed quiet for a long time before she finally cleared her throat. "It's just… It's hard, Merry."

"I know." She sighed. Maybe being terrible at dating was a genetic trait. "I'd just like to see a man in your life, Mom. I didn't need a dad, and I know you don't *need* a husband, but I used to imagine that someday you'd fall in love with a big strong guy. Someone who could fix things around the house and mow the lawn and get stuff off the top shelf, not because you can't, but because you deserve a break. Don't you want that?"

"Oh, Merry." She sighed, her voice sounding a little shaky. "I don't know what to say to that. I wish I could've given you that when you were a little girl. A nuclear family. The American dream."

"I didn't need that."

"When you were little, you used to make your Barbie and Ken get married every day."

"I did not!"

"Yes, you did. I'd hear voices in your room, and I'd go listen to you act it out. And the boy doll would…" Her voice cracked before she could speak again. "Ken would always say, 'You and your little girl don't need to worry anymore, sweetheart. I'll take care of you now.'"

Merry pressed a hand to her parted lips. "No." She shook her head in horrified shock. "I did not."

"Yes, you did. And I would try to make myself imagine that I could meet someone and give you a family, but I just…I couldn't. I don't know why. I wanted to, for you."

"Oh, Mom, no. I didn't need that. I must have been really small, because I don't remember even playing with Barbies."

"You gave them up when you discovered *Star Wars*. Well, you didn't give them up. You made them play Princess Leia and Han Solo and then there was a tragic crash onto an ice planet pond that wasn't quite frozen, and they were lost forever."

Merry laughed past the tears that thickened her throat. "I remember that!"

"It was big news in the neighborhood. You told everybody you saw. You were so excited."

They were both laughing now, thank God. Merry sighed. "I remember after that you saved up and bought me action figures."

"You were a good girl. You deserved them."

"I feel the same way about you and dating."

"Oh, let's forget that. I don't need a date. I'm wonderful. I was only calling to let you know about your cousin."

Jesus, Merry had forgotten for a moment, and she groaned in remembered dread. Her mom offered yet another scolding about appreciating your family, but as soon as they said goodbye, Merry called Grace.

"Can I pretend your apartment is mine?" she asked without explanation.

Grace didn't hesitate. "Sure. Anytime."

"Thank God." She dropped into a chair on the porch and groaned. "Crystal is coming tomorrow."

"Why?" Grace had met Crystal one time and they'd

taken an instant dislike to each other. Merry had been secretly thrilled.

"Ugh, I don't know. She's going mountain climbing or something amazing like that. She probably just found out I was living here and wants to show off."

"And you want to use *my* place to impress her?"

"I just don't want her to know that I'm sleeping on a couch or that I'm—" Merry snapped her mouth shut. She hadn't said a word about her trouble with the board to Grace. It was too embarrassing, and Grace would get really outraged and possibly violent, and Merry didn't want to upset her when everything was going so well with Cole.

"Will you do my makeup tonight?"

"Hell, yes. And then I'll clear out. You can have my place, and I'll get to spend the evening away from Crystal."

"Good. You can't afford to be arrested twice in one calendar year."

Grace snorted. "Be nice or I'll make you look like a cheap prostitute."

"I wish." She hung up and slumped into the chair to glare out at the clouds hanging above the hills. "Damn it." The only good news was that Crystal probably had plenty of wealthy, glamorous friends to hang out with in Jackson. She'd be too busy to bother Merry much. But this was going to be one painful night. And another night she wouldn't be able to get herself off.

After Shane had left last night, she'd been too morti-fied and guilt-ridden to even try. She'd just shoved her vibrator deep into the box it had come from, thinking to herself that she'd never need it again. But then on the drive to work, she'd found herself daydreaming about Providence in a way she never had before. Not about the buildings or its past or the brochure she'd worked so hard on. Instead she'd thought about working late with Shane. In the last cloying rays of the sun, he'd gotten hot and stripped off his shirt, seeming unconcerned that she was standing only a few feet away. She'd watched, of course, and he'd glanced up and caught her looking. Instead of embarrassment, anger had flashed over his face. Merry had taken a step back, but he followed.

"I always catch you looking, but you never touch," he'd growled.

God, she wanted to touch. She did. She wanted to touch him everywhere and not be the least bit hesitant. She wanted to stroke him. Squeeze him. Taste his skin. In real life, she'd never have the nerve, but in her fantasies, she could have him any way she wanted. He'd never find out, would he?

And as she'd driven, she'd decided to give herself another try. He couldn't possibly interrupt again, and she needed it. She was tense. Stressed. She deserved a little guilty pleasure.

But instead of getting off to thoughts of Cole unbuttoning his jeans for her impatient hands, she'd get to walk through a minefield of conversation with Crystal.

Despite that she was almost done with her rough mock-up of the brochure, Merry felt suddenly hopeless. If she were smart and ambitious and full of self worth, she'd turn in her notice and move on. She'd tell those old bastards to stick it where the sun doesn't shine.

But that wasn't her, and plus…she didn't want to leave. As sad is it was to be only half-wanted, she loved it here. She was going to make this work, and she was awesome enough to deal with Crystal for a couple of hours. After all, even Crystal must have bad days occasionally. She wasn't perfect.

"It'll be fine," Merry said aloud, repeating her mother's words to herself. Yes. It would be fine.

CHAPTER SEVEN

"Merry!" her cousin exclaimed in an ingratiatingly kind voice. "It's so wonderful to see you!"

"Hi, Crystal." Just opening the door had been a blow. Crystal had bleached her dark blond hair to a sleek platinum bob. She looked amazing. Slim and tall and stylish. She wore a sleeveless linen dress and coffee-colored heels. Merry felt clumsy and lumbering in comparison as she stepped back and waved Crystal in.

But at least Grace had helped her clean up. Merry still wore jeans and black and pink sneakers, only because Grace's cute boots were too tiny to stuff onto her feet. But Grace had forced her out of a T-shirt and into a tight black tank top that looked almost elegant when paired with the thick rope of silver that Grace had looped around Merry's neck.

She glanced down at the glinting metal and told herself to feel confidence.

"You look amazing," Merry made herself say. "I love the hair."

"Thank you, darling. And you. Love the shoes."

The words sounded completely sincere. Merry knew they weren't, but her cousin was never sarcastic enough to be called on it. Ever. The woman was smart, and if

Merry's mom had been watching, she'd say, "But honey! She said she loved your shoes!"

"Is this your place?" Crystal asked, making a slow turn on her beautiful spike heels.

"It is!" Merry thought the apartment was beautiful, with its old hardwood floors and dark woodwork and windows open to the evening. Aspen trees whispered in the breeze that snuck past the white curtains, and she could hear the occasional laughter of kids playing in the front yard across the street.

But from her expression, she could tell that Crystal saw the old couch and the tiny kitchen and the walls that didn't display beautiful artwork. "Well, the town is gorgeous. You're so lucky to live here."

"Thank you. Would you like to walk into town and get dinner?"

"Oh, I never eat after six." She ran a hand down her nonexistent abdomen.

"Right. A drink, then? There's a place right next door."

"Perfect. But don't you want to give me the tour first?"

Merry made herself smile brightly. "This is it! Living room, kitchen, there's the bedroom. Great light here, huh? Are you still in Chicago?"

"I am. I love living downtown. Everything I could ever want is right there."

"Except rock climbing?"

"Oh, it's just a little sport climbing." She waved a hand. "Jake took it up at the gym and convinced me to try it. Our best friends have a little villa up on Teton

Mountain, and they're letting us use it, so we've come out to give it a try on real rock."

"Sounds fun." It did, honestly. A few days at a gorgeous mountain lodge. An exciting new hobby.

She led Crystal outside and started across the lawn before she remembered the heels. "Sorry," she murmured, cutting back to the sidewalk.

"It's really a saloon?" Crystal asked. "I thought it was actually a little gift shop or something."

"No, it's a saloon." Country music blared out when someone opened a door and Crystal's eyes widened with a little trepidation.

"Come on. It's fun. I know the owner." Merry was also scared to death of the owner, but she left that out. "And the bartender, if Jenny's working tonight."

She didn't see Jenny when they walked in, but the place was packed with cowboys. Several of their heads turned, and a few of those actually took off their hats and smoothed their hair down at the sight of Crystal. She looked fantastically out of place in her cool cream linen, and Merry would have been squirming with discomfort if she'd been the one wearing it, but Crystal just swept a serene gaze over the room.

Merry didn't see an empty table, but when they headed to the bar, two cowboys stood up in their path and waved a hand at the table. "Ma'am," the closest one said to Crystal.

Merry was in the middle of declining the kind offer when Crystal interrupted with an easy thank-you and took a seat.

"Oh." Merry stood there and stared at the men. "Well…" She had no choice but to sit, as well.

No one had ever sacrificed his table for her when she was on her own. Things worked differently for beautiful women who looked as if their very presence was a gift to you.

Crystal gingerly swiped at the table with the side of her hand before setting her clutch purse on the table. "I'm so glad I was able to stop by and see you, Merry. How are you?"

"Wonderful!"

"So your mom told me you're working in a little ghost town?"

Merry knew for a fact that wasn't what her mom had said. "I'm the curator of a beautiful little town called Providence. It's currently under restoration and I'm hoping to get it open to the public soon."

"Wow. Pretty impressive for the Merry Slacker."

"Yeah. Thanks a lot." She was saved from having to say more when she spotted Jenny pop up from behind the bar. "Oh, there's Jenny! She's the blonde in the apron. I don't see Rayleen, but—"

"Looking for me, Christmas?" a voice growled from directly behind her.

Merry jumped and bit back a yelp of fear. Rayleen was scary as hell even when she wasn't sneaking up from behind.

"Hey," Rayleen said when Merry turned around. "I see Grace helped you out with your makeup. You look nice for once."

Merry grimaced. "Crystal, this is Rayleen Kisler, she's Grace's great-aunt. Rayleen, this is my cousin Crystal Waterton."

"Pleased to meet you," Crystal said. "Is Grace here?" She looked around with more than a little nervousness.

"Nah," Rayleen said. "She's probably off riding that stallion of hers. It's her only hobby, far as I can tell."

Crystal's perfectly plucked eyebrows rose. "I can't imagine Grace on a horse."

Merry choked and shook her head. "She's talking about Grace's boyfriend."

"Oh." Crystal's confusion turned to a distasteful frown as Rayleen howled with laughter.

"Look at that face!" Rayleen crowed. "Christmas, I never thought you'd have a cousin with a stick up her ass."

Much as she hated being called Christmas, Merry almost laughed at that. Crystal did have a stick up her ass. So did Crystal's mom. Merry had never been able to understand how her mother and her aunt could be sisters raised in the same household. It made no sense.

Then again, they'd come from a very poor family. Merry's mom had learned how to work hard and persevere. Crystal's mom had been ambitious and determined never to be poor again. They'd taken different paths with their similar strengths. But they'd come from the same place, so they had that in common. Merry and Crystal, on the other hand...

Merry slapped her hands together and stood. "I'll grab some drinks from the bar! What would you like?"

"Gin and tonic, please." She arched a look toward the bar. "See if they have Hendricks at least."

Rayleen snorted and walked away, muttering something that sounded suspiciously like "prissy bitch" under her breath. Merry pretended that she hadn't heard, but

Crystal's tight look caused her forehead to wrinkle. Must be time for more Botox.

"God, Jenny," she groaned when she got to the bar. "Make me something strong. I don't care what it is, as long as I can get it down fast."

"Hmm. Cosmo strong or something more substantial like a Long Island Tea?"

"Yes, the tea. Hit me."

The blonde laughed as she pulled a glass from beneath the bar. "And your friend?"

"She's not my friend. She's my cousin Crystal, and she wants a gin and tonic with the fanciest gin you've got."

"Whatever you say." She held three bottles and tipped them all over Merry's glass at the same time. "So you seem a little stressed."

"God, you think so? My bitchy cousin showed up to visit, I'm freaked out about work and I haven't had an or—" An alarm flashed in her head just in time. Or not just in time.

Jenny raised one eyebrow. "Been a while?"

"God, you have no idea."

"Oh, I had a bit of a dry spell myself. But that's over now. Yours will be soon, too."

Merry was damn sure the sweet, funny blonde had never had a dry spell that lasted any longer than she wanted it to, and now she had a cute cop for a boyfriend. Merry told herself not to feel jealous. It didn't help, but the drink would.

"Thank you!" she said when Jenny popped a maraschino cherry in the glass and handed it over. The first swallow tasted strong, but the second was much smoother. The third went down like silk. "Bless you, woman."

"And the fancy gin and tonic."

Wincing at the loss, Merry slid over a twenty. Jenny pushed back a ten. "Yours is on the house. With my sympathies."

"You're the best, Jenny."

"Anytime."

Merry felt so much more relaxed as she wove her way back to the table. Relaxed and maybe even willing to stand up for herself. "Don't call me the Merry Slacker anymore," she said as she sat back down.

"Fine." Crystal didn't look obnoxiously friendly now, just obnoxious. "Tell your friends to stop calling me names."

"Stop acting like you're better than this place."

Crystal smirked. "It's not an act."

Merry close her eyes and took a long draw of her drink through the tiny red straw. Then she sighed. "Why did you come here, Crystal?"

"I came to rock climb."

"And just be generally rich?"

"Look, I'm sorry if you have a chip on your shoulder, Merry, but I'm doing well. It's a good time to be a lawyer in Chicago. Do you want me to apologize?"

No. No, but Crystal's success made Merry feel like shit, and sometimes she couldn't tell if Crystal intended it to or if it was all in Merry's head. The paranoia drove her to distraction whenever her cousins were around. "Why did you want to see me?"

There it was. That arrogant glint in her eyes. That flash before she said something really—

"You're my cousin, Merry. I worry about you. I know how hard it can be for you to find your footing sometimes, and I wanted to be sure you were…okay."

"I don't have trouble finding my footing," Merry said, sinking lower in her seat to get more comfortable while she stared into her disappearing drink. "I like to take chances. I like new experiences. There's nothing wrong with that."

"No, there's not. As long as you're happy."

"Exactly," Merry snapped, as if she weren't sleeping on a pull-out couch in her best friend's living room. As if she weren't actually a glorified temp worker.

"Great!" Crystal patted her hand. "I'm glad you've finally found a good situation."

Yes. *Finally.* As if Merry had stumbled over a lucky coin in the dirt. "Well." She set down her empty drink. "It's been great catching up, but you should probably get back to the villa."

Crystal looked shocked. Merry was usually more timid around her, afraid to push back out of fear that Crystal would point out just how inferior she was. The problem wasn't her pointing it out, of course. The problem was that Merry found herself believing it.

Not anymore. She couldn't do it anymore.

"Merry—" Crystal started, but Merry cut her off.

"I'm sorry, Crystal. I'm tired. I'm starting this place from scratch and it's a lot of work. Let's just leave it at that."

Crystal set down her drink with a shrug. "Whatever you say. I'll tell my mom I did my duty."

"Perfect."

On their way out, Merry already felt guilty. She was

no good at being mean to people. It felt awful, and she worried that Crystal might actually have feelings and that Merry had hurt them.

"I do hope you have a great trip, Crystal," she said over her shoulder. "The rock climbing sounds amazing."

Crystal said something back, but Merry didn't hear her, because she was just registering that Shane's truck was parked at the curb ahead, and he was walking around the bumper.

Oh, shit. She didn't want him to see Crystal.

But of course, he wasn't blind, and he looked up and caught sight of Merry just as he stepped onto the sidewalk. "Hey! I was just coming to knock on your door. I thought I'd see you on-site tonight."

"Sorry, I…"

His eyes slid past her and locked on Crystal.

"My cousin's in town," she said quietly. "Shane, Crystal. Crystal, this is Shane."

"Pleasure to meet you, ma'am."

"The pleasure's all mine," she purred.

God. He was probably eating this up. Platinum-blonde beauty with a husky voice. Merry hated that she was standing right next to her. "Thanks again for coming, Crystal."

Her cousin smiled at Shane as she walked past him, but she left without another word to Merry. Shane watched her go, of course.

When he turned back to Merry, he frowned. "You okay?"

She realized she'd poked her lip out in a pout. Apparently alcohol did not make for a great poker face.

When she nodded, Shane shoved his hands in his

pockets and rocked back on his heels. "So I found that show you told me about. I downloaded the first two episodes. I thought we could order a pizza. But you're all dressed up, so maybe you've got other plans."

"Are you kidding?" Keeping with the theme of not hiding her emotions, Merry clapped and squealed like a five-year-old presented with a princess dress. "I'd love to. Just let me—" She dragged a hand over the silver rope around her neck, meaning to say "get this stuff off," but his eyes followed the slow slide of her hand, and Merry immediately changed her mind. She wasn't exactly comfortable in jewelry and makeup, but she always felt some level of awkwardness around men. Better to feel the I'm-too-sparkly kind.

"Sure." He finally focused on her face again. "I need to take a shower, so maybe in fifteen?"

They walked into the Stud Farm together, and Merry gave him an enthusiastic wave just before she closed her door, likely looking as nervous as she felt.

"Stop it," she told herself as soon as she was alone. Her stern words didn't work. In fact, she leaned against the door with a dreamy sigh. Thanks to Grace, she felt pretty tonight, and that illusion was making her stupid.

This wasn't a date. It was nothing more than two friends hanging out. If it were a date, he would've asked her out earlier, maybe even the day before. He wouldn't have just come upon her on the street and asked if she wanted pizza. In fact, he wouldn't have mentioned pizza at all. He'd take her to a restaurant. He'd try to impress her. This was nothing more than watching a TV show with a friend.

Her grin finally faded at that, because it was so damn

familiar. She'd fallen for that mix-up a dozen times already. It was the same every time: guy asks her over to watch a movie or play video games, she gets excited and hopeful, and then...nothing. Worse than nothing, actually. Oftentimes he wanted to talk about problems with the girl he was really interested in. Or worse yet, he wanted to feel Merry out about one of her cute friends.

There was nothing worse than being felt out when you really wanted to be felt up. Nothing.

She almost changed into her normal look. She almost scrubbed off the makeup and shucked the jewelry. But what the hell. If she were just going to be a buddy, she could look cute while doing it.

So instead of changing anything, Merry checked her email and loaded the dishwasher and then added a tiny bit more lip gloss before crossing the hall to knock on his door.

He didn't answer, so she knocked again, then worried he wasn't ready yet. Maybe she had the time wrong. Maybe— The door opened. Shane might be ready, but she wasn't. She hadn't braced herself for the sight of him in just jeans and a black T-shirt. No hat, no boots, just bare feet and damp hair and over six feet of clean man in between. She was suddenly assaulted with the fictional memory of him in the shower, naked and aroused. Soapy water streaming down his chest, sneaking lower over his abdomen and then...

"Hi," he said.

"Oh," she answered.

Shane's smile faltered but he stepped aside to let her in. "What kind of pizza do you like? There's a pretty good local place."

"Anything except peppers. Actually jalapeño peppers are fine."

"Yeah? You like a little heat, huh?"

Her blushing face got even warmer. Apparently she did. Apparently she liked a *lot* of heat when it came to Shane Harcourt. God, she was turning into a creepy, perverted neighbor.

"Me, too," he said, then called to order the pizza.

While he was on the phone, she took the chance to look around. He had more furniture than she and Grace did. A coffee table made out of a wide slab of polished wood. A beautiful old bookshelf made of something that looked like ancient pine. She walked over to examine the books, all of them worn paperbacks that looked like they'd been read a hundred times. Westerns, of course, but not very many. Most of them were thrillers and spy novels and biographies, with a few surprising choices mixed in: vampire sagas and historical novels. No sci-fi, but maybe she'd turn him tonight.

Merry took a step back and found herself flush against a very warm body. "Oh, shit," she gasped, lurching away. She spun around so quickly that she had to reach out to balance herself on his arm. But she missed his arm and found her hand pressed to his chest. "I'm sorry," she choked out and jerked her hand from its hot, solid resting place. "I didn't… I'm not trying to molest you, I promise."

His eyebrows flew up. "That's a strange promise."

"I know! I'm so sorry! I just don't want you to think I think that we…that this… I know it's not, all right? So don't worry."

"Not…what?"

"Anything!"

He was too close. She couldn't back up without running into the bookshelf. But he was watching her so strangely and her heart tripped into a panicked beat. She slipped past him as quickly as she could and moved to the couch. "Let's watch the show!"

He turned to stare at her for a long moment, and she knew she'd revealed too much. The cocktail she'd downed had combined with her natural awkwardness with disastrous results. She'd blurted out all the things she never should have said, and now he knew she was thinking them. The sudden, awful urge to confess that she'd indulged in a dirty fantasy about him hovered on her tongue, as if it wanted to escape and free her from the last of her secret guilt. *Don't say it. Don't say it.*

She swallowed hard, forcing down the compulsion to confess. "I'll sit over here," she said instead, pointing at the far end of the couch.

He blinked slowly. Blinked again. Then nodded. "Okay. Sure. How about a beer?"

"Please. Yes." She sat in mortified tension through the first ten minutes of the show, clutching her beer like a lifeline that was her last link to dignity. Silly, of course. There was no chance she had any dignity left, but at least the rush of new alcohol let her hold on to the fantasy.

She relaxed a little as the magic of the show pulled her in and she forgot to be hyperaware of Shane sitting two feet away. The show was too damn good to ignore. She laughed out loud at a joke, and glanced over to find Shane smiling at her. Something deep inside her belly tightened with wistful yearning.

"This is good," he said.

It was good. It was nice having him as a friend, her physical attraction aside. If she could just learn to relax around him, it would be even better.

"A space Western," he said, turning back to the TV.

She smiled at his profile and pretended that she wasn't wishing she could snuggle up to his neck. "Pretty cool, huh?"

"Pretty damn cool," he agreed.

By the time the pizza came, she felt almost normal again. She took off her shoes and curled her bare feet beneath her and tried to pretend she was with Grace. "Did you make this table?"

"No, a friend made that for me. But the bookshelf is mine."

"They're both beautiful."

"Thanks."

"Is it strange to be a carpenter living in an apartment? Do you secretly build cabinets in the middle of the night?"

He laughed. "You think I have an untamable need to renovate?"

"I know you do," she said, narrowing her eyes. "How do you handle it? Custom closet shelves? Refinishing the wood floor?"

"If I tell you, I'd have to kill you."

"Or you could just buy my silence with some furniture. In case you hadn't noticed, our place is a little spare."

He shot her a hooded look. "There might be something I can do for you."

This time, Merry didn't give in to the embarrassment that wanted to rise up. She didn't blush at the brush of his eyes down her body. He was teasing her, so she stretched out a leg and kicked his hip with her toes. "Shut up."

"I'm serious." His hand closed over her ankle when she tried to pull her foot back. Merry would've been a trembling mess at this point if she hadn't finished her beer. But instead of holding her breath and noting every nerve he touched with his callused fingers, Merry poked his leg with her toes again. He playfully tugged her ankle before letting her go.

"Come on. I'll show you."

He got up and walked toward the bedroom, and she followed him. "Are you luring me to your room?"

"Sure. I'm not the one who promised no molesting."

If he could laugh about it, maybe she hadn't freaked him out so badly after all.

When he stepped into the bedroom and out of the doorway, Merry gasped. "Oh, my God, Shane! Did you make that?"

A tall headboard of solid wood rose high above the bed. The warm stain showed off the scene that had been carved in relief into the arch of wood.

"It's a little clumsy," he said, tipping his chin toward the scene of mountains and trees.

"Are you kidding me? It's amazing, Shane! Look at it!"

A big grin spread over his face. "I see it every morning." He tipped an imaginary hat. "Ma'am."

She couldn't help but giggle at his exaggerated flirtation. "Seriously, Shane. It's the most beautiful thing I've ever seen."

"Now that is just blatant ego stroking."

"It is not!"

"Right. You think that headboard is more beautiful than a work of art? Hell, I bet it doesn't even measure up to your romantic view of Providence."

"Dude, if I found something like this in Providence, it would be on the front of the brochure. *That's* how much I like it."

"'Dude,' huh?"

"Well, you told me not to call you cowboy."

He smiled and her stomach fluttered. It felt…secret, somehow, this smile. And when he spoke, his voice was softer. "I'd rather you just called me Shane," he said.

She could've sworn his gaze dipped down to her mouth, but she was so nervous, she focused on the headboard instead of him. "Well, it's amazing. What you did. It's…"

"Rough." When had he gotten so close? His biceps brushed her shoulder as he turned toward her. "This light is a little more generous. If you see it in the morning light, all the flaws stand out, at least to me."

"You want me to sneak in and surprise you at dawn?"

"No, that's not what I was thinking."

She'd been in denial, staring at the bed and ignoring that he was looking at her as he spoke. But there was no way to ignore him when his hand touched her shoulder. She looked up, her heart pounding so hard that she couldn't hear, couldn't think. Even as he bent his head toward her, she knew it wasn't *really* happening, he wasn't really about to kiss her. But her eyelids fluttered closed and then his lips brushed hers, and Merry wanted to weep.

His mouth was gentle, as if it were asking her a question, but she had no idea how to answer. He was so gorgeous. So damn sexy he'd inspired fantasies she hadn't bothered with in more than six months. But…did he like her? Did he really want her that way, or was it just that she was in his bedroom and she had breasts and all the other important female parts that made a bedroom more fun?

She didn't want it to matter. She wanted to just open for him, part her lips and take him inside, but it'd been too long for her. After two long years, she suddenly realized she didn't want to be another notch in someone's bedpost, even if it was handcrafted, because this would mean something to her. She couldn't bear it being one meaningless night in a guy's memory.

But when his mouth whispered over hers with the slightest bit more pressure, she gave in with a sigh that seemed to part his lips. His tongue touched hers, his arms pulled her closer.

She was in his grip, in his arms, in his room, and Shane Harcourt was exploring her mouth with a slow determination that weakened her knees. She had to stop him, but not…quite…yet. Not yet. She just wanted a little more of this. A little more of his tongue, sliding over hers. A little more of his hands as they slipped down her back and settled on her hips.

Oh, God. Her *hips*. His hands rested there, shaping to the curve of her body, then gripping her. As if he *liked* that. As if he needed to touch her.

Merry sighed into his mouth and his hands tugged her closer. Their hips were almost flush. If she eased forward, she would feel him. Right there. Against her.

She wanted to feel him. She wanted it desperately. And if she did that, she knew that would be a signal. He'd ease her shirt up. Touch her naked skin. He'd undress her and they'd fall into bed and then…

Merry pulled back. "I'm sorry," she whispered.

"It's okay," he said, eyes a little unfocused as he started to bend toward her again.

She couldn't pull away, couldn't force her body away from his, but she did manage to turn her head. His mouth settled on her neck, and that was just as good. Better, even, as nerves screamed to life and stretched beneath her skin, lusting for his touch. His tongue touched her skin. And then his teeth.

"Oh, God," she groaned out loud.

"Merry," he said against her neck.

The power of that, the ability to make him growl her name like a spoken wish… And then he tugged her hips closer and she knew he wanted her. He wanted this. They could be naked in moments. She could send the signal, reach for his shirt or lift her own. She could touch him and say yes and he'd be hers for a little while. It was so good to be touched this way. She wanted it so badly.

His hand slipped toward the small of her back, and she felt a startling jolt of wicked pleasure as his thumb snuck beneath fabric to slide against bare skin.

But when she gasped, the pleasure was swallowed by self-consciousness. Yes, in a few moments she could be naked with him. Too naked. Vulnerable and lost in what he'd do to her, gasping and needing and too damn aware that he did this all the time with all sorts of women. He was smooth, after all. Grace had warned her, and Merry had seen it herself when he'd made a point of turning on the charm.

That was what he was doing now, wasn't it? Seducing a willing partner. Because she was here. Because there was a bed. Because she had all the needed parts. And maybe, if she'd never see him again, she could deal with that, but she couldn't let him know her like this and then live with casual hellos and awkward conversations over the woodpile. It would mean too much to her and too little to him.

"Shane," she whispered.

He hummed an approving sound against her neck just as his hand spread over her bare back.

"We can't."

His mouth froze against her. His shoulders tensed. Neither of them moved. He was probably still processing her words, and Merry didn't want to give up this last contact. For one last moment, she was still in his arms, he was still hard against her, and his hands still hoped to coax pleasure from her body. But then he stepped away, his hands raised slightly as if to show he'd meant no harm.

"I'm sorry," he said. "I thought…"

"No, I'm sorry. It's just that we probably shouldn't…"

"Of course. You're right. Bad idea."

She nodded, crossing her arms to hide the sight of her body, which was still yearning toward him, still eager and aroused. "But the bed! It's really awesome."

"Yeah. Thanks." He shoved his hands in his pockets.

"So…" Her own nervous laughter made her cringe. "Anyway. I should probably go."

"You don't have to go. We could watch more of the show. I like it."

"But what if I molest you again?" she said with forced humor.

"Oh, I don't think you were... I mean, I think I—"

"I was just kidding!" Her smile felt like the grin of a madman. "Anyway, I'll see you later. Tomorrow, maybe. In Providence, I mean. Not here."

She rushed out before she babbled some terrible secret, grabbing her shoes before she raced for the door. Shane stood outside his bedroom, watching, but she kept him in her peripheral vision as she called another goodbye and escaped.

But she didn't have the chance to breathe a sigh of relief, because she opened her door to find Grace waiting for her. For a moment, Grace looked cheerful and waved hello. "Hi, Merry. I hope you don't mind me stopping by, I—"

Her gaze fell to Merry's bare feet as Merry shut the door. The smile snapped to a frown. "Where were you? I thought you were with Crystal."

"I was."

Grace eyed her bare feet again. "Without shoes?"

Merry cleared her throat. "I thought you were staying at Cole's tonight."

"I was, but I'm out on a site tomorrow and I forgot to pack boots. So what's up?"

"Nothing!"

Grace was more than familiar with Merry's nervous reactions, but they both knew that Merry was never nervous when they were alone. Her eyes went from

Merry to the door, then back to Merry's feet again. "That bastard."

Merry sighed and rolled her eyes. "We watched a show at his place."

"I leave you alone for two hours and that asshole swoops in and makes a move on you."

Merry dropped her shoes and dropped onto the couch. "Cut it out, Grace. We watched TV. That's it."

"My ass! Are you telling me that Shane Harcourt wants to be friends with you?"

"Why wouldn't he? I'm a pretty awesome friend."

"You're an amazing friend. You've also got a pretty spectacular ass."

"I do?" Merry craned her neck to try to see her backside.

"What happened?"

"Nothing! God, what is your problem with Shane? He seems perfectly nice and he's funny and he wanted to see *Firefly*. What did he do to piss you off so much?"

Grace shrugged and looked a tiny bit chastened. "I don't know. I can't figure him out. Cole obviously trusts him, but Shane never really tries to get to know me better. I can't read him. I don't know what his deal is."

"Do you try to get to know him better?"

She scowled, answering Merry's question.

"I'm a big girl, you know," Merry said softly. "I know I act like a clueless idiot sometimes, but I've managed to navigate my way through a pretty complicated life."

"I know that! You're just a little…innocent about guys sometimes."

"I'm not innocent! I'm not too trusting. I know what men can be like. It's not naïveté, Grace, it's just celibacy. And if I want to have sex with Shane, I'll have sex with him."

Grace's scowl returned with a vengeance. "Fine. Whatever you want. Did you do it?"

"No!"

"Good."

Merry groaned. "Oh, my God. Even if you thought it'd be a mistake for me to sleep with Shane, how many mistakes have you made with men? Don't I get to take the same chances?"

"No," Grace said sullenly. She dropped onto the couch with a huff. "No, I won't let you make the same mistakes. You don't deserve that."

"And you did?"

"Yes," Grace said without even thinking.

Merry's throat thickened. "Oh, fuck you," she said softly, taking Grace's hand. "That's not even close to true."

"I'm not kind like you are, Merry. You're *good*. And I don't want anything bad to happen to you. Not if I can stop it." Grace's hand tightened around Merry's.

"You know bad things have already happened to me, and I'm fine. We come from the same place. You know that. I might seem like a helpless dork, but I'm not. And if I want to get boned like crazy by the hot guy next door, I will."

A smile tugged at Grace's scowl. "Yeah? What happened to 'No one ever wants me'? Did he make a move?"

"No," Merry lied.

Grace smiled. "Good. Because I'll totally kick his ass no matter what you say."

Merry rolled her eyes. "God! I'd like a penis inside me sometime in this decade, thank you very much."

"Overrated."

"Yeah, right. That's why you have finger shaped bruises on your upper arms, huh? Because of your passion for Greco-Roman wrestling?"

Grace snatched her hand away and covered her arm. Her cheeks turned pink. Merry couldn't believe it. "Are you blushing?"

"No."

"You are! Grace Barrett is blushing like a little schoolgirl! I can't even begin to imagine what kind of filthy memories would make you blush. You'd better keep it quiet. Not just for my sanity, but also because it's probably illegal in this state."

"And several others," Grace muttered.

"Well, this is exactly my point. You get to act out your sluttiest fantasies every night. I want to be a slut, too."

Grace sighed. "But that's the thing, Merry. You're not a slut. I was never bothered by men using me for sex, because I was using them, too. But you aren't like me. Not in that way. You're strong and amazing, but you have a soul you need to protect."

"Oh, please. So do you."

"Maybe I do now. *Maybe*. But it's tough as hide."

Merry laughed and elbowed her friend. "You're starting to sound like your cowboy."

"You're so annoying," Grace scoffed.

"Oh, *I'm* annoying? You're the one trying to keep my bed empty. Cut it out, okay? Just…trust me."

"I do trust you. It's everyone else I don't trust. Especially Shane."

Merry leaned in and gave Grace a kiss on the cheek just to annoy her, but it didn't seem to work. Instead of making a face, Grace grabbed her and gave her a hug. "Just *try* to keep it in your pants?"

"Believe me, it doesn't take any effort. Nobody's trying to cross this border."

But that wasn't true anymore, and Merry fell asleep that night with spinning thoughts of just what might have happened if she'd whispered yes instead of saying no.

CHAPTER EIGHT

JESUS CHRIST, THIS was just what he needed to cap off a shitty day. He was working on a complicated two-story wooden mantel in a new lodge being built for some damn multimillionaire who'd likely spend five nights a year there. It was his least favorite type of work. First off, he was stuck inside, and second, these types of clients often complained just to make sure you never forgot who was in charge.

To be fair, so far the project was going well. His work was good. But after eight hours at the site, he was exhausted. He'd hardly slept at all the night before, tossing and turning with worry about Merry Kade.

Merry, who'd tempted him with her laughter and the low scoop of her tank top. Who'd made the nicest little noises when he'd kissed her. Who'd seemed to melt softly into him even as she made him painfully hard. Who'd suddenly said no and left as quickly as possible.

And now this. This huge white SUV pulling into the parking lot just as he left his lawyer's office.

He saw the moment the driver spotted him. Then the moment when she recognized him. His grandmother's eyes went wide.

Shane pushed through the glass door and headed for his truck. He almost made it.

"Shane!" she snapped. He heard her truck door slam just as he hit the unlock button on his truck. "Shane, just what are you up to?"

He stopped and let his head drop, praying for patience. Jeanine Bishop was actually his stepgrandmother, and she'd made that clear for as long as he could remember. She'd never had any of her own children, and she didn't seem to know what to do with the few she'd inherited. His grandfather hadn't been any sort of example of grandparenting, either. He'd been impatient with kids and hot-tempered with everyone. Visits out at the Bishop ranch had been unbearably quiet and tense.

Jeanine Bishop's footsteps stopped just behind him. Shane took off his hat and turned. "Grandmother," he said, even as he wondered what his real grandma had been like. She'd died young. Or hell, maybe that was a lie. Maybe she'd run off like half the other members of his family.

"Are you engaging in a campaign of vandalism to discourage the board?"

"What?" he snapped, shocked despite himself. He shouldn't be surprised by anything at this point. These people were insane.

"Well? Are you?"

"I have no idea what you're talking about."

"The mailbox was destroyed out on the homestead."

"And why would I do something like that?"

"I have no idea!" she spat. "Why would you sue for your grandfather's money after everything he did for you? He didn't have to leave you that land, you know."

"Oh, I know. In fact, I never asked for it. I never asked for anything."

"Your grandfather honored you with—"

"Right. You've told me this before, remember? But we both know Gideon Bishop left me this land because he couldn't stand to see it sold off and he'd be damned if he'd give it to the state for preservation. So it came to me."

She sniffed. "And yet it's not enough for you."

"The money would've been mine, too, if I'd changed my name back to Bishop. He didn't give a shit about that old ghost town. Grandpa gave the money to the trust to teach me a lesson. He was a spiteful old goat."

"Don't you speak that way about him! You should've been proud of that name! Taking your mother's name was nothing more than a long-term tantrum. Your mother's people never contributed anything to this community."

Shane shoved his hat back on his head and sneered. "Maybe not, but they helped raise me, which is a damn sight more than I can say for anybody in the Bishop family."

"Your grandfather wasn't responsible for your father's failings."

"You're right. He wasn't. But even the smallest gesture would've meant a lot to my brother and me. To my mom. A little help with money. Some sympathy. One goddamned kind word. The only words your husband ever offered were advice about how my mom could've held on to her man."

"Maybe it was good advice."

"Yeah? Did he offer the same helpful suggestions to you when he kicked you out and moved his new wife in?"

She gasped and pressed a hand to her chest. "Shane Bishop! How dare you!"

"It's Harcourt," he muttered, already pissed at himself for lashing out at an old woman. He opened the door of his truck and slid in. "I know you hired a curator for Providence, and I know why you did it. A cute move, but a waste of money."

"It's what your grandfather wanted!" she yelled, any pretense of civility gone.

"What he wanted was to piss me off. So I guess he wins again."

Shane slammed the door and drove away, leaving Jeanine Bishop glaring after him. God, he sometimes wondered if he ever should've started this. He hadn't wanted anything from the Bishop family, and when he'd been informed about the land inheritance, his first word had been *no*.

No, he didn't need anything from his grandfather. More than that, he didn't *want* anything. He'd told the lawyer to start the process of selling the land. But in the days that had followed, Shane had reconsidered. Why shouldn't he get the land? Didn't he deserve something to go along with all the pain of being his father's son? And if his brother ever reappeared, he'd deserve something, too. Shane had been named the sole heir, but did he have the right to give it all away without even talking to Alex?

That was when the insult had sunk in. The sharp stab of his grandfather's final stubborn point. The land, but not the money. The Bishop legacy, but not the comfort.

That was when Shane had gotten pissed.

If his only recourse had been to sell it, he would

have. But his lawyer had presented another possibility, to challenge the change to the will, and Shane had jumped on it. Hell, maybe he didn't deserve the money, but he knew for damn sure that a bunch of falling-down buildings didn't need it more than he did.

No matter what Merry Kade might think.

Shit. He'd known better than to touch her. She was going to be pissed enough when she found out who he was. And now there was *this* between them? Thank God she'd stopped him before it had gone any further.

He had to talk to her tonight. He'd been too busy to go out to Providence this morning. Or else he'd been too chicken, still uncertain exactly what had happened the night before. Had he pushed her too hard? Had he misread the signals?

He'd also been painfully conscious of the fact that at 2:00 a.m., desperate for sleep, he'd finally let himself imagine what might have happened. He'd imagined her beneath him, her nails digging into his back, her voice crying his name as he buried himself deep inside her. Now he'd have to face her as a friend, and pretend that hadn't happened, and hope that the sight and sound of her didn't arouse him.

He growled as he pulled up to the curb of the Stud Farm. Cole's truck was there as well, so he wasn't the least bit surprised when his best friend popped through the front door and raised his hand in greeting.

"Hey," Shane said as he got out of his truck. "I guess it's been a couple of weeks. How's it going?"

Cole's limp seemed to have completely disappeared, and Shane nodded as his friend walked down the sidewalk. "It's great," he said. "Sold off most of the yearlings and moved the rest of the herd up to the high pasture, so I can take an hour or two off. How about you?"

"Busy season, but it's good. Listen, is Merry home? I need to talk to her."

Those words wiped all the open friendliness from Cole's face. His jaw clenched and he stared hard at Shane. "Christ, man."

"What?"

"I thought Grace was just being paranoid. Damn it, Shane, are you moving in on Merry?"

"No!" he said automatically. Then, "Wait. What do you mean, 'Damn it, Shane'?"

"Come on. You're not exactly the kind of guy we'd choose for Merry."

"We?"

"Yes. We. Merry's kind of a little sister to me now."

"And what the hell am I?"

Cole crossed his arms and glared at him. "You're my friend, but you don't exactly have a great history with relationships."

"I don't have any history with relationships, so what the hell does that mean?"

"Exactly what you just said."

Shane really couldn't believe this. He knew Grace wasn't crazy about him, but Cole was his best friend. Cole knew him like… Well, shit. He knew Shane well enough to know the same things that Shane knew about himself.

All his outrage escaped as he exhaled and felt his shoulders slump. He wasn't the guy anyone would want a friend or sister dating. Fuck, he didn't think he was a dog. He never promised anything more than he had to give, but what he had to give was lacking. Sex, not love. Momentary company, not commitment. He knew these things. So did Cole.

"It doesn't matter," he said, holding up his hand like a flag of surrender. "It's not like that. She's a neighbor. We had pizza."

"Yeah? You sure?" Cole's raised eyebrows spoke a soliloquy of doubt.

"I'm sure. Merry is just…a buddy, you know? That's all. Someone to hang out with."

Cole apparently found that easy to believe, because his tension melted into a relieved smile. "Good. Because I don't want to have to kick your ass over this. Or shovel you into an ambulance after Grace gets a hold of you."

"Got it."

"Because you know she would stuff your balls down your throat, right? After she cut off your dick."

"I've kind of been getting that feeling. But it's not going to be an issue. We're friends. That's it."

Cole slapped his shoulder. "Perfect. Easy's having us over on Sunday evening and asked if you'd come out. This'll be much more relaxing if I'm not guarding you from the gelding knife Grace has been eyeing."

"I'll be there." Easy was a damned master of the grill pit. Shane wouldn't miss it for the world. And it would be a damn sight more comfortable if he could get past this apology to Merry. "So is she home?"

"Yep."

He said goodbye and steeled himself for the next few minutes. Best to apologize and get it over quickly, like peeling off a bandage. Still, it went more quickly than he'd planned. His knuckles had just barely hit the door to her apartment when she yanked it open and greeted him with a bright smile.

"Hi!"

Shane had just barely formed the worry that Merry was a little too excited to see him when she corrected his panicked thoughts.

"I'm sorry about last night," she said on a rush. "I shouldn't have gotten so flustered. I know it didn't mean anything."

"Oh. Right. Yes, I'm sorry." His mind tried to find the right words. "It was just the beer and the, um…"

"I know. There was a bed right there, so why not? Right?"

"Uh. Sure. Of course. And you looked different last night. I just got a little…"

"I wiled you!"

Shane blinked. "Huh?"

"I wore shiny stuff and showed some skin, and listen, I totally get the friends with benefits thing. It's cool."

"Oh." What was she saying? The conversation was quicksand beneath his feet. "Friends with benefits? Was that what you were thinking?"

"No!" She laughed. Hard. "No way! Oh, God, I'm sorry. It's not that I wouldn't want to. I swear. You're super hot. And really sexy. And I'd be up for it. I really would. But it would be too weird."

"Weird," he repeated, but what he was really thinking was *hot. Sexy.*

"Not weird because of you! No. You're not weird. I'm weird. Or, I mean, I'm not weird. Well, I probably am. But it would be weird because I haven't had sex in a really long time."

"Oh." Shane's brain felt as if it had shattered into a hundred pieces that were all flying in different directions. "I see. I think."

Merry cringed and covered her eyes. "Oh, God. I don't mean like a decade or something. I wasn't even having sex a decade ago. It's only been two years. That's a long time, right? But not freakishly long?"

"Two *years?*"

She peeked at him past her fingers. "What?"

"Nothing," he said, shaking his head.

"Is that awful?"

"No! Not at all. Anyway, I just wanted to be sure you weren't pissed off. If I made you uncomfortable or I was out of line last night, I'm sorry."

"No big deal! We'll do it again sometime. The pizza and a show. Not, you know, the benefits. Which would be lovely and all, but… Goodbye!"

She closed the door on his face, and Shane just stood there staring at the wood. *Two years?* He told himself not to think about how hard he could make her come, how tight she'd be, how much she must need it. And he failed miserably.

CHAPTER NINE

MERRY IS JUST A BUDDY.

Yes. Good. Thank God she'd stood in the window and eavesdropped on Shane and Cole. Rude, of course, but she was clear on their relationship now. She was a buddy, her normal position. She was used to that and she could deal with it. It was the uncertainty that had tormented her.

This morning she'd woken up confused by the kissing. The touching. She'd let herself wonder if she'd been wrong about him. Maybe she should've been braver and taken a chance. Maybe, despite Grace's suspicions, Shane Harcourt really was interested in her and wanted something more with her.

But no. She was a buddy. What had thrown her off was the friends with benefits thing. It wasn't some exotic phenomenon she'd never heard of, it had just never been something a man had wanted with her.

With Grace, certainly. And every other cute, cool girl she'd ever known. But Merry had always been a buddy in the truest sense of the word. Buddies didn't have touchable breasts or intriguing vaginas. Buddies were people you burped around and bragged to about other women.

So this was a promotion, really! She was not just a

friend, but also a sexual being. It felt nice. Or she told herself it felt nice. And it was an option if she really needed access to a friendly penis in the future. She could check that off her worry list.

"Whew," she said out loud.

She heard the *thunk* of the pipes shutting off. Grace was done with her shower. There was another thing to be thankful for. Merry had managed to straighten out her relationship with Shane without inciting another lecture from Grace.

"I'm off to the museum!" she shouted toward the bathroom.

"Have fun!"

Fun. Right. A fund-raising party for the Jackson Historical Society. She'd be the youngest one there, aside from the kids dragged along by parents. And sadly, she *would* have fun. She'd always loved listening to stories from older generations, and she'd feel more comfortable than she would among her peers. But it was a really terrible way to meet men, unless you didn't mind the forty-five-minute wait for Viagra to work.

But she turned out to be glad she'd worn tight jeans and her favorite black T-shirt for the party, not to mention some dangly earrings Grace had made her buy at some point, because as soon as she opened the apartment door, she ran into a tall, handsome cowboy. A *new* tall, handsome cowboy.

"Hi!" she chirped in surprise. He froze in the act of starting up the stairs. His boot hovered for a moment, and then he spun to face her, a smile spreading over his face. His neatly trimmed beard couldn't dim the beauty of that grin.

"Hi yourself. I'm Walker. I've been meaning to introduce myself." He took her hand in a firm grip and tipped his hat with the other. "I just rented a place upstairs."

"Oh, welcome to the Stud Farm." Rayleen certainly had damn good taste. Walker's broad shoulders loomed so far above her that Merry felt a little woozy.

"Thanks. Are you Grace?"

"Sorry, no. I'm Merry. I'm staying with Grace for a while."

"Ah. I thought you looked a little softer than the description Rayleen gave."

"Oh, I'm definitely softer by about thirty pounds."

"Yeah?" His eyes swept down her body. "Nothing wrong with that, Miss Merry."

"No?" Merry found herself giggling, and couldn't believe she'd actually managed to flirt with this adorable man. She hadn't mentioned *Star Wars,* historical societies or her two-year drought. Amazing. "That's good to know."

"Well, tell Grace to take it easy on me when we meet. I'm moving the rest of my stuff in this weekend, so I'll be sure to see you around, all right?"

"That's definitely all right," she said just as Shane opened his door. His eyes caught hers for a moment, and then he tossed Walker a quick frown before stepping forward to shake his hand.

"Walker," Shane said. "You all moved in?"

Merry left them with a wave, but she could've sworn she felt Shane's eyes on her as she left. Wishful thinking, probably, but as she strolled down the sidewalk, she had a bounce in her step that had nothing to do with the beautiful evening.

The Jackson Museum was almost a mile away, but at this time of night there were so many tourists out looking for dinner that it was almost quicker to walk than drive. Plus, she loved the town. The wooden walkways and Old West charm had completely seduced her with her very first glimpse.

She loved it even more now, because whenever she walked through the town square with its strange arches made of thousands of elk antlers, she thought to herself *I live here. I actually live here.* Jackson felt like hers, in the same way Providence felt like hers. A silly feeling, though. She was only a subrenter in both places. But hell, what did she care? It was a beautiful night, Merry was on her way to her favorite kind of party, and a really cute guy had flirted with her. Oh, and she'd been upgraded to possible friend with benefits. Life could be worse. In fact, it had been just a few weeks before.

So Merry breezed into the Jackson Museum with a big smile and a hopeful outlook. It didn't last long.

"I'm still not convinced he didn't do it," Kristen Bishop said with a sigh that made clear she'd been suffering. "I feel so vulnerable out there all by myself."

"I never said he didn't do it," Jeanine snapped. "And if you're so terrified out there, just sell the house and move to town. It was always a bit too much for you to care for, anyway."

Kristen forgot her suffering pout and stood straight in outrage. "I've always loved the house, and I've always taken good care of it."

"I'd hardly call five years 'always.'"

Merry had hoped to edge past Mrs. Bishops numbers two and three, but Jeanine looked up and caught her eye. "I had the most upsetting encounter," she said. "I ran into Gideon's grandson coming out of the office of that awful lawyer, and he was so nasty to me. And ungrateful. If he were my grandson, I'd have made sure he had manners."

"I'm sorry," Merry said. "Did he mention the lawsuit?"

"Not per se. But he did say he knew we'd hired a curator. I'm not surprised. This is a small town and he probably knew the moment we hired you, but it does confirm the possibility that he vandalized that mailbox in retaliation."

Merry's stomach turned with guilt. She couldn't shift the blame to that young man, whoever he was. "If there haven't been any other instances, I'm sure it was nothing. Heck, maybe it just fell over. Maybe the, uh, gophers got at it or something."

Gophers and their damned reckless driving.

Merry smiled. "So has Levi talked to you about maybe releasing more funds for—"

"Oh, honey, I'm too upset to talk shop tonight. Maybe at the next meeting."

Kristen nodded frantically. "I'm too upset, as well. This has all been so much to handle only months after my husband's death."

Jeanine shot her rival a look that could have frozen water, but Merry just pointed her smile at the two women. "Would it be possible to call an earlier meeting? I'd really love to show all of you the brochure I've come up with."

"Oh, an emergency meeting?" Kristen gasped. "I'm sure those should only be called in the case of an actual emergency. For example, if something more happens out at the house. What a nightmare this has all been."

Merry was starting to feel a little less guilty about the damned mailbox.

She escaped the orbit of self-absorbed pity and made her way toward a woman she recognized as a guide at the museum, then discovered an elderly man who was a descendant of the Smiths, one of the founding families of Providence. Merry quickly forgot her frustrations and settled into a chair in the corner of the room to listen to Wilfred Smith tell his oral history.

An hour later, Merry had regained all her enthusiasm for Providence, and she'd found new determination that had nothing to do with her own personal goals. Providence had meant something once. It had been important to people, and she wanted it to be important again.

By the end of the evening, she had a plan.

COME TO THE SALOON.

Well, it was Friday night, and she was wearing dangly earrings, so Merry obeyed the note Grace had taped to their door and headed to the saloon. Now she could get her fix of olden days' stories *and* still tell herself she was young and hip. Or as young and hip as one could get at a saloon.

Perfect.

The place was packed when she walked in, but she spotted Grace over in Rayleen's designated corner of the bar and worked her way through the crowd.

"Hey, you made it!" Grace cried. She was obviously already tipsy. "How was your museum thing?"

"Fascinating!"

"Good. Have a drink. Jenny's making us some sort of special martinis." She pointed to the bar and Merry turned to see Jenny holding out a pink martini.

"Thank you!" she shouted as she took the drink. With one tiny sip she gave Jenny an enthusiastic thumbs-up. The martini was delicious and had just enough sweetness to mask the fact that they were nearly pure alcohol. No wonder Grace was in such a good mood.

"Have you met Walker yet?" Grace said over the music.

Merry turned to find that Walker was standing on the other side of Rayleen's chair, a delicate pink martini in his big hand. "Howdy," he said with a wink.

"We met earlier," she said, "but I don't mind running into him again."

He took her offered hand and turned it up to kiss her knuckles. "Good to hear, Miss Merry."

Grace raised her chin even as the edges of her mouth lowered. "And Shane's here." She left off the last word of that sentence, which was obviously supposed to be *unfortunately*.

Shane was frowning even harder than Grace, his eyes on the way Walker still held Merry's hand.

But screw Shane. She couldn't be a buddy to every man just because she was a buddy to him. If Walker thought she was nice and soft and worthy of flirtation, she was going to enjoy the hell out of it. Heck, maybe after a martini or three, she'd take it even further. He was hot as hell, and somehow didn't make her feel nervous the way Shane did. She felt more in control with Walker. More confident. Like she could be friends with benefits and it'd be no big deal. No pressure. No awkward hurt she'd have to hide.

"Hey, Christmas!" Rayleen said. "Get your hands off the real tenants. I ain't running a community exchange program."

Walker finally let her go then bent down to give Rayleen a kiss on the cheek. "Come on, Rayleen. You know you're my gal."

"Jesus Christ and cheese and crackers," Rayleen snarled, but her cheeks went as pink as the martini. "You're the most ridiculous man I've ever met. I bet there's naked photos of you on the internets."

Walker made a strange choking sound and his hands jerked away from Rayleen's shoulders.

The old woman's face brightened and she hooted. "There are, aren't there?"

"No!" he said emphatically.

"Young man, did you send out some of them cock shots to your lady friends?"

He shook his head, his cheeks heating as Merry pressed a hand to her mouth to hide her hysterical giggles. She couldn't tell if he was horrified to hear this seventy-year-old lady talk about cock shots or if he was mortified because he'd done exactly what she'd accused him of.

"Hoo boy," Rayleen crowed. "I'm going to do an image search as soon as I get home tonight. Get a better feel for my new tenant."

His wide eyes caught Merry's. "I swear it's not true."

"I believe you," she said, but she'd do a quick search herself. She could see the tiniest glimmer of doubt in his eyes, as if he couldn't quite remember if a lover had ever snapped a nude pic of him. Poor guy. Merry had better check just so she could reassure him.

She and Grace grinned at each other. "Where's your man?" Merry asked.

"Working late. He'll be here soon. You're coming out on Sunday, right?"

"I am. I love Cole's house. It's so cute." Cole lived in the ranch manager's house, set just a little apart from the "big house" on the Easy Creek Ranch. Cole owned the ranch now, but he seemed more than happy with keeping the old arrangement with Easy, who was like a father to him.

Merry edged a little closer to her friend. "Are you thinking about moving? You sure spend a lot of nights out there."

Grace shook her head. "You just want my place."

"Well, the views get better every day."

"Yeah." They both took a moment to stare at the latest big hunk of manflesh to move in. When her gaze swept over to find Shane glaring at her from his post against the wall, she raised her drink and sipped from it. He took a long draw from his beer and turned away.

"But seriously," she said softly to Grace, "things seem really good with Cole."

Her words prompted a soft, secret smile that she'd never seen on Grace's face, and Merry's heart melted. Grace deserved this. After the life she'd had, she deserved everything. Merry grabbed her in a quick hug. "I'm so happy for you," she whispered in her ear. "And only the tiniest bit jealous."

"You'll meet a great guy one day," Grace said. "Soon."

"A guy like Walker?"

"Oh, God, no. He's a little too much fun."

"But good for scratching an itch, maybe."

"No," Grace said flatly.

"Jeez! I guess I never needed a dad, after all. I expect to find you standing in the door with a shotgun the next time I come home from a date."

"What date?" Grace growled.

"Seriously, Grace! I just want to get laid!"

Of course, the jukebox took that moment to switch songs. And of course, Merry had shouted that way too loudly. Not loudly enough for the whole bar to hear, but if the wide eyes of Shane and Walker were any indication, her words had easily reached their ears.

Rayleen howled. "Girl, you just hung out the blinking Christmas lights! Merry, merry! Taking all volunteers!"

"Oh, God," she groaned, forcing herself not to cover her face and crouch on the floor. Instead she turned around and downed her drink. Jenny was right there with another.

"Seems like you might need this," she said with a wink.

"Oh, God," Merry repeated.

Jenny smiled. "That Walker seems like a tall drink of water. Why don't you take him home for a ride?"

She shook her head.

"Seriously. He looks...*big*."

Merry finally found the will to smile. And then laugh. "You're awful."

"No, I'm not. I'm a bartender. I hear things. Important things."

"Stop it! I don't want to know this!"

"Sure you do. Knowledge is power. The power to get it on."

Merry nearly collapsed in giggles, but then she sobered just the tiniest bit. That was probably the wrong word, though, because she'd never get the nerve to ask her next question sober. She leaned closer to Jenny. "What do you hear about Shane?"

"Shane Harcourt?" Her eyes focused past Merry's shoulder and she cocked her head. "There's not a lot of gossip about him, actually. No long-term relationships that I've ever known. He dates around a little, but he doesn't troll the bar every weekend or anything. I think he was seeing Paulette Jameson after her divorce. That was a while ago."

So Grace was right. Shane was a tough guy to read. Even Jenny didn't know much about him.

Merry looked over to see him talking to Walker and a petite blonde who'd wandered over at some point. She had no reason to think the girl was anything but perfectly nice, but Merry still wanted to snatch her hair off. She was everything Merry wasn't. Petite and tan and perfectly made up to accent her big blue eyes and high cheekbones.

Fucking cheekbones. Merry had cheekbones, too, if she held her head at just the right angle in perfect lighting.

And Shane was doing his charming thing again, offering an easy smile and eyes that practically twinkled. He'd tried that on her a couple of times, but he didn't bother with it anymore. People didn't twinkle for buddies, after all. But that blonde girl, he wanted to be smooth for.

And why not? The girl was pretty. Shane was gorgeous. They were a lovely contrast to each other. A perfect pair. All Merry could do was sip her drink and hope he didn't want to tell her all about it later.

For a moment, she wished she was back at the museum party, chatting up old men about their families. At least she'd felt adequate there. But then Grace made a joke about blow jobs and Rayleen chimed in with a helpful tip, and Merry was laughing so hard, she felt like a fool for even considering being sad.

She had good friends, and a happy place here in Jackson, and she could be satisfied with that even if she never had sex again.

CHAPTER TEN

THE GIRL AT HIS SIDE was talking so much that Shane couldn't eavesdrop on what Merry was saying anymore. Oh, he'd heard her plea for sex clearly enough, along with every other man in a ten-foot radius. And her flirtation with Walker had been obvious. But now her head was dipped toward Grace as they whispered and laughed about something, and he had no idea what it was.

"And of course, I love the rodeo," the blonde said.

Shane perked up. "Yeah? I heard Walker is a damn good cowboy, aren't you, Walker?"

The woman's eyes lit up and she shifted toward Walker. A stroke of genius on Shane's part. Now he could ease closer to Merry and the big cowboy would be too busy to flirt with her anymore.

Merry ran a hand through her hair, and it slid back, dragging over her shoulders. They weren't bare tonight, but he could picture them easily. She was tall and strong, her shoulders perfectly proportioned to curvy hips, and her skin had been so smooth under his hands. It had looked even softer where her breasts had risen oh so slightly up above the neckline of her tank top. He wanted to see that again. He wanted to see more than that, and apparently she was horny. Of course she was. It had been two years.

God, she was a damned torture device. Had she known how insane that would make him? Had she said that on purpose just to drive him crazy? Because he felt crazy now, imagining slipping a hand between her legs. How wet she'd be. Her gasps of need as he stroked her.

Shane shifted and cleared his throat.

He knew he shouldn't sleep with her. Hell, everyone seemed to know he shouldn't sleep with her. And on top of his own failings in relationships, he was lying to her about something big. But the lie didn't feel like something real. It didn't have anything to do with who he was or what he wanted from her.

There was something about her. Something sweet and right that had crept inside him over the days he'd known her. And then that kiss… Even though he was the one who'd initiated it, even though he'd been standing there, staring at her beautiful skin and thinking that he wanted to touch it, the kiss had still surprised him. Wanting to kiss her had felt like curiosity, but the taste of her mouth had overtaken him, had pulled him under, and turned him inside out. He'd wanted more. So much more.

Merry looked up and caught him watching. Her eyes slid to the blonde, then back to him and she offered a wide smile, as if she were happy to find him alone again. When he smiled back, her cheeks flushed and she looked away. He wanted to see her blush like that in his bed. Naked and pink and modest even as he put his mouth to her breast and made her sigh. He wanted to push her past her natural self-consciousness, arouse her so thoroughly that she forgot to be embarrassed.

"I'd better go," he heard her say to Grace. "I've got to get up early tomorrow."

"But tomorrow is Saturday! And what will I do without you here?"

Merry smiled. "Cole just walked in. I think you'll do fine."

"Oh!" Grace looked up with happiness in her dark eyes. She might not like Shane all that much, but he was happy for her, and even happier for Cole. Cole had almost lost everything, including Grace, but it had worked out. Of course, Cole was a great guy. Steady. Responsible. The kind of guy who'd make a good husband some day. The kind of man who'd never walk away.

For a moment, Shane wanted that for himself, and as Merry moved toward the door with a farewell wave for the whole group, he followed her. "Hey," he said as he held the door open for her.

She looked up at him in surprise. "Oh, hi!"

"I thought maybe I should walk you home after your declaration. You might have a following."

"Don't tease me!"

"Sorry," he said, offering her a wink. "What are you up to so early tomorrow?"

"Just work in Providence. I heard the best story tonight from a descendent of one of the Smith settlers. Did you know there was an ice house just inside the canyon beyond the town? I think I'll go look for it tomorrow. This man was telling me how they used to cut ice during the winter and store it there in a little shack they built around a natural depression in the stone. It never got any sunlight, so it would stay cold all summer long, and sometimes the kids would sit in there on really hot days. They'd play games and hide from their parents."

She gestured as she spoke, her eyes bright with happiness. Shane nodded politely as he opened the door of the Stud Farm and waved her in. He didn't care about Providence stories, but he loved watching her tell them. He couldn't take his eyes off her as she laughed with delight at something about raspberries and fresh cow's milk. Her teeth caught her bottom lip as she smiled, and Shane watched that tender flesh give to the pressure as she stopped in front of his door.

"Merry," he murmured.

"I know. I'll shut up. I just love all the—"

He dipped his head and stopped her words with his mouth. Her voice died on a small gasp then the gasp turned into a tiny little moan as she opened for him and took him in.

He stroked her tongue with his, tasting her and the sweet drink she'd been sipping. His body responded immediately, reminding him that he'd tasted her before and that he wanted more. He spread his hands over her waist and her warmth seeped into his hands. It was like a drug, the feel of her, penetrating his skin and going immediately to his bloodstream. His heart beat harder. When Merry's arms went around his neck and she deepened the kiss, Shane nearly groaned with relief.

Keeping her tight against him with a firm hand across her back, he reached past her to open his door, relieved that he hadn't bothered locking it earlier. He walked her backward and kicked the door shut behind him.

Her nails dug into his neck. She pressed her hips to his and the pressure made his cock swell. He suddenly felt like he was the one who hadn't had sex in two years…desperate and wild.

Breathing her name again, he slid his mouth to her neck and sucked at her skin as he slipped his hands beneath the back of her shirt.

"Oh, God. Shane. That feels…"

Yes. It felt too good for words. It felt right and he spread his fingers over her back and moved them higher. "I can't stop thinking about you," he said against her neck before he bit her and felt her shiver in his arms.

"Oh," she breathed.

When he pushed his hands higher, she lifted her arms, and suddenly her shirt was off and Shane felt stunned. He kissed her shoulder, breathed in her scent. "Is this okay? Please tell me it's okay."

"It's okay," she said, a smile in her voice.

"Thank God." He moved a hand behind her legs and picked her up, laughing when she screamed. "Have I ever shown you my hand-carved headboard?" he growled.

"Ha! I bet you use that line on all the girls."

He didn't, actually. He wasn't usually friends with the women he slept with. Just long-term acquaintances. Or short-term ones.

He laid her on the bed and laid himself on top of her, his hand sweeping down her belly just to feel her skin. Her hair fanned across his pillow in a dark sweep. "I'll go slow, all right? I'll go slow, just…let me, Merry."

"Yes." Her eyes dropped shyly away, but she reached for the buttons of his shirt.

Shane held himself still and watched her fingers work, freeing first the top button, then the next. It was a terrible pleasure, watching her move so slowly, knowing that when she was done she'd touch him. When had he become so desperate for this? When had it changed from idle curiosity about a cute woman to a need that made him shake?

She finally pulled his shirt free of his jeans and spread it open, her fingers trailing pleasure over his shoulders and down his arms. Then she really touched him. She pressed her palms to his chest and smiled. "You're kind of...furry."

He looked down at his chest as if he'd never seen it before. "I guess I am."

"I like it."

He glanced up and smiled into her shy eyes. "Good." He kissed her while she was still laughing, and then each touch blurred together into the next. His belly against hers, her ribs beneath his hand. And then he unclasped her bra and swept a palm over her breasts as her breath came harder.

Oh, God, she was soft and sweet and her rose-brown nipples puckered under his touch. They tightened even further when he dipped his head and kissed her, circling her with his tongue before he sucked gently. He loved that. The way she arched into him, the way her hands clasped his head as he rolled that deliciously hard nub against his tongue.

He wanted inside her. Now. *Needed* it. But he'd promised to go slow. She deserved that. If he couldn't give her a commitment, he could at least make this good for her. As good as he possibly could, his own needs be damned.

And fuck, this was pleasure on its own, listening to her soft sounds of need, teasing her until she tightened her hold and pulled him closer. He pressed his teeth gently against her nipple and was rewarded with a tight gasp. When he lifted his mouth, she whispered, "Don't stop. Please," and he smiled as he tipped his head to her other breast and sucked her into his mouth.

This sigh was louder and edged with a high note that gratified the animal howling inside him. This time, as he teased her, he slid his hand down her belly and un-buttoned her jeans. Her stomach sucked in in surprise. He felt her tense, but when he scraped his teeth over her nipple, she grew wild again, and seemed to forget that he was pulling her zipper down.

"God, your mouth," she moaned. "It feels so good."

Shane's pulse drummed so hard it almost drowned out her words, but he heard them and they twisted through his head and joined up with the knowledge that he was about to touch her. He felt mad. Tortured. His hand shook against her stomach as he flattened it to her skin and slid it beneath her panties.

His fingers touched soft hair as her belly pulled in again. Shane raised his head and looked at her. Her wide eyes watched him with a slightly unfocused gaze. Her pink lips were parted, her breath coming fast. Shane's hand slid lower. He brushed her wet heat, and her eyes squeezed tightly shut as her hips tipped up. "Oh," she said, her mouth forming a perfect circle of surprise. "Oh," she gasped again as he slipped his fingers along her.

He watched her face, stunned by the beauty of her pleasure as he touched her clit. She looked young and somehow pure. It made no sense, of course. There was nothing pure about the wetness that soaked his fingers or the way his cock throbbed with every heartbeat. There was nothing pure about the way her neck arched as her hand curled around his biceps. She clutched him as if she were falling. It was lust on her face. Need. Hunger. But it still managed to be *pure*.

"God, you're beautiful," he growled.

She shook her head and spread her knees wider.

Merry needed more and so did he. He needed her naked and open for him, but it was damned hard to stop touching her. To tear himself away from the sight of her face, flushed and tight with gorgeous tension. But he was going to have to force himself if he wanted inside her, and he wanted that more than anything in the world. More than life. Because he'd die if he didn't feel her. Soon.

He went to his knees to tug her jeans down. Merry didn't stop him. In fact, she lifted her hips and twisted as he pulled, and then she was all bare legs and black panties. Jesus, she was lovely.

Looking down at her, he slowly eased her panties down, hardly able to breathe when she was finally naked before him. Her thighs were the color of cream and looked like they were made to cradle a man's hips. And just above, a dark triangle of curls that made his mouth water.

She'd pressed her thighs tight together, as if she wanted to hide from his gaze, but that only made him want her more. Made him want to tease her, coax her, touch her until she lost all sense of modesty and begged him.

The thought of that made every nerve in his body strain toward her. He wanted to shove his jeans down, free his cock and be inside her *now*. He needed it. But he clenched his jaw and lay beside her again.

Slow. Slow.

Her eyes were still closed, as if she didn't want to see him, but this time when he touched her, she sighed with relief and her legs parted. He stroked her, coaxing those gorgeous soft sounds from her again, but this time, when her hips tipped desperately up, Shane slid a finger inside her.

She cried out, and his heart tripped over itself. She was hot and wet and tight around his finger, and Shane groaned. Oh, God. How had he imagined he could go without this? How could he have walked away?

He pushed slowly in and out of her, feeling her relax for him. He tipped his head down and kissed her neck as he eased another finger inside her. God, she was tight. He didn't want to hurt her, so he slipped out and touched her clit again, circling her with his wet fingers until her hips pushed toward him again. When she seemed desperate, he eased his fingers deep, loving the way she cried out.

"Does that feel good, sweetheart?" he whispered.

She nodded, her lips pressing tight together to try to stop a moan.

He smiled against her skin. For once, Merry was speechless. Working his fingers slowly in and out, he listened to every sigh, every trapped groan. She didn't want him to hear, but he needed those sounds. He fed on them until he couldn't think anymore, until her hips worked rhythmically to take his fingers deeper. She was so wet for him. So lost.

"I want to be inside you, Merry."

She nodded again, eyes still squeezed tightly shut.

Shane unbuttoned his jeans and dug a condom from his wallet as he toed off his boots. When he was finally naked, he eased between her legs. "Merry."

She kept her eyes shut, but her hands clasped his back to pull him closer.

His cock brushed her heat and Shane had to close his own eyes for a moment, fighting the impulse to surge forward, to take her like some caveman staking a claim.

"God, Merry." He took himself in hand and stroked his cock over her. "Open your eyes."

She shook her head. "Please, just…" She gasped when he dragged himself along her clit.

"Look at me. Please. Look at me." He needed that. Needed her to know who was inside her. Needed to see her eyes as her body took him in. No one had touched her this way in so long, and he wanted to know that she'd chosen *him*.

Her eyes finally fluttered open. She watched him with worry or doubt or some other sorrow. He notched himself against her and pushed gently in. "Shane," she gasped, her fingers digging into his shoulders.

He hissed at the feel of her. The tightness and heat that squeezed him until it was a pleasure close to pain. He eased out after only a couple of inches and pushed slowly in.

"Oh, God." She sighed. "Yes. Just… *Yes*."

Yes. *Hell,* yes. He pushed deeper and deeper still,

slowly sinking himself inside her delicious body. "Jesus," he growled, "you feel so damn sweet."

"You feel...*big*."

He couldn't believe she could drag a laugh from him at this point, but she did. "Is it okay?"

She nodded and buried her face in his neck, but he couldn't complain that she'd looked away. He needed to look away himself. If he kept watching the gorgeous pleasure on her face, he'd come right away.

Slow, he reminded himself. Go slow.

And he was glad for that, because she responded to every slow slide of his cock like it was a wonder. She sighed and gasped and made a sexy humming sound that shivered over his skin. And she was so damn wet that he knew he didn't need to be careful, he knew it'd be good for her no matter what. He kept a slow pace, but he took her harder, deeper.

She threw her head back and pulled her knees up so he could settle deeper into her body. "God," he ground out between clenched teeth. "That's so good." He pressed her knee higher and fucked her harder, loving the way she cried out for him, loving that she wanted more.

He raised up on his arms to look down at her, and that was a brutal mistake. The sight of her was too much. Her white skin and dark nipples and her lip caught between her teeth as she fought for her pleasure. It was an image he'd never forget. Sweet Merry, wicked and wanton as she took his cock.

Fuck. His body tightened in warning. But he couldn't come yet. Not yet.

Shane pressed her knee back down to his hip and

slowed his strokes. He eased his body higher on hers, changing the angle until he could feel his shaft rub tight against her every time he thrust. A trick he'd learned from an old lover, and he was damned thankful for it now.

She gasped in surprise, and he clenched his jaw and told himself not to hear her, not to see her, not to indulge in the exquisite pleasure of watching her get off as his cock rubbed her clit with each stroke.

But oh, fuck, she sounded so damn sweet. Her hands slid down his back to clutch his ass and pull him tighter. Her nails dug into his skin. "Yes," she moaned. "Shane. Oh, God, Shane. Fuck me."

Christ, was she trying to destroy him? Had anything ever sounded so filthy as Merry Kade begging to be fucked? He couldn't hold on. He couldn't. She was so hot and tight and her nails carved tiny bites of pain into his body, and she needed this. She needed him and he was—

"Oh, God, *yes*," she screamed. When her hips jerked against his thrusts, Shane opened his eyes and let himself go. He fucked her harder and let it take him under. His cock pulsed and jumped and he groaned in desperate release.

Thank God. Thank God he'd held out. He wasn't sure how long it took him to come back to his senses, but when he did, he could feel Merry trembling beneath him.

He raised his head from the pillow. "Merry? You okay?"

"I think so," she whispered.

"I didn't hurt you?"

A shy smile flashed over her face. "I think I'll re-cover."

He collapsed beside her, shaking himself, although he was shaking with laughter. "Are you putting me in my place?"

"No!" She covered her face with her hands then seemed to remember she had other parts to cover as well. He watched her cover her breasts, then a help-less hand hovered over that lovely triangle of hair for a moment.

"Could you, um…." She tugged desperately at the covers. "Could you get up for a second?"

He wanted to say no and make her lounge naked for an hour, but instead he got up and went to the bath-room. The bedroom was dim in the evening light, and when he came back he switched on the light, but Merry squealed. "Turn that off!"

"Are you shy?" he teased.

She threw a pillow at his head. Shane caught it and tossed it back, but he switched off the light. That was the extent of his concession, though. He slipped under the covers with her, but tugged them down to expose her breasts. Merry immediately snatched them back up.

"Come on. I want to see you."

"Shut up."

"You've got nothing to hide now. I've seen it all."

"Shut up!"

"From a couple of different angles."

The pillow hit him smack in the face. Shane brushed it aside and kissed her. She still wouldn't let go of the blanket.

"Please?" he coaxed. "If you pull down the blanket,

I'll be topless, too." He raised his eyebrows. "Are you going to pass up the chance to ogle my chest?"

Merry finally peeked up at him. Her grip loosened. "Well…" When her gaze drifted to his chest, she finally let go of the blanket to brush her palm softly over his chest. "It is very nice."

Shane eased the blanket down to her waist and cupped her breast gently in his hand. But then he forgot what his point had been, because instead of looking at her, he found himself watching her hands as they skimmed lightly over the hair on his chest, then settled right over his heart. She seemed fascinated, and he felt…strange. Giddy and overwhelmed in a way he hadn't felt since he was thirteen and had his first uncertain crush on a pretty girl.

His heart raced under her fingers. He hoped she didn't notice.

"You sure you won't let me turn on the light?" he asked.

"Are you always like this after sex?"

His thumb caught on her nipple and he circled it carefully, watching as it tightened again at the renewed attention. "Like what?"

"You're so relaxed and…"

He leaned down and put his open mouth to her nipple.

"And you keep…teasing me."

He was teasing her. He didn't know why. But he did know he wasn't usually like this. He kissed her one last time. "You're cute when you laugh," he said, which was true enough, but not the whole story. Her smile made him happy, but he couldn't say that. Ever.

"Only when I laugh, huh?"

"Oh, also when you say my name and beg me to fuck you."

"Jesus, Shane!" She shoved him hard and dragged the covers up over her head.

He laughed. Hard. And he only laughed harder when one of her fists emerged from the covers to punch his shoulder. But he finally took pity and lay down next to her, mostly because he was suddenly exhausted. He hadn't come that hard in a very long time, if ever. And it had been much longer since he'd laughed that hard. He felt as if his muscles had melted into pools of warm liquid.

"Christ, Merry," he breathed. "That was good."

She was silent for a long moment, and he was beginning to worry she didn't agree. But then he heard her draw a deep breath. "Was it good? It felt really good."

He smiled at the ceiling. "I think that's the only measure."

"I've never…"

Those two words trailed over his skin as they disappeared into silence. He turned toward her, but in the dark room he couldn't see anything more than a faint glimmer of her eyes in the shadow of the blankets.

"I've never come like that before."

"Like what?"

"During sex like that. With you inside me. It was…" Her smile flashed white for a moment. "Nice."

Shane grinned. He couldn't help it. If he had more energy, he would have jumped up on the bed and hooted while he beat his chest. Thank God his exhaustion could masquerade as dignity.

"I'm glad," he murmured. "Because it was pretty high up in great moments of my life."

Merry laughed so hard she snorted, which gave him another thing to tease her about. But his amusement died when she snuggled close. Shane put his arm around her and pulled her head to his chest. And as her breath chased over his skin in gentle puffs, he didn't feel like laughing at all. He just stared into the darkness and wondered what the hell he'd done.

MERRY SNUCK INTO Grace's apartment, sure that dirty guilt was written all over her face. Her clothes probably looked normal, but she felt generally rumpled, and she was certain she could smell Shane on her skin.

God. She blushed at the very thought of his name, but the warmth kept traveling over her skin, falling from her face to her neck and her chest and all the way down to her thighs.

She'd been very thoroughly fucked, and she felt it in every inch of her body. There was no way she looked the same.

Luckily the apartment was empty. A glance at the clock revealed that only sixty minutes had passed since she'd left the bar. How was that possible? It had felt like hours. She shook her head in surprise but grabbed a pair of sweatpants and moved quickly to the bathroom. She needed to wash off the invisible depravity that covered her skin.

Yes, she thought to herself as she let the shower heat up. That was how she felt. Depraved. Dirty. Wonderful.

And still embarrassed. She couldn't help it. Being naked like that, being exposed…it felt so vulnerable.

She'd always been in awe of Grace, who used her body for pleasure whenever the urge struck. Merry could never be that brave. To let a man *inside* her and just accept that as her right. It felt scary. And she couldn't tell if it was scarier that she hardly knew Shane or terrifying because she knew him at all.

She stepped beneath the hot water with a groan of relief.

Thank God she'd gone to the saloon. Thank God she'd had those two martinis, or she'd never have been able to let that happen.

She cringed at her own thought. That she had to *let* it happen. That she was barely an active participant. But right now she couldn't make the semantics matter, because it had been fucking *fabulous*.

Merry looked around the shower as if someone else would be watching, then she took a deep breath, balled her hands into fists and danced on her tiptoes to a silent squeal of triumph.

"Ohmigod," she panted, covering her open mouth with her hands to keep the water out. "Ohmigod."

He'd been perfect. And big. And perfect. And he'd made her feel beautiful for a few minutes. He'd made her feel like she was the woman he wanted.

God. If this was only friends with benefits, she'd take it. She'd take it and she'd worship him from across the hall and swallow her worries for her heart and she would take it *all*.

"Okay," she whispered. "Okay, be cool."

She could be cool. She'd kill herself being cool about it if she had to. She'd taken a chance and it had been worth every second.

Merry washed up and when she got out of the bathroom, she felt more in control. She tucked her wet hair up into a bun and fired up her iPad to send an email. If she didn't get the answer she wanted, then she'd take one more chance. What the hell.

Life was good today. And Merry was determined to make tomorrow even better.

CHAPTER ELEVEN

MERRY LOOKED AT EACH of their faces, Levi and Harry, both creased and leathered by the sun, Marvin, still plump and pale under his standard fisherman's hat, and the women: Kristen, a handsome sixty-two-year-old woman with carefully styled hair, and Jeanine, starting to stoop a little with age. To a person, each of them stood in the bright morning sun and stared open-mouthed at the sign.

Black paint had dripped from the crude letters and stained the rough grass beneath the fence.

"Oh, my word," Kristen said for the third time since she'd stepped from Levi's car.

"I know," Merry said solemnly. "It's crazy. You should probably call an emergency meeting and decide how to proceed from here."

"What we should do," insisted Jeanine, "is call the sheriff!"

Merry's stomach twisted as the whole group murmured agreement. "Call the sheriff? I wouldn't say this was a crime."

"It's vandalism!" Harry said.

"Well… It's really just an old scrap of wood nailed to an even older fence post. I don't think anything's been damaged."

Jeanine sniffed. "Maybe not, but it's a threat."

"Yes!" Kristen added. "It's intimidation!"

Merry felt her fingers go numb and looked down to see that she'd twisted them into a knot. She forced herself to let go. "It only says No More Tourists! That's not exactly threatening anything. The sheriff has real crime to fight. We shouldn't bother him."

They all looked at her like she was crazy. Merry squirmed and fought the urge to blurt out a confession. "How about we take pictures of it? File a report so there's a record."

Levi seemed to consider it. "There could be fingerprints. Tire prints."

Oh, good Lord. Why did they have to make everything so difficult? "As far as I know, that doesn't really happen in a case like this. My car was stolen two years ago, and when they found it, even then they didn't take fingerprints. Department funding and things like that. But you guys do whatever you think is best."

"I'll call the sheriff," Jeanine said firmly.

Merry felt sweat drip down her neck and sneak past her shoulder blades.

She hadn't done anything illegal, per se. A sign wasn't vandalism. She'd been careful not to make the message scary. And she wasn't the one reporting it as a crime. Surely she couldn't go to jail. How would they even know it was her?

Her mind latched with a vengeance onto the hundreds of hours of television she'd watched over her life. The little clues that TV detectives always found. A hairpin. A stray drop of paint. A certain curlicue in the letter

E that she couldn't help but make even when she was trying to disguise her writing.

Oh, God. Merry ran a surreptitious hand through her hair just to reassure herself that she hadn't worn any barrettes or ponytail holders. No. Her hair was just long and straight as usual. And she'd already checked for paint drops like she was looking for ticks after a camping trip.

Still… She stared down at her hands. Did paint traces show up under a blacklight like blood? There were no telltale smudges of black, but would she stand up to a good swabbing? What if they could test for latex paint the same way they tested for gunpowder residue? What if—?

Jeanine snapped her phone closed and walked back to the group with a frown. "The dispatcher said there's a grassfire outside town and we should just take pictures and file a report."

"Oh, thank God," Merry gasped.

Five pairs of eyes looked straight at her.

"I mean, I'm glad we can report this without having to pull them away from the fire. Good news. Boys in blue, saving lives." She was in full-on flop sweat now. "Okay! I'll take the photos! In HD, of course."

The group backed away while Merry snapped away with her phone. She took a few pictures of the ground around the sign, then about a dozen of the sign itself, then two from the other side of the fence, just to be sure she looked enthusiastic.

"All right!" She dusted off her hands and waited for them to figure out the meeting schedule. But apparently they'd been having a totally different discussion.

"Who knows a reporter with the paper? I bet we can get someone out here this afternoon."

What the hell? She'd only stepped away from them for a few minutes.

"Whoa, whoa! A reporter? I don't think that's a good idea at all."

Jeanine crossed her arms. "We need to make clear that we won't put up with this. If that little ingrate thinks he can—"

"We don't know who did this. It could've been anyone. And if you start throwing accusations around, the board could be sued! This guy has already proven he's litigious, right? Bad idea. We could lose everything."

"She's got a good point," Levi said. Harry grunted in agreement.

The women did not agree. Kristen swept her manicured hands in a wide sweep. "So we're supposed to just put up with this? I can hardly sleep at night! This is awful!"

Apparently Kristen Bishop hadn't faced very many scary situations in her life. A broken mailbox and vague sign wouldn't have even registered on Merry's radar as a kid. Still, she felt terrible about her distress.

"I have an idea," she said, trying to sound calm. "Maybe we should fight vinegar with honey. If that's a thing people say. Do people say that? Anyway." She cleared her throat and tried again. "Calling a reporter is a great idea, but instead of focusing on the negative, maybe we could get someone to do a whole write-up about Providence. About the trust. About what Gideon Bishop was trying to do and what this community meant to the area."

"Hmm," Levi responded, rocking back on his heels.

"Public opinion," she pressed. "I'm not saying we don't mention the troubles we've had with the lawsuit, but the best thing we can do for the case is create goodwill, don't you think? Get the town on our side."

"But what about the sign?" Kristen asked. "What about the mailbox?"

"Listen, if the town is on our side, I bet no one would dare to try anything else."

Harry nodded. "It's not a bad idea."

Jeanine looked doubtful, but she held her tongue, and with Jeanine, that was nearly enthusiastic agreement.

"This is all so awful," Kristen said again, defaulting to her martyr role. Merry could hardly resent it, though. She'd helped to create it.

Levi clapped his hands together. "Well, this is clearly an emergency situation. We'll email you the meeting details when we have them, Merry. Ladies, let's get you back in the car and out of this sun."

They all turned away, murmuring to each other about the horror of it all. She was almost in the clear when Levi turned back. "I'd better take the sign as evidence."

"Oh, I can do it. I'll take it in and send them the pictures, too."

"No, that's too upsetting for a young woman like yourself." She wouldn't have been surprised if he'd offered smelling salts at that point, but she couldn't take offense. Not when she was trying to keep a low profile. So instead of objecting, she watched Mr. Cannon pry the sign off the fence post and tuck it under his arm. "See?" He gestured toward the post. "Good as new. If you want to take a few days off, feel free. At the very least, you should probably work from home until this dies down."

"Oh, maybe. We'll see. Thank you, Mr. Cannon."

She watched him toss the sign in the trunk and wished she could snatch it back.

Despite the problem of kidnapped evidence, Merry breathed a huge sigh of relief as the car rolled away. Then she coughed up some gravel dust and told herself not to feel proud. She'd done something awful. Terrible. She'd perpetuated a con.

But she had her meeting.

"All's fair in love and war," she muttered to herself. And ghost towns, apparently.

Or she'd just done the worst thing of her life and she'd regret it later. She'd find out soon enough.

CHAPTER TWELVE

"OH, PLEASE," NATE HENDRICKS said as they walked down the block toward the Stud Farm. "That chase scene sucked it, big time."

Shane rolled his eyes. "I don't think it was written to stand up to the analysis of actual cops. Come on, when that train flew over the road? That was awesome."

"It was pretty damn awesome," Walker agreed.

Shane tried not to shoot the guy a glare. When Cole had suggested catching a movie on Saturday afternoon, he'd invited both Shane and Jenny's new boyfriend, Nate. But on their way out of the apartment building, they'd run into Walker, and Cole had invited him, as well.

The guy was fine. Shane had known him for a few years, and he seemed decent enough. Except for the fact that he'd flirted with Merry. And she'd flirted back.

Shane bit back a growl. He'd sat on the far side of their group at the theater, three seats away from Walker.

But there was no reason for jealousy. Flirtation meant nothing after what he and Merry had done. She'd flirted with Walker, yes, but she hadn't had sex with him. *That* she'd saved for Shane.

So it didn't matter. But he was still happy when Walker said a quick goodbye and jogged up the steps of the Stud Farm. Nate said goodbye as well, and Shane and Cole dropped into the two ancient metal chairs that sat beside the front steps.

"So when are you planning to build the house?" Cole asked.

Shane had told him that he'd inherited land from his grandfather and planned to build on it, but he hadn't said more than that. "Everything's still caught up in probate, but hopefully this fall."

"That'll be great for you. Are you still renting storage space for your carpentry stuff?"

"Yeah. Not to mention boarding my horse. It might take me a couple of years to get it built, but it'll get there. How's life as a ranch owner?"

Cole smiled with the satisfaction of a man whose life was falling perfectly into place. Shane wasn't sure how much of that satisfaction could be credited to the ranch. "I can't complain. Took a damn long time, but I'm finally just where I want to be. Don't sweat a couple of years. It took me a dozen."

"Yeah, but you're an old man now. Hardly able to enjoy life at all."

There was no mistaking Cole's grin this time. He definitely wasn't thinking about the ranch. And hell, if Shane could have that kind of happiness every night, he'd be smiling, too. Hell, one night of it and he already found his gaze going a little hazy at the memory.

"Still no word from your brother?" Cole asked.

"No. Nothing." He and Cole had been acquaintances in high school and friends later. Cole knew part of the story. Hell, everyone who'd lived in Jackson then knew that Shane's dad had disappeared. It had been a much smaller town.

"What do you think he's up to?"

"Hell, I have no idea. He was really into motorcycles. Maybe he's working in a shop. Maybe he's been cruising around the country this whole time. Maybe he's dead."

"Fuck, man. He's not dead. You would've heard something."

"Yeah," Shane said, but he didn't believe that. Anything could've happened to Alex in fifteen years. If he'd fallen into drugs and died on the streets, no one would've bothered tracking down his long-lost family.

No, Alex was gone. Maybe not dead, but just as out of reach as their father had been for all these years. It was just Shane and a mother who couldn't get out of her own head long enough to live a life.

Whatever pleasure he'd had with Merry last night, whatever joy he found in her presence, he couldn't have more than that. Maybe he'd never leave Jackson, maybe he'd never run, but just staying in one place was hardly a commitment. Hell, even when his dad had been here, he'd had a girlfriend. Dorothy Heyer, otherwise known as Mrs. Greg Heyer. There'd been rumors about them for months, about all the time Shane's dad had spent with the young woman married to a rich old rancher. It had been an open secret confirmed by their disappearance together.

And Shane's grandfather hadn't been any better. His first wife had died in a car accident, but not before she'd walked out on Gideon and his cheating ways. Jeanine had lasted much longer, but only because she'd turned a blind eye, ignoring his philandering until he'd finally kicked her out for "the love of his life," Kristen.

Shane's own history didn't inspire confidence, either. He'd never been in love. He'd never even been close. Hell, he could barely stand to be around his own mother anymore. No, despite the temptation to make it something more with Merry, he was destined for a solitary life. He'd build his house out in the middle of nowhere. He'd have a place to work. A shop. A barn and pasture for horses. That was all he needed. It was all he could handle. A wife and kids would be nothing but a long-term investment in disappointment and hurt. It would only be that much worse if he fell for a nice girl like Merry.

He and Cole sat under the blue sky, wrapped up in what must be very different thoughts. Cole was a man who would settle down. His biggest challenge would be talking Grace into it, but Shane had a feeling he'd succeed. Grace was damned prickly and tough to deal with, but she'd gentled a little in the past few months.

As if to refute his very thoughts, Grace exploded out the front door, the red tips of her hair flying as she looked back and forth. When her eyes locked on Cole, she bounded down the stairs. "I need a ride!"

"Okay. Where?"

"Merry had some trouble out at the ghost town and I've been trying to call her for two hours but the call won't go through. I'm worried."

Shane shot to his feet before Cole could stand. "What? What kind of trouble?"

"Vandalism, I think," Grace said in a distracted tone. "Someone posted an antitourism sign or something. I'm sure it's no big deal, and her phone goes out a lot, but I'd like to check on her."

"I'll do it," Shane volunteered.

Grace narrowed her eyes at him.

"Look, I go out there every day. I'm familiar with the place and where she might be working if she's not in her office."

Cole nodded. "Good. Call us when you get there. If you're okay with that, Grace?"

She watched him for a long moment, but then she nodded. "Okay. Thanks, Shane."

He would've felt triumphant about her softening toward him if he hadn't known that he didn't deserve it. After all, she was worried that he was going to use her friend and walk away. He might not be using Merry, but he was lying to her, and there was no doubt he'd walk away at some point.

But none of that mattered as he got into his truck and headed toward Providence. He tried her on his cell and the call went straight to voice mail. Maybe she'd just forgotten to charge it. Maybe she'd gotten excited about some new ridiculous story and lost track of everything else.

But what about that sign? Shane shifted and rubbed a hand over the back of his neck, trying to push some of the tension out. He'd have thought nothing of it, except for that weird accusation Jeanine Bishop had thrown at him. Was he being set up?

It wasn't beyond possibility. After all, two million dollars was at stake here. There wouldn't be any proof he'd done it, because he hadn't, but maybe suspicion would be all it took. If they could paint him as the bad

YOUR PARTICIPATION IS REQUESTED!

Dear Reader,

Since you are a lover of romance fiction – we would like to get to know you!

Inside you will find a short Reader's Survey. Sharing your answers with us will help our editorial staff understand who you are and what activities you enjoy.

To thank you for your participation, we would like to send you 2 books and 2 gifts – **ABSOLUTELY FREE!**

Enjoy your gifts with our appreciation,

Pam Powers

SEE INSIDE FOR READER'S SURVEY

For Your Romance Reading Pleasure...

Get 2 FREE BOOKS that will fuel your imagination with intensely moving stories about life, love and relationships.

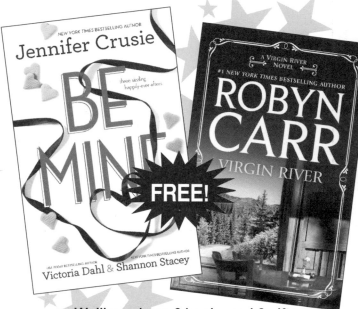

YOUR READER'S SURVEY
"THANK YOU" FREE GIFTS INCLUDE:
- ▶ 2 Romance books
- ▶ 2 lovely surprise gifts

PLEASE FILL IN THE CIRCLES COMPLETELY TO RESPOND

1) What type of fiction books do you enjoy reading? (Check all that apply)
   ○ Suspense/Thrillers ○ Action/Adventure ○ Modern-day Romances
   ○ Historical Romance ○ Humour ○ Paranormal Romance

2) What attracted you most to the last fiction book you purchased on impulse?
   ○ The Title ○ The Cover ○ The Author ○ The Story

3) What is usually the greatest influencer when you <u>plan</u> to buy a book?
   ○ Advertising ○ Referral ○ Book Review

4) How often do you access the internet?
   ○ Daily ○ Weekly ○ Monthly ○ Rarely or never.

5) How many NEW paperback fiction novels have you purchased in the past 3 months?
   ○ 0-2 ○ 3-6 ○ 7 or more

YES! I have completed the Reader's Survey. Please send me the 2 FREE books and 2 FREE gifts (gifts are worth about $10) for which I qualify. I understand that I am under no obligation to purchase any books, as explained on the back of this card.

194/394 MDL FVVW

FIRST NAME	LAST NAME

ADDRESS

APT.#	CITY

STATE/PROV.	ZIP/POSTAL CODE

If offer card is missing write to: Harlequin Reader Service, P.O. Box 1867, Buffalo, NY 14240-1867 or visit: www.ReaderService.com

BUSINESS REPLY MAIL
FIRST-CLASS MAIL   PERMIT NO. 717   BUFFALO, NY

POSTAGE WILL BE PAID BY ADDRESSEE

HARLEQUIN READER SERVICE
PO BOX 1341
BUFFALO NY 14240-8571

NO POSTAGE
NECESSARY
IF MAILED
IN THE
UNITED STATES

guy in a town this small, his case would have less of a chance.

More importantly, he knew he hadn't threatened the Providence operation, so who had?

Shane pushed the truck faster, risking a hefty ticket if he got caught. Merry still wasn't answering her phone. And she couldn't be much more alone than she was out there.

Even aside from what had happened between them last night, he couldn't stand the thought of Merry being in any danger. She was just so…unprotected. It wasn't just the fact that she was alone in a deserted town, but in the rest of her life, as well. It was as if she'd somehow grown up with no shell. No armor.

He wasn't sure how that could be true for a girl who'd grown up poor with no father around, but he couldn't shake the feeling that she needed protecting. Maybe that was only because he knew he was hurting her himself.

Yeah. That felt about right. He was worried for her, because he should be. Because he knew he was going to hurt her.

"Fuck," he cursed, slamming a hand against the steering wheel.

How the hell had he let this happen? Why couldn't he control himself around her? She was so harmless and nice; it should've been easy to treat her as nothing more than a friend. But somehow she'd snuck inside and become something dangerous.

Not that resisting her would've absolved him. Even if they'd stayed just friends, he'd lied to her. Used her trust to get something he wanted. And shit, it wasn't even worth it. What had he learned aside from the board's tactics? He could've gleaned those from afar, and his lawyer had barely been interested.

He was going to have to stop coming out here. He'd check on her, be sure she was fine and then he'd tell her he didn't have time to keep working on the saloon. Too little too late, but the best he could do at this point.

Once on the gravel road, the slower pace wound his gut up in knots, but he finally caught sight of Providence after what felt like eons. There was no gravel dust in the air ahead of his truck, which meant no one had driven through in the past half hour. He tried to make himself see that as a good sign.

And when he pulled into the parking area, he spotted Merry's car and no others. Another good sign, surely.

"Merry!" he called when he got out of the truck. He slammed the door and heard it echo for miles, but there was no response from Merry.

He called her name again, moving steadily toward the little house she'd claimed for work, but keeping his eyes moving, just in case. He made it all the way to the porch without any sign of her, but when he rushed into the small room, he saw her iPad right away, and his heart froze. She never went anywhere without that damned thing. So where was she?

The saloon. She had to be there, but he rushed over to find that building was deserted, too. What the hell had happened to her? For the first time since Grace had asked for help, Shane's worry turned to true alarm.

There weren't too many natural dangers that would cause her to disappear. A mountain lion, maybe, but not in the middle of the afternoon. So could it have been the vandal? Or had she just wandered off?

A thought suddenly freed itself from the fog of erotic memories of last night. When he'd been staring at Merry and wishing he could kiss her, she'd been talking about…something. It must have been Providence; there was no question of that. She'd been excited and babbling and bright with curiosity.

An ice house, she'd said. Somewhere at the start of the canyon.

"Thank God," he muttered as he took off at a jog. That had to be it. Her phone wouldn't work up there, and she probably wouldn't have carried her iPad along. Hopefully she was just caught up in her explorations and wasn't hurt.

He knew from his childhood that the trail that followed the canyon actually skirted above it, so Shane ignored the packed dirt trail and cut into the narrow canyon itself. At this time of year, the stream was still a fairly healthy flow. In another month it would decrease to a trickle. But at least it wasn't spring. Merry would have to work pretty hard to be swept away in this water, but during a wet spring, it would be damned hazardous.

"Merry!" he called again. He had to keep a close eye on his footing as the place was strewn with loose rocks and boulders that seemed to have been stacked on top of crumbling slate, but he stopped every dozen yards or so to sweep the area with his gaze.

Finally, about fifty yards up the canyon, he heard a voice. Singing. Shane sucked in a deep breath and sighed with relief. Okay. She was fine.

He rounded an outcropping of rock and found her walking toward him, singing a pop song he recognized from the radio. When she finally glanced up, the song turned into a screech of horror and she stumbled back so quickly she nearly fell on her ass in the narrow stream.

Shane jumped forward to steady her, but she waved him off. "Holy crap, you scared me!"

"Are you okay?"

"Aside from the fact that I almost wet my pants, yes."

"Grace was worried about you. She said there was some kind of vandalism up here, and then neither of us could get a hold of you."

"Oh." She looked guiltily away. "I'm sorry. Yeah. There's no signal up here. Thank you for coming to check on me."

"It's no problem. You're sure you're fine?"

"I'm good. In fact…" She brightened up and waved her hands. "Come back with me! I found the ice house! Or what's left of it. I think. It's pretty cool."

He started to demur, but she was already scrambling back up the canyon, so he had no choice but to follow. Plus, he didn't mind looking at her curvy hips ahead of him. Or the plump ass he'd curved his hand around when he'd kissed her good-night. A mix of relief over her safety and watching her swaying hips combined to cause him a problem he'd never experienced before: hiking with an erection.

"Christ, man," he muttered. "Get a grip."

After all, Merry didn't seem the least bit aware of him as she rushed ahead. She was too busy being excited about the two decaying boards of wood she pointed toward. "Look!"

"Uh," he responded, doing his best not to tell her it didn't look anything like an ice house.

"It's pretty broken down," she explained unnecessarily.

"Yeah."

"But look at the flat stones laid out here in this notch. I'm pretty sure this was the floor. See how it's set down below the level of the dirt? And there's still a board wedged in here."

"Very cool."

"Yeah." She sighed, kneeling down to put her hands to the stones. Half of them were buried in silt from some long ago flood, but Merry didn't seem to see that. She seemed to see a complete ice house here, newly built by hardworking folk and used as a summer playroom for mischievous children. "So cool," she whispered. "We can't make it part of the tour, obviously. It's too treacherous up here, but I've got a lot of pictures. I can make a little display about it, use some quotes from the story I heard."

"Right."

She looked up at him with a huge grin, and Shane felt a now familiar rush of warmth fall through him. He knelt next to her.

"See this?"

"Merry."

When she turned back to him, he kissed her, aware that he always had to draw her attention before he could claim her mouth. But that didn't matter. What mattered was that when his lips touched hers, she always melted into him. She always wanted more.

But why the hell did her greatest passion have to be the one thing he couldn't support? If it was anything else, he could happily play second fiddle as long as she sighed like this when he touched her. As long as her shy tongue snuck in to taste him and drive him wild.

"Oh," she said when he finally let her go.

"We should get back. The sun's setting."

"Okay." She sighed, taking his hand when he stood to pull her up.

She followed him, quiet for once, in that way she only seemed to get around him. He liked her shyness around him, but he was happy when she finally spoke.

"Shane?"

"Yeah?"

"Thanks for coming to check on me."

"No problem. Just be sure to tell people when you're heading into the hills, all right? We were worried."

She got quiet again, and despite the beauty around them, the running water and deep shadows and dancing Aspen leaves, Shane couldn't take the quiet. He'd gotten used to her voice.

"You okay, Merry?"

"Sure."

He stopped and pulled her around to look at him. "I feel like I should say something about last night. So you'll know it wasn't…"

"I know! I know it wasn't some big declaration. I'm not your girlfriend. And I'm good with that. I swear. I needed that. Big time."

He answered her smile, but that hadn't been what he'd meant. He'd wanted to say… Well, fuck, he'd wanted to say it had meant something, that it hadn't been just some attempt to get laid. But how could he tell her it had been meaningful without implying that he'd want something more?

"I don't think I can do the friends with benefits thing if you're dating around," she said. "That's too much for me. But last night? With you? That was so good, Shane."

"I'm not dating around," he growled, strangely angry that she might think that. "Look, I'm not the settling down type, but I'm not a player. I'm not sleeping with anyone else."

"Oh, good!" she said brightly, then a blush climbed her cheeks. "Maybe we could…"

He raised his eyebrows, wondering what she was about to say.

Merry covered her face and took a deep breath, then seemed to brace herself and stand straighter. "Maybe we could do it again? Just once more? Or more than that? I don't know how these things work. Would that make me a booty call?"

"What? No!" He shook his head and then saw the way her face fell. "I mean, *yes* we can do it again. Christ, Merry."

She crossed her arms. "What?"

"You're not a booty call, all right? I want to sleep with you again, but not like that."

"Okay," she said cautiously.

"It's just that you're nice. I like you. And I don't know how to say that I want to sleep with you, but I don't want any…"

"More?" she offered softly.

Jesus. How could he even answer that? What kind of man was he? "It's not that I wouldn't want more. You're a great girl. I like you."

"I get it," she said and flashed him a comforting smile. "I feel the same way."

Her voice wasn't quite convincing. He studied her carefully.

She covered her eyes. "Stop looking at me. I want to have sex with you, okay? Can we stop talking about this?"

Well, fuck, he couldn't argue with that. "Okay," he finally said.

She dropped her hand and smiled. "Just don't tell Grace."

"I value my male anatomy way too much for that."

"Hey, me, too!"

His laughter winged through the narrow canyon, joining up with hers when she laughed, too.

"Seriously," he said as they began picking their way down loose rock again, "that girl scares me."

"She should."

"How did you two meet?"

"Grace was in school to become a makeup artist. She was already amazing, though, she just needed the certificate to get her foot in the door. I had the great idea that I'd learn to do hair, which doesn't make any sense. I can't even do my own hair. She came across me practicing layering on a wig and told me to give it up."

"Ouch."

"In a nice way, though. Well, not in a nice way, but I could tell she felt bad about breaking the truth to me like that. I dropped out and went back to work as a waitress, but I stayed in touch with Grace. She let me live with her for a month, and we've been best friends ever since, no matter where we lived or what we were doing."

"Opposites attract, I guess."

"Yeah. We take care of each other. And we're more alike than you could know."

Shane couldn't see it, but he didn't argue. Grace was all fists and fire, and Merry was like some sort of funny earth mother, if earth mother types were sexy. But he was smart enough not to say any of that to her.

"Be sure to call Grace as soon as we get out of the canyon. I hope finding that ice house was worth risking her wrath."

"She'll be fine. And it was!"

Shane had inadvertently triggered another enthusiastic description of a Providence story she'd heard, but he smiled as he followed her over a pile of boulders, then hopped down to put his hands around her waist and ease her down. She didn't stop talking.

"These people were so amazing. Can you imagine coming here when it took a whole day on horseback just to run across the closest neighbor? When there were no doctors? No hospitals? They brought their children here and built these houses from scratch."

"And then they left."

"Oh, no. It wasn't that simple."

"There was a flood and they picked up and scattered. I'm not sure how admirable that is. Practical, yes. I can't say I wouldn't have done the same." No, he definitely couldn't say that.

"No, Shane. You don't understand. It wasn't just the flood. Granted, that was catastrophic. Five people in Providence died, including a little girl, and three houses and a granary were destroyed. But they rebuilt. They kept going. But the flood had swept a wall of debris into the canyon. The first year, the stream's flow was cut in half. They tried to move some of the boulders. One of the founders lost his arm in an accident when rocks shifted onto him. Then the next year, more spring flooding pushed everything farther into a narrow funnel in the rock. The water dried up. Completely. Even then, they kept the town alive for two more years. They dug wells. They tried to redirect the stream farther north. But when a drought hit, they couldn't sustain themselves. They couldn't do it."

They'd finally reached the mouth of the canyon, and she stopped and spread her arms to encompass the town. It lay below them like an Old West model, like a toy.

"This was their home. These people held on as long as they could. They loved this place, and they wanted it, but they couldn't live here without water. All but one of them moved on. Gideon Bishop's great-grandfather held out for five more years, then he moved a few miles south near the current Bishop ranch house. There was water there. It was easier. But he never gave up. That's why the land is still in that family."

Shane shoved his hands into his pockets and glared at the town. He'd never heard that story before. All he'd ever heard about was the flood. Not that it made a difference. These people really had nothing to do with him. It was still just a dead town his grandfather had funded in a fit of spite. It was nothing more than a two million dollar dollhouse collection for tourists.

"I wish I could have seen what it was like when it was alive," Merry said softly. "Kids running through the streets. Men and women plowing the fields. The houses whitewashed and flowers planted. Can you imagine?"

He couldn't, but he could see the beauty of it on her

face. The wonder. The possibility of what it could've been if tragedy hadn't struck.

Shane wondered if he looked the same way when he stared at her.

CHAPTER THIRTEEN

MERRY WASN'T IN THE RIGHT frame of mind to talk to her mom. She wasn't even in the right mood to deal with waking up to Grace falling onto the bouncy mattress of the sofa bed. She definitely wasn't prepared to do a video chat. But here she was.

"Say, 'Hi, Mom!'" Grace urged, annoyingly chipper at 8:00 a.m.

Merry peeked over the covers. "Hi, Mom."

"Hi, Mom!" Grace repeated, waving at the screen of Merry's iPad.

Merry's mom and Grace began chatting, thank God, because Merry needed a few moments to collect herself. She'd been deep in a dream involving Shane and a horseback ride and a few gymnastic-like moves that were only possible on horseback during REM sleep.

She was so grateful for the minute to collect herself and drag her focus away from that insane sex dream that she couldn't even be annoyed at the happy chatter occurring five inches from her ear.

Grace was strangely easy with Merry's mom. She always had been, and it made Merry's heart swell every time she saw it. Something about her mom seemed to put Grace at ease and always had.

"Cole's doing great," Grace was saying.

"I hope he's good to you, sweetheart."

"Oh, he is. He really, truly is."

"I'm so happy for you." Merry's mom sighed. "What about my sweet girl? Has she met a nice cowboy yet?"

"Not if I have anything to say about it," Grace answered. She tipped the screen toward Merry who finally got a look at her mom's face, which was a rounder, older version of her own.

"Grace is cock-blocking me, Mom."

"Merry!" her mom shrieked, disappearing from the screen as it wobbled from her laughter.

"It's true! I need that old copy of *Our Bodies, Ourselves* you gave me when I was twelve. I need to explain to Grace what my vagina is for."

True to her old hippie roots, her mom just waved an amused hand. "You can get all that on the internet now, honey."

"I've heard rumors about that." Merry snuggled up next to Grace so they could both be on the screen. It felt a little like a slumber party, and Merry's heart filled with love. "Hey, Mom. Ask Grace about her boyfriend again so you can see her face melt into starry-eyed mush. Can you even believe it?"

"It's beautiful."

Beautiful or not, Grace still punched her shoulder.

"But I want to find out what's going on with you, Merry. Did you see Crystal?"

Merry groaned and Grace disappeared from camera with an eye-roll. "That's my cue to go make coffee."

"Yes," Merry finally answered. "I saw her. And she was a bitch."

"Your cousin is not a bitch," her mom scolded.

"She is."

"It's not true. And even if she was a bitch, she's still your family. There's love there."

Merry groaned. "There's no love there, Mom. I know you love your sister. And you should. But however different your lives are now, you two came from the same place. Crystal and her brother were raised in a McMansion in a gated community on the lake in Chicago. I've never even lived in a *house*. We have nothing in common. She thinks I'm slacker white trash and I think she's a snooty bitch."

"Oh, honey. We don't have much family left. I really wished you'd try."

"I've tried. I swear. But I'm not like them. And now even you seem to have bought into their crap about success and jobs and education."

Her mom shook her head. "I don't know what you're talking about."

Merry slumped. She didn't want to have this conversation. Ever. She'd rather just do well and never have to consider it again. She'd make Providence a success. She'd have a respectable job and live in a beautiful place, and then she wouldn't have to worry that even her loving mother considered her a disappointment.

"Never mind, Mom. I need to get up and have some coffee. Big day today."

In reality, she had nothing on her schedule except dinner out at the Easy Creek Ranch, but it was too early in the morning to play the part of disappointing child. "I love you," she added, which was always true, no matter what. But Merry couldn't disappoint everyone again. This was her last chance to make it.

"Ugh!" she groaned as soon as she'd hit End. "What is her deal about family?"

"Don't ask me," Grace said. "I don't know anything about family crap. But she looked great."

"She did. I wish she'd find someone. She seemed a little lonely the last time I saw her."

"Oh. Well."

Merry sat up and looked at Grace. "What?"

"Nothing!" Grace yelped. "I hope she finds someone, too."

Merry collapsed back to the bed and checked her email. And there it was. An emergency meeting of the board on Monday afternoon. The brochure was being printed on gorgeous glossy paper on Monday morning. Merry could force the board to take a look, she could present all her ideas for the fluff piece with the local paper, and then she'd free up some funds for renovations.

Everything was coming together. She was going to be a legend. Or at least not a wandering slacker who'd never held down a real job. And, damn it, that was good enough for her.

THIS WAS STUPID. It was pointless. And Shane had no idea what he was doing here.

His horse shifted impatiently, as unsure of her purpose as Shane was of his. Usually when Shane loaded her onto the horse trailer, there was hard work ahead. Hours of riding. Work to be done. But now they just stood here, looking over Providence as if it were dangerous.

It wasn't, but somehow Shane felt afraid.

He shouldn't have come here. There was no reason.

But he finally shifted forward, and his horse walked slowly through the town.

Nothing looked different. The town was the same, but he wasn't as quick to dismiss the buildings as he usually was.

This was their home, Merry had said. They didn't want to leave.

The idea of it meant nothing to him. It changed nothing. But somehow her words had opened up memories of the time he'd spent here with his father. The mornings when they'd pull up so early Shane could see his breath in the air even in September. The way his dad would let him explore and poke around no matter now long Shane wanted to take. He might've been through the church twice already, but there was that one snake that kept escaping, sliding between the broken floorboards to hide.

His dad hadn't been much of a talker. He hadn't told stories about Providence. But he would point out an old horseshoe or a broken wagon wheel, and in Shane's eyes they'd been archaeological wonders. Relics of a past filled with Native American wars and brave cowboys and shoot-outs with horse thieves.

Now Shane knew that life in Providence had been nothing like that. Any nearby Native Americans had been traders and hunters passing through, and the cowboys had been quiet, hard men who didn't ride out in posses and probably spent more time farming than ranching. But as a kid... My God, these people had been heroes. And best of all, they'd been related to him.

Blood relations had seemed a good thing back then.

At some point, it had damned them in his mind. He'd damned them along with his father.

Shane didn't need to stop and poke around this time. The place held no romance for him, but he rode on toward the old trail.

He passed into the trees, a stiffness in his spine, jaw aching. How many hours had he spent on horseback here, following close behind his dad? Silent rides through bright green aspens just starting to edge toward yellow.

Oh, there was a road. They could have driven up to the ancient log cabin high in the trees, but that hadn't been the point. The point had been the task of packing it up. Of learning how to travel light and load the horse just as Shane's dad had done when he was little. Not with his father. Grandpa Bishop wasn't a man who tolerated kids or had the patience to teach them. No, Shane's dad had ridden with his grandfather, an old-time cowboy whom Shane had never met.

He eased his mare up the trail, so ancient and hardpacked that it was still clear of grass and brush even all these years later. They'd always come here alone, he and his dad. Alex hadn't liked horseback riding or camping. He'd much rather have ridden a bike with his friends or raced ATVs. He'd never been here, never seen the cabin.

If Shane wanted to see Merry's eyes light up, he could tell her about the cabin. He didn't know who'd lived here, but judging by the state of the place twenty-five years before, it was damn old. She'd be over the moon about it. Exploring it. Researching. Solving the past like a mystery, as if finding the original owner's name would make something right with the world.

But the world wasn't right. He didn't understand how she couldn't see that. Her own father had left her without a backward glance. Was that why she wanted to see the past as romantic? Did that excuse her own father, because he must have had his reasons? He must have had troubles?

But that didn't explain her love for this place. She'd been tricked into watching over Providence by people with an ulterior motive. How could she still see such good things? It was as if she willfully ignored all the shadows in life and claimed they were only there to set off the brightness of things.

He'd protect her from such foolishness if he could, but there was no way to do that. Because the world wasn't right. His own role in Merry's life was proof of that. He wished it wasn't.

The trail drew close enough to the edge of the narrow canyon that he could see part of the stream bed where he and Merry had walked the day before, and he missed her in that moment. He'd have to bring her up here. She'd be so happy.

But then the trail was swallowed by the trees, and Shane was with his dad again. The ride to the cabin had only been about ninety minutes, but it had felt like a day long journey to a place no one had seen in a hundred years. This had been the point where Shane would settle from babbling excitement into quiet. Here in these shadows.

The sounds were the same. And he could feel his father. He could feel that memory, and then all the grief and hope of the next few years. Fuck, that man had broken them all. Him and his brother. And his mom most of all. Like Merry, she had a way of seeing only brightness, too, the difference being that she would look into utter blackness and deny the dark. She'd claim she'd seen a glimmer of something. If only Shane looked harder, he'd see it, too.

He had. For years.

He wished he could have those years back. Wished he could watch out for his little brother instead of indulging his mom.

He could've done so much more. He could've made his little brother's life better, but he'd been too damn busy shoring up his own false hope. "When Dad comes back…" Shane had said a thousand times, putting every opportunity on hold. When Dad comes back, this is how it'll be. When Dad comes back, we'll all do this together.

No wonder Alex had run.

Their father wasn't coming back. But on this trail, beneath these trees, Shane was able to think of him in an almost normal way for the first time since he'd disappeared. It hurt. It felt awful. But the memory was still there beneath it, instead of being obscured by a thick fog of grief and hate and anger. The abandonment had been monstrous, but that didn't mean the man had been a monster. He'd done something awful, something Shane could never understand, but for a decade, he'd been a good father.

For years, that truth had made his disappearance worse. But right now, in this moment, it actually made things better.

By the time he reached the cabin, Shane was exhausted. Not by the ride, but from having let his dad back into his life for a moment. But even past his weariness, he smiled when he saw the half-collapsed structure. Yeah, Merry would love this. Maybe he'd hang around long enough to show it to her. Or he could offer it as consolation when she decided she hated him, as she would. He could give her this place as a way to heal her wounds.

But he didn't want her up here by herself. Even back then the road had barely been safe, and today he'd passed a washed out section of it where the trail crossed.

He tied off his horse beneath a shady tree and walked the open area around the cabin. The fire pit was still there, and even the area where they'd always set up camp was still relatively cleared, but the years had taken a toll. A corner of the cabin that had once been straight and sturdy was now collapsed. Branches littered the tall grass of the makeshift yard, broken off the trees over years of storm and wind. But a few of the old apple trees still stood at the side of the house, tiny, hard apples peeking pale green between the leaves.

Yes, he wanted to show this place to Merry. While she still liked him. While she would still share that blinding smile and crack her strange jokes. He wanted to see her happy and unguarded, not for some old man who'd told her a story, but for *him*. For something he'd given her. Maybe it would make up for what he was going to take away.

He explored the place, finding memories he'd lost, and thinking about his dad, and by the time he looked up at the sky, he realized it was past time to go.

He didn't want to rush his horse on the steep trail, so he turned her down the road instead. He had to get back to Providence, load up his mare and then drive her back to the farm where he boarded her. It wasn't too far from Easy's, though. He should make it fine.

Rushed as he was, he wasn't feeling reckless. When he got to another stretch of road that had been washed out to little more than four feet wide, Shane dismounted and walked. This road was a hazard. He wondered if anyone had been up here in the past decade.

That would probably please Merry. She'd know no one had been bothering the site of the cabin, pulling out artifacts and doing damage.

As he eased along the final few feet of the wash out, Shane caught sight of something glinting down below. He edged closer to the drop-off and tried to get a better look, but he couldn't see anything more than the flash of sunlight on something reflective when the leaves below shifted in the breeze.

Maybe it was just water dancing on some offshoot of the stream, but he didn't hear water and he thought he could see something white down there, a corner that could be rock, but seemed awfully straight and sharp for that.

Shane walked a little farther on, looking for a path down, but he didn't find one, and there wasn't time anyway. He'd come back again. With Merry. Or maybe without her. Maybe there was some structure down there even he didn't know about and he could surprise her with that as well.

Shane mounted his horse and urged her to a trot, all his tiredness gone at the thought of seeing Merry again He had to end it, but not tonight.

Not tonight.

CHAPTER FOURTEEN

MERRY HAD NEVER seen this side of Rayleen before. Oh, she'd heard rumors about a budding romance between Rayleen and Easy, but she'd understood it to be an ornery, adversarial romance. A dance like two old dogs circling each other. She hadn't expected this.

She stole another glance in the rearview mirror.

Grace had crossed the yard to Rayleen's house an hour earlier, and when the two women had reappeared, Rayleen had looked fresh and bright and ten years younger. Her long white hair was pulled into a loose chignon at the base of her neck, and makeup brightened her eyes and softened her skin.

She still wore her standard jeans and boots, but Grace had apparently talked her into a pretty pink gingham blouse. The unlit cigarette, however, was still in evidence, but at least it had been tucked into the breast pocket of the blouse and wasn't clasped between Rayleen's tinted lips.

Merry looked up at her own face and wished she'd thought to have Grace help her with makeup, too. She just looked like normal old Merry, round-faced and harmless and plain. And the thing was…she didn't feel like that anymore. She should look different, shouldn't she?

She was a covert vandal. A deceptive manipulator.

And now…a wild, sexual woman who'd taken a secret lover. But she still looked like the girl you'd hire to housesit for you and walk your dog while you went somewhere exotic and dangerous.

Damn. Maybe eyeliner would have made all the difference. Or maybe she would've just looked like plain old Merry who'd gotten into the makeup drawer.

It didn't matter, she told herself as she drove beneath the Easy Creek Ranch sign and spotted the men standing in the shade of a huge cottonwood tree that nearly filled the space between Easy's house and Cole's.

Grace smiled. Merry felt a smile tugging at her own lips as well, but she tried to fight it. She didn't have an excuse for a goofy, lovesick grin. She wouldn't be able to explain why her eyes went so bright at the sight of the three men in cowboy hats, each of them with a beer in their grasp. When she glanced at the mirror, she saw Rayleen scowling and felt better. Things weren't as topsy-turvy as they seemed. She could pull this off. Everything was normal.

But when she parked and got out of the car and met Shane's eyes, there was no stopping her smile. Oh, God. All she could do was duck her head and pray that everyone else was too wrapped up in their own greetings to notice.

They were. Cole moved forward to kiss Grace, and Rayleen stalked toward Easy. "That beer for me?" she barked.

Easy sighed as if he were already exasperated, but he handed over the open beer.

Shane watched Merry and very slowly raised a hand

up to tip his hat in greeting. She blushed. He smiled. "Can I get you other ladies a beer?"

"Yes!" she said too urgently and he winked before he turned to walk to the half barrel that was filled with ice. "Easy, you need another one, too?"

"Apparently," he groused, but Merry caught him watching Rayleen with a sidelong look. "You ladies look real nice tonight," he said, including them all, but Rayleen flushed at the words.

Merry wished she had a right to flush herself, but she was just wearing jeans and a T-shirt again, though she had purposefully chosen her Wonder Woman shirt. Men thought Wonder Woman was hot, with her all-American bustier and high-heeled boots. Plus, it was tighter than her other T-shirts, and she wanted Shane looking at her breasts. And her waist. The curve of her hips. He'd liked them okay, hadn't he? He'd told her she was beautiful. He'd seemed enthusiastic.

"Were you working today?" she asked when he handed her a beer.

"A little. And I went for a ride. I apologize if I look rough. I didn't have time to stop for a shower. Maybe I should ask Cole if I can use the bunkhouse bathroom."

"No, you look great. I mean, you look fine." But he did look great. A little dusty, and his hair looked slightly damp with sweat against his nape. He looked…dirty. Like a gorgeous dirty cowboy who wanted to do filthy things to her in the barn or…

Merry cleared her throat and forced herself to stop staring at the wisp of hair she could see just past the open collar of his shirt. He probably smelled like sweat. Somehow that made her mouth water.

"So," he said, as if she'd lapsed into silence for too long. "What did you do today?"

"Oh, I was finishing up the brochure. It's going to be amazing. The board's meeting tomorrow, and I'm going to make them take a look at it then, and I'm already planning what we'll say to the reporter about—"

"Reporter?"

"Yes, we're hoping to get a really solid piece written up."

"About the vandalism?"

"Oh, God, no." She felt the color draining from her cheeks. Cole joined them, and Grace smiled to cover her nervousness. "It was no big deal. Just a sign."

"What did it say?" he pressed.

"Uh. Something like No More Tourists."

"Huh." Shane rocked back on his heels. "Any idea who it could be?"

"No!"

Cole frowned. "That's really strange. There are people who oppose new development here, obviously, but I've never heard about anything like that. And it doesn't make much sense. Why post a sign where no one's going to see it? Usually people just send a letter to the editor of the paper."

"Maybe it has to do with the lawsuit!" she said, throwing that poor guy under the bus when she'd vowed not to do it. But she couldn't handle pressure. She felt like there was a bright light shining right on her and every nervous blink of her eyes was giving her away.

"Lawsuit?" Cole asked.

Shane cleared his throat and started to say something, but Merry was in full-on babble mode.

"I'm sure it's not that, either. The guy who inherited the rest of the land is suing over the money left to Providence. It's no big deal. Standard stuff, I'm sure. No vandalism."

"Right," Shane interrupted. "I'm sure it's nothing. But you need to be careful out there from now on, okay? No more working with your earphones on."

She nodded, and then grabbed on to the first out she could think of. "Oh! We left the food in the car. I'll go get it."

"I'll help," Shane volunteered.

Cole was frowning at him, seemingly suspicious about Shane's quick offer to help, but Shane just started toward her car. Merry followed, relieved the interrogation was over.

"We brought pies. And Rayleen brought potato salad. None of it's homemade, I'm afraid. Grace and I are a little hopeless in the kitchen, and Rayleen said she hadn't worked her whole life so she could slave over a kitchen stove to please a bunch of clueless cowboys. Oh, sorry. I'm sure she didn't mean you."

"No?"

She met his smile. "Okay, she probably did."

"So you can't cook? Have you been living in your mom's basement your whole life?"

"No! Of course not! Why would you think that?"

He blinked at her response and shook his head. "I'm just wondering what you eat."

"Oh." Right. He didn't know she was a slacker loser with no career path. "Sandwiches. Salads. I can cook up some mean nachos if I need to. And by 'need to' I mean every Friday night."

He laughed. "You sound like a few cowboys I know. Aside from the salads, I mean."

"Can you cook?"

He shrugged. "A little, but I'm a meat and potatoes kind of guy. I'll make you pot roast sometime if you're nice."

"Then I'll be nice."

"Yeah?" He waited as she opened the trunk, and as soon as it swung up and blocked the others' view, Shane stepped closer and rested his hands on her hips. "Damn, I've been wanting to touch you since I saw you."

"Oh." Her pulse hammered, pushed on by the danger of being seen and the thrill of him wanting her.

"You look so…"

She waited for him to say sexy. Or hot. Or beautiful.

"Sweet."

She shook her head.

"You do. You look cute and untouchable. Like someone I shouldn't think dirty thoughts about."

God, what was she supposed to think about that? She wanted to be sexy and hot and beautiful. She didn't want to be sweet and cute like a cozy little friend. But his hands tightened on her hips and he kissed her, and what the hell did she care how she turned him on, as long as she did? He shouldn't be doing this, shouldn't be touching her here, only a few feet away from everyone, but he couldn't resist.

Merry smiled against his mouth and he pulled back.

"Damn, you're adorable," he said, answering her smile. "I guess we'd better get this food?"

"I suppose it shouldn't take quite this long to gather up potato salad."

"Maybe." He touched her jaw, brushed his thumb over her mouth, then dared one last quick kiss before he let her go. When he closed the trunk, Merry expected everyone to be looking at them, but no one seemed to have noticed their strange behavior. No one except Cole, whose intent gaze made her cringe.

But Cole wouldn't say anything. He wouldn't want his best friend neutered.

And after that one close call, the barbecue was lovely and fun. The men were adorable, sitting down at the table and taking off their hats, looking half naked without them.

Even Rayleen seemed on her best behavior, complimenting Easy on the ribs and only complaining about the bright red highlights in Grace's hair three times.

Easy told stories about Cole as a boy, and Grace hung on every word, looking so soft and happy that Merry curved an arm around her waist and hugged her.

Grace laid her head on Merry's shoulder. "What is it?" she whispered.

"Nothing. This is just so nice. So…right. It feels like home here, doesn't it?"

Grace was quiet for a long moment. They both watched Easy as he told a story about a snowstorm that dumped four feet of snow in one night. "Yes," Grace finally said. "It does."

Merry hadn't formed bonds here as deep as Grace's but she felt that, too. That sense that these people liked her for herself and didn't expect something else. They certainly liked her more than her own cousins ever had. Cole was like a big brother to her now, the kind of role she'd always wanted Crystal's brother to play. And hell, Grace had always been like a sister.

And despite the fact that they'd never even dated, Rayleen and Easy perfectly fit the role of quirky grandparents. Even as she thought that, Rayleen was poking at Easy. "I bet there was nothing to do but fiddle and fornicate for days!" she said.

Easy shook his head. "Weren't any women on the ranch. It was just us cowhands."

"That's what I meant. Don't tell me you never got up to a little bunkhouse slap and tickle."

Easy's face turned bright red. "Woman, there are ladies here, even if you don't qualify."

"Well, they've got all the parts, I guess, but they're the ones laughing."

Merry tried her best to stifle her giggles when Easy shot them a look of accusation, but she couldn't. In fact, her laughter escaped on a muffled snort that made Grace collapse in hysterics. Easy shook his head and turned to glare at Rayleen.

"You're incorrigible."

"Then maybe you'd better go on and find yourself someone corrigible to play cards with!" she snapped. "Because I'm damn sure tired of hearing about it."

They glared at each other so long that Merry's giggles finally faded away. She cleared her throat. "Do you play the fiddle, Easy?"

"Just campfire style," he muttered.

"Will you play? I love fiddle music."

"Oh, no one wants to hear that."

They all urged him to play. Finally even Rayleen said, "Just go get it, you old coot."

Easy looked at her one last, long time, then nodded and headed for the house. Cole lit the fire in the pit and passed out beers, and they settled in to listen to Easy play through his repertoire of Western jigs and range ballads. It was beautiful. A perfect night with the last red glow of the sun outlining the dark crags of the Tetons. Merry's only unanswered wish was that she could lean against Shane the way Grace had snuggled into Cole's arms.

But it wasn't like that for them. Not really. Though it was nice to look over and catch him stealing a glance of her. She blushed and felt awkward in the very best possible way.

Rayleen leaned close. "I think that boy's about to stamp your ass with a brand, Christmas."

Merry choked on her beer and leaned over to cough as Rayleen pounded her back. "No," she gasped.

"Oh, he wants it," Rayleen insisted. "I'd bend over and let him call me Sally if I were you."

"No! Whatever that means, I'm not going to bend over and…anything!"

"Your loss, Christmas. You young girls don't know how to jump on a red-hot opportunity."

Merry rolled her eyes. "I'm not sure you should be the one telling me that."

Rayleen snorted, but her eyes went to Easy as he finished his last song with a flourish. "Hell," she murmured. "I'd break his hip."

"Then maybe you should jump softly."

For a moment, her eyes went a little…sad. But then she shook her head and raised her chin. "Not bad for an old fart," she called out. "You all worn-out, Easy, or do you have enough energy to get your butt kicked at rummy?"

"Lady—" he sighed "—I've got enough energy to make you eat those words."

"Once again, you've forgotten what a woman's mouth is for, old man."

"Damn it, Rayleen," he groused.

Rayleen howled. Easy stalked off to get the cards, muttering something about loose old women.

Shane stood, drawing Merry's eye. "I've got an early day tomorrow. I hope you all won't mind if I head on home."

Her brain spun. She wanted to go with him, but she couldn't. She'd driven Rayleen and Grace here. He must know that.

So maybe Shane didn't want her with him. Maybe he was tired and he wanted to go home and sleep.

Crap. She perched on the edge of the bench and tried not to scowl.

"Anyone want a ride back?" he asked.

Merry looked around, but Grace was clearly planning on spending the night with her man, and Rayleen was settling into her seat, ready for a game of gin rummy with Easy.

Shane raised his eyebrows and cut his eyes toward his truck.

"Oh. I…I'm actually really tired. Rayleen, can you drive my car back for me when you're ready? I'm gonna head home now."

Rayleen was in the middle of shuffling cards, and paused to wave an impatient hand. "Sure. Go on. I'll put your keys in the mailbox." Luckily she was too focused on gearing up to beat Easy to make a dirty remark or encourage Merry to get laid. And even Grace seemed too content and happy to be suspicious.

Merry handed her keys to Rayleen, they said their goodbyes and then she was in Shane's truck and on her way home.

"Jesus," he said, "I was afraid you wouldn't come."

"I thought maybe you wanted to get to bed."

"I did. Was I not clear?"

Her own laughter surprised her. It was deep and husky and pleased, but she wasn't used to this. She wasn't used to being someone's secret. Or an object of desire. It was really…really…

Completely fucking awesome.

Her Wonder Woman T-shirt had worked its charm. Best superhero ever.

Shane reached across the truck to put his hand on her thigh. Merry watched his wide hand settle on her leg. She wanted this image in her mind forever. His tanned fingers, slightly dusted with hair, spread across her thigh. The fingertips blunt and wide and rough from work. They looked so beautiful and unfamiliar, despite that they'd already been inside her body.

The last glimmer of evening light caught his face, the shadows making his jaw even harder, and Merry watched him for a dozen heartbeats. More. This was a scene from someone else's life. A handsome man in a cowboy hat driving a pickup truck through the mountains. His hand on the thigh of his lover. The moonless night hiding their secrets.

Her window was cracked, but Merry rolled it all the way down. She wanted to feel everything tonight, so she let her arm slide out the window and cupped her hand to catch the bright cold of the air. And her other hand... Her other hand she slid down Shane's arm, over his warm skin and soft hair and flexing muscles. She spread her fingers over his and held his hand to her leg.

She had no idea why, but this moment felt important. A stolen breath between before and after.

His hand turned up and he folded her fingers into his. "Will you be in Providence tomorrow?"

"Not until late. I've got to get to the printer's first thing. I'm trying to cobble together a press package before the board meeting tomorrow."

"I'm not sure how much more time I'll be able to put in on the saloon. Work is getting tight. I thought I'd finish up the floor tomorrow, but after that..."

She squeezed his hand. "I understand." She did, but her chest still ached a little. He wasn't there often, but she'd liked that promise. Of knowing he might surprise her. Of wondering when he would show up. Usually he'd just gone straight to the saloon, but sometimes he'd stopped in to say hi. And now that they were lovers, she realized she'd been crafting moments in her head, assigning him lines and stolen kisses and afternoons when he couldn't keep his hands off her. "I'm thankful for what you've done," she said, instead of asking him to keep coming every day.

"Do you think you could come by after the board meeting? I wanted to show you something."

She forgot her strange mood and turned toward him. "What?"

"It's a surprise."

She shook his hand like a rag. "What surprise?"

Shane laughed and twisted free of her grip to squeeze her thigh. "You'll have to wait and see."

"Noooo! No fair! I'm going before the board tomorrow! If it's something I can—"

"No. It's just for you. Not for the board. Not for the paper."

He sounded serious, so Merry tried to contain her excitement. And failed. "Just give me a hint. Please? I can't take it. What is it? Did you find something? Is it in the saloon? Was there something hidden under the floorboards? Is it treasure?"

"God, Merry." He chuckled. "You're like a kid."

"I'm not! I just love surprises."

"She says in her Wonder Woman shirt."

Her happiness froze and turned into something heavy and cold. "Hey." She let go of his arm and faced straight again, and suddenly the crisp air pouring through the window was too cold. "Wonder Woman is sexy."

"True." He smiled at her.

She folded her arms.

"Come on, Merry. I like your shirt."

"Sure. Thanks." Now she knew why tonight had felt like a scene from someone else's movie. Because it was. Someone who wasn't a girl who floated through life on cartoon clouds and goofball dreams.

"Hey." Shane stopped just before the highway and put the truck in Park. "I was only teasing you. Wonder Woman *is* sexy."

"Right. I'll be sure to wear something that shows off my tits next time. Would that be more grown-up?"

"First of all, your tits look amazing in that shirt, and you know it."

She shrugged, pretending like she hadn't worn an extra tight shirt on purpose.

"Second, there are a dozen women at the saloon every Saturday night in shirts that show off way more than they cover. You're the one I can't keep my hands off."

"Right. You think I'm cute."

"You are cute."

"Great!" She turned her head to stare out into the night, pissed off and feeling stupid as hell for being pissed. Which only made it worse.

"Merry."

She crossed her arms tighter.

"I don't get it. Is there something wrong with thinking you're cute?"

Crap. She was being ridiculous. She didn't know why she felt hurt. He wanted her. She wanted him. So why did she need him to say it a certain way? To look at her a certain way? "No, it's good. Let's go."

"Okay," he said, but instead of putting the truck in gear, he leaned closer and tipped her head toward him. He kissed her, softly at first, then with increasing urgency. When he pulled back, her arms were clutching his shoulders and they were both breathing hard. "You're cute, Merry. And you turn me on like crazy. If you can't tell, maybe I'm the one who should be upset."

She rolled her eyes.

"You're not just cute, you also look sweet and harmless, and when I see you I remember how it felt to be inside you and to see you naked beneath me. I remember how you looked as you came, and it drives me insane. Like I know something about you that no one else does."

She tried to hide her delighted smile. All her hurt had disappeared and now she was just turned on and trying not to feel anything else for him. Anything scary. "Well, a couple of other people know."

"Just a couple?"

Oh, God. Now she'd let that slip, too? "Let's go already. I've got secrets I want to show you, too."

He watched her for a long moment, but then he finally shook his head and put the truck in gear. "There's no way I can say no to that. Hang on."

He peeled out, gravel flying as he turned onto the highway. Merry let her hang-ups go. She let her worries fly out the open window into the night. She could be worried about looks and sexiness when she was alone again. Why bother with worrying about them right now when she had a big, hot man driving her home for illicit sex? That was the definition of screwed up and self-destructive. Grace wouldn't need to bother with cock-blocking if Merry was going to do it for herself.

"I need a shower," Shane said apologetically as they approached the lights of town. "Can you give me a minute?"

"Oh," she breathed. "I guess."

"You can't wait one minute for me?" he asked with a huge grin.

Her heart thumped hard as she thought of what she really wanted. What she'd say if she were bold and brave and more confident about sex. "It's not that," she whispered.

He shot her a questioning glance.

"It's just that I…" Oh, fuck. What the hell. She took

a deep breath. "I'd like to see you in the shower. I've thought about it."

"You've *thought* about it?" He sounded shocked, but surely he was a little pleased. He was a man, after all.

"Yes."

"You've thought about me showering?" They'd reached town, finally, and she could see the surprise on his face. And the delight.

Wishing it were still dark, Merry decided that if she wanted to be seen as sexy, she had to be sexy. There was no way around it. "Yes. I fantasized about that. Watching you. In the shower."

When he looked at her, she kept her face straight ahead, but she couldn't stop the smile that spread over her face. His voice held an entirely different timbre when he spoke. "You fantasized about me, Merry?"

"Yes," she said, her own voice hoarse with embarrassment and excitement.

"Did you touch yourself?"

"Um… Yes."

When he had to stop at the first light, Shane's thumb tapped impatiently at the steering wheel. Merry pressed her lips together and held her breath.

"Christ," he finally cursed. He didn't say another word as he drove through the crowded streets of town. But his thumb tapped. Over and over. Faster.

The truck jerked to a stop when he parked in front of the Stud Farm. He quickly circled to open her door.

Merry smiled up at him as she hopped down. He slammed the door and followed her into the building. She got her keys out and tossed him a look over her shoulder. "Anyway, did you want to shower or did you want to come in with—?"

She'd barely turned the key in the lock when Shane pushed her door open with a growl. His body moved her in. He slammed the door behind her and reached for the hem of her shirt. "Get naked," he ordered.

Merry giggled. She couldn't help it. Shane growled again and pulled her shirt up. A second later, he had her bra unclasped. "Stop!" she shrieked, laughing as she covered her bare breasts.

"Oh, sure," he said, walking her backward toward the bathroom. He tossed his hat to the couch. "You tell me you want to shower with me. Tell me you've fantasized about it, that you fucking touched yourself and fantasized about it, and now you want me to *stop?*"

Oh, God. He backed her against the bathroom wall and braced one hand next to her head. His brown eyes burned, brushing her skin with heat.

"Did you touch your breasts, Merry?"

She opened her mouth, meaning to answer, but her throat dried to dust.

"Did you?"

She nodded.

"Show me."

She couldn't. She couldn't. But she was already cupping her breasts, trying to hide, and Shane just put a hand over hers and slipped her fingers a little lower. "Show me, Merry."

Her lungs couldn't hold enough breath. There wasn't enough air in the room. She was panting now. So was he. His eyes watched her hand as if she held the key to some treasure.

Merry brushed her fingers over her nipple and watched his jaw jump. Terrified power exploded through her body. She rolled her nipple between her fingers. His lips parted. She squeezed and gasped, and Shane groaned.

"What else?" he rasped.

She shook her head again. "No. I can't."

"You can. Please. Please. Show me."

She had to look away from him. She couldn't watch his face. Instead she looked down to her own trembling hands as she reached for the button of her jeans. She pulled the zipper down slowly then slid her fingers down her belly, beneath her underwear. When she touched her clit, her breath broke in her throat.

Shane's hand spread over her shoulder, his thumb tracing her collarbone. "You thought of me?" he asked as she slowly slipped her fingers deeper.

"Yes."

His fingertips trailed down her skin and circled her nipple. She groaned and arched her head back.

"God, Merry. You make me insane."

She'd never done anything like this. Never. But she kept touching herself as Shane shrugged out of his shirt and stood bare-chested before her. He kissed her, making her whimper against his mouth then reached over to turn on the shower.

"Let's make your fantasy come true."

Oh, this was already way better than her fantasy, but she wasn't going to stop now. They both stripped down to nothing, and she couldn't believe how hard he was. How big already. The head swollen and skin stretched tight. She almost groaned again and she wasn't even touching herself anymore.

Shane stepped into the shower and held out a hand to pull Merry in after him. The water was hot, but what made her gasp was the searing heat of his skin as he pressed himself to her. His cock lay against her belly like a brand.

"Is this how you thought of it?" he asked, his mouth dragging down her neck. "Us together? Under the water? Like this?"

She pushed her hips tighter against him, loving the way the length of him slipped against her slick belly. She didn't want to say no. Didn't want him to step away. But she'd give him the truth about this. "No," she whispered against his dampening hair. He smelled like sweat, but she liked it. A more potent version of his natural scent.

"No?"

"I just…watched you. You were washing yourself, and you…"

She couldn't say it, but she felt the breath shudder from his chest as his teeth pressed her neck.

"Is that what you want?"

"Yes," she breathed.

He stepped back and reached for the body wash. She felt dizzy. Her heart fluttered like a trapped bird in her chest, and she had to lean against the shower wall as Shane spread dripped soap over his chest.

"Touch yourself," he said as he soaped his chest.

She touched herself. He spread the soap down to his thick cock. "Oh, God," she breathed as a bolt of lust shot through her body and ended right between her thighs. She'd never seen a man do that before. She'd never seen a man's fist around his shaft, slowly stroking. "Oh, God. Shane."

She edged her foot up to the rim of the tub and rubbed herself, painfully aware of his eyes on her as she did. But if he could offer her a show, she could let him watch, couldn't she? She could do that.

And damn, it felt so good. So good to touch herself and watch Shane's arm flex as he worked his cock. This was insane. Reckless. And so, so dirty. She couldn't believe it was her. Couldn't believe it was real.

But it felt real. She felt tight and swollen and so close already.

Shane shifted, angling his body closer to her, bracing an arm above her head. His tension and size added danger to the mix, and Merry felt everything inside her wind tighter. His fist stroked faster. She looked up and found him watching her intently, each of his breaths edged with a low growl.

"Watch me," he ordered. "This is what you wanted, Merry. Wasn't it? Is this what you wanted?"

"Yes. Please. Yes." Her gaze swept down his wet body, over the soap suds stuck in his chest hair, down to the rivulets that snaked down his stomach, and finally to his hard cock. Oh, God. He was so thick. The head so tight and plump and darkly flushed with need.

"Watch," he growled, tightening his fist just as Merry's own body tightened.

"Oh, God," she groaned, her voice breaking into a cry as she came. Her hips jerked against her own hand. Her cry crashed through the tiny space as she screamed.

"Oh, fuck," Shane whispered. "Merry. That was…"

His mouth closed over hers and he took her hand and closed it over his shaft. "Touch me. Please."

Her fingers tightened around him as the last spasms rolled through her. He kept his grip over hers, getting himself off with her hand. Urging her faster. Faster. Merry couldn't catch her breath. She was too caught up in watching him use her. Watching until—

"Ah, fuck yes," he groaned, "Yes." His hips flexed, pushing toward her, and then he was coming, his body a line of taut muscle as his cock pulsed in her hand. Come dripped hot down her hip.

She was shaking. From the shock. The pleasure. The weakness in her thighs. Merry closed her eyes and leaned her head against the wall.

She could feel everything. Water snaked down her side and over her thighs. Steam tickled the hair at her nape. And then Shane's mouth touched her shoulder, pressing heat deep into her skin. Her grasp loosened. She set him free with a sigh that was half relief and half sorrow.

"I can't believe we just did that," she breathed.

"Hey, it was your fantasy." His deep voice vibrated through her.

"I didn't… God, I'd never have actually *done* it."

"Well, then…" He kissed her mouth one last time. "I guess you should be glad I was around to help."

Merry collapsed in laughter, finally giving in to her weakness and letting Shane support her weight. "You're awful."

"Am I?"

"Yes!"

"Naw. I'm pretty sure I deserve an award for lasting longer than you, Miss Kade. That was a goddamn miracle. I expect a plaque or something. Maybe a nice big commemorative belt buckle."

She laughed harder, loving the way the water slid down his shoulder and over her lips, connecting the two of them. "Sexual rodeo?" she asked.

"Yeah. I held out longer than eight seconds."

"Oh, God. You're killing me."

"No. Not even close. You're killing me, Merry."

Her heart swelled up so quickly, so sharply, that she had to swallow a gasp. That was alarming. She didn't want to feel so much for Shane. He was just a lover. Just a man who lived across the hall and stopped by occasionally to bring her pleasure. That was it. She couldn't feel this terrible density in her chest. Not for him.

"I think I have to clean up again," he whispered.

"Ha. I never got clean in the first place."

He handed her the body wash, and she couldn't stop her laughter. There was nothing to laugh about, really. Nothing truly funny. But their chuckles filled the room as they washed. And she didn't stop smiling once.

Until some small sound made her peek around the curtain.

And there was Grace, framed in the doorway, her face a blank of shock and surprise, her hand clutching the shirt Merry had dropped on the living room floor.

"Oh, no," Merry breathed.

Grace closed the door.

"Grace is here," Merry whispered to Shane, whose responding grimace of terror was probably only half feigned.

Merry didn't exactly fear facing Grace. That wasn't

the feeling that sank over her. Mostly it was regret that she'd lost this secret. That it was known now, and therefore something much more complicated. It wasn't just pure sex and honest desire anymore.

Shit.

Shane turned off the water, and Merry realized she had nothing to put on but a pair of jeans and her shoes. Grace had taken the shirt with her.

The jig was very, very up indeed.

MERRY WAS THANKFUL for one thing, at least. Shane had all of his clothes. Hell, he was even wearing his boots when he stepped out of the bathroom. Aside from his wet hair, there was no hint that they'd showered together. If Grace hadn't opened the door, Merry could've claimed he was just helping with some plumbing emergency she'd encountered midshower. Awkward, but these things happened.

He'd offered his shirt to Merry, but she hadn't wanted him walking out bare-chested, so she wrapped a towel around her chest and followed him out.

Grace stood at the kitchen counter, beer in hand and eyebrow raised in cold judgment.

"Grace," Shane said evenly. "Good evening." She just took a swig from her beer and said nothing as he grabbed his hat from the couch. "Merry, I'll call you tomorrow."

Merry half expected the beer bottle to crash against the door as Shane closed it, but Grace remained calm.

Too calm.

"So," Merry said.

"So."

"I'm sorry you had to see that."

Grace took another drink of beer then shrugged. "I'm just glad the curtain is opaque."

Merry casually strolled over to the couch and grabbed her shirt. "Excuse me," she said as she turned her back and pulled it over her head.

"Rayleen got a little too into the card game and sucked down three more beers, so I had to drive her home." She pushed Grace's keys across the counter. "Sorry if I surprised you."

"Well, obviously, I wouldn't have..." Merry felt a sudden crash of thankfulness that she and Shane hadn't been on the pull-out couch.

"Look, Merry, I don't like him. And I don't want you to get hurt. But you have every right to have sex with anyone you want, and I just hope it's good for you. Okay?"

Merry watched her closely, waiting for a crack in her calm facade, but it didn't come. "Okay," she said, a grin escaping her control and spreading across her face.

"Well, you're smiling. That's something." Grace reached into the fridge and handed Merry a beer.

"Oh, I'm smiling." She sighed.

"So Shane Harcourt is all right in bed, huh? I guess I can live with that."

"He's great in bed. And truly spectacular in the shower."

"Fine." Grace laughed. "But you're in charge of scrubbing the tub tomorrow, okay?"

"Ah, right. It probably needs it. Sorry."

"Oh, my *God!*" Grace pretended to cover her ears. "I'm not sure I can hear this."

"It's okay." Merry meant to sit on the sofa, but her thighs were still shaky and she half collapsed. "I don't kiss and tell. Actually maybe I do and I just never had anything to tell before. He's just… He treats me like I'm sexy, Grace."

"You are sexy."

"I'm not. I'm just me. You don't know what that's like, because men look at you and they see danger and sex."

"Thanks," Grace said dryly.

"Oh, please. That's exactly what you want them to see. What they don't see is how sweet you are. How much you feel. No one saw that until Cole, and that's why you love him."

Grace shot her a look. "Don't tell me you love Shane."

"No. I don't know him well enough. And it's not like that between us. But he sees something in me that I've wanted someone to see. So as much as you don't trust him, can you try to cut him a break for my sake? And for the sake of my poor, neglected erogenous zones?"

Grace had been maintaining neutrality, and doing an admirable job, but some of the worry finally cleared from her face and she sighed. "All right. But only for your erogenous zones."

"Thank you." Merry gave her a kiss on the cheek and clinked their bottles together. "From the bottom of my, um…yeah."

"God," Grace moaned.

"And look, I know he can be a little cool and hard to read, but when we're alone, he's funny. And sweet. And really, really hot."

"Considering how happy you look right now, I suppose I can learn to like him. You always just looked confused when you got home from a date with old what's-his-name."

"Kenneth? Yeah. He was kind of into dirty talking in a really weird way. I thought I wasn't experienced enough to deal with it."

Grace's nose crinkled. "What kind of weird way? Baby talk?"

"God, no! Even I would've known that wasn't sexy. He would just mutter things all the time. Like, 'Yeah. That's it, baby. Do it just like that. You're so good. You make me so hot.' Except I wouldn't even be doing anything. I'd just be lying there and his eyes would be closed, and I always suspected he was imagining an entirely different scene, with a different girl. I felt like a blow-up doll."

"Ew."

"But I kept telling myself to loosen up. Other women like dirty talk."

"Not like that! That's not dirty talk. That's more like a running monologue."

"Maybe I'm not as frigid as I thought."

"You're not frigid! Good dirty talk isn't about fulfilling the talker's fantasy. Jeez. It's about making both of you feel, well, dirty. In a really hot way."

"Yeah, I…" Merry's face went hot as fire. "I kind of get that now."

Grace slapped her arm and laughed in horror. "God, I'd be happy for you if I didn't feel like I was talking to my little girl."

"I think my mom would be cooler about this, actually."

"Damn hippies," Grace muttered.

Merry grabbed her in a hug, noticing that Grace barely stiffened at all these days. "I love you. Thanks for not being pissed."

"I wasn't going to be pissed, hon. I just worry about you. You're not hard like me."

"I'm pretty tough."

"I know." Grace kissed Merry's cheek and then shoved her away. "I'll try to be cool with him, okay? But when you're ready for me to shiv his ass, you just give the word. I've usually got a blade in my boot."

"Deal. But it won't be necessary. We're just…friends with benefits."

Grace gave her a doubtful look, but Merry ignored it. If other people could do it, so could she. She'd keep her heart out of it and have a good time.

No problem.

CHAPTER FIFTEEN

"FIRST OF ALL," Jeanine Bishop intoned in her most self-important voice, "I want to assure all of you that the police are fully caught up on all the frightening events we've suffered in the past week."

Merry squirmed.

"All evidence has been turned over, and, Ms. Kade, I believe you said you sent in the photos this morning?"

"Yes, ma'am. The detective called and I emailed them right to him." Much to Merry's relief he'd sounded bored out of his mind and hadn't even replied to her email.

"Whoever has done this, the police now have a file and I'm sure they will diligently pursue all leads."

"Great," she said.

Kristen leaned forward. "I'm almost sure I heard a noise last night. Someone sneaking around the barn."

Oh, no. Merry had given this poor woman a complex. She was about to reassure her and was reaching out to pat her hand when Levi snorted.

"Good Lord, woman, there were thirty-mile-per-hour winds when that storm blew through at midnight. Not to mention you've got ten horses in that barn and a groom living in an apartment above the stables. What exactly did you hear that sounded like sneaking around?"

"I know the sounds of my own house, Levi!" she snapped.

Jeanine scowled the way she always did when reminded it was no longer her house.

"So!" Merry interrupted, just as Jeanine was drawing that distinctive deep breath that indicated she was about to get self-righteous. "That's great news about the police. I'm glad they're taking this seriously. But moving on to something more uplifting, I've put together a press kit. If you'd all open up your folders…" She passed folders around the table. They weren't customized with images of Providence, but the clean white gloss looked nice.

"Press kits," exclaimed Harry. "That sounds serious."

"Oh, I am dead serious," Merry said. "The first thing you'll notice is the brochure. Now please keep in mind that the font and layout of 'Providence Ghost Town' is just an idea. I think it's perfect, but the graphic designer is more than willing to make changes."

"Graphic designer?" gasped Kristen. "I'm sure we didn't authorize that expense."

"The initial cost was only seventy-five dollars. If we want a logo, it'll be about $150 more. It's really not a big expense."

Kristen stared her down.

"I…" Merry sat straighter. "I understand that the board hasn't approved a budget for me, and this isn't a cost of normal operation. I'm willing to cover the seventy-five dollars myself."

Levi waved her off.

Merry nodded. "The brochure is just a mock-up,

but I had a short run printed so you could get a better idea of—"

"Another unapproved expense?"

Merry met Kristen's eyes and nodded. "Yes. But if we're going to have a press kit, we need something to show. And if we're going to move forward with this project, we need a press kit."

"The brochure is damn pretty," Harry said, cutting a little of the tension in the room.

"Thank you. I think it gives you a good idea of my plans for Providence. I envision weather-resistant placards in front of each building printed with information about the place. What it was used for or who lived there. We can include earlier photos of the building, if we have them, or photos of the building before it was restored, if that's applicable. And pictures of the families and founders, of course. In the main building—"

"Ms. Kade," Jeanine snapped. "This meeting was called to address the threats we've received. Not to come up with a plan for steps we haven't even decided to take."

Crap. She'd noticed that, had she?

"Okay. That's fair enough. But we do all agree we should move forward with a story in the local paper?"

Jeanine and Kristen didn't look pleased, exactly, but who could object to a favorable news story? Levi and Harry were still looking eagerly through the brochure. Marvin might have been sleeping, but Merry would take that as agreement.

"There's also a nice bio sheet in the folder about Gideon Bishop and his statements about why he wanted to open Providence to the public." Both women immediately tore the sheet from their folders and began to scan it. "That's open to correction, of course."

"Yes," Jeanine said tightly. "There are a few mistakes here."

Kristen tossed her a glare and went back to reading.

"So," Merry said, folding her hands on top of the table. "Does anyone have a good contact at the paper?"

Harry looked up. "My niece works at the paper. She's a darn good writer, too."

"Now, wait a minute," Jeanine interrupted. "We need to decide what we'd even want to present to a reporter. This organization is still in its planning stages."

Merry pressed her hands flat to the folder. "It doesn't have to be. I understand why you're taking it slow, but maybe the best way to ensure success is to press forward as if you intend for this town to open. To set a date, even."

"But the funds—"

"All the more reason to go big with this news story."

Marvin seemed to wake suddenly and slapped the table. "I like it. This cautious, wait-and-see approach really chaps my hide. I say we go for it. Get aggressive."

The other men nodded. Even Kristen seemed a little roused at the excitement.

"All well and good, gentlemen, but…" Jeanine shot Merry a sidelong look. "We've already decided on a slow course. A plan for aggressive development would need more—" she cleared her throat and looked straight at Merry "—*consideration*."

Merry felt heat climb from her chest to her neck to her face. All five of them were looking at her, most with some measure of pity, all with discomfort. "I'll work hard for you in whatever capacity I can unless you decide I'm no longer the right fit for Providence. But please keep in mind that if you find the funds to hire someone new and that's the course you decide upon, recruitment could take months. You'll need an interim curator at least. I'd be honored to—" She swallowed a strange thickness in her throat. "I'd be honored to work in Providence as long as you'll have me."

Levi dropped his head for a moment then met her eyes. "We'll take that into consideration."

"Thank you."

"All right, Ms. Kade," Jeanine said, tapping the folder against her hand. "I think we have everything we need here. We'll let you know what we decide about the reporter."

Well, that was that. She was being dismissed. She wasn't part of the board, and if they were going to vote, she didn't need to be there. But what they were really going to do, she understood, was discuss the problem of *her*.

She gathered up her papers, acutely aware that this was likely not the first time people had had this discussion. What are we going to do about Merry? She's sweet, but not quite *right*.

As if to confirm her fears, her phone rang and Crystal's name appeared.

"Really?" she groaned as she hurried from the building. *"Really?"* She wanted to ignore the call. She desperately wanted not to answer, but what if Crystal was lost on a back road somewhere, surrounded by a rogue herd of buffalo? It could happen.

Forcing herself to cut off her moan, Merry answered. "Hi, Crystal."

"Merry!" God, she was so fake. She always sounded surprised to hear Merry's voice, as if she weren't the one calling. "We're having a little party. I'd love it if you could come."

"I'm sorry. I'm so busy tonight. I just got out of a meeting of the museum board, and now I have to meet someone in Providence." That felt good. Being professional and busy. She grinned in triumph.

"That's no problem. The party is tomorrow. I'd invite you to bring a guest, but you know how terrible Grace and I are together, and I'm sure you don't have a gentleman you'd like to—"

"Actually I do."

"You have a boyfriend already? Didn't you just move to town?"

"Well, he's not my boyfriend, exactly. But I'm seeing someone, and I'm sure he'd love to—"

"Perfect. Then we'll see you tomorrow around nine. I'll text you the details."

"Oh, I—"

"Bye!"

Merry held the phone to her ear for a few more seconds. Had she just accidently agreed to attend Crystal's party? Because she'd jumped at the chance to be petty? Oh, God.

She should cancel. Right now. Call and make up some commitment she'd forgotten. But she knew it would look like Shane had said no and she was too embarrassed to go alone.

So now she'd have to actually attend Crystal's party. Which meant she'd have to ask Shane.

This was horrifying.

He wasn't her boyfriend, and the truth was that they weren't dating, either. "No," she bleated, pressing her fist to her forehead. Maybe Grace would let her borrow Cole. Crystal would never know.

Or she could just be brave and ask Shane. It wasn't the damn prom. It was just…an evening with her family.

"You are a terrible coward," she told herself. And it was the most honest thing she'd said to anyone all day.

But she wasn't going to let Crystal ruin her day. She'd done a good job with the board and now she was meeting Shane for a surprise.

That cheered her up. She got in her car and drove away with a big smile. No point being honest now. Everything was going her way today. And a surprise in Providence meant things were only going to get better.

SHANE LOOKED UP from his work at the sound of wheels on gravel. A car door closed. Merry was here.

He took a deep breath, set down his hammer and slipped off his gloves.

Why did he feel nervous? This made no sense. He was leading her to a broken down cabin in the woods, not presenting a ring. But he still had to wipe his hands on his jeans as he stood.

Maybe it was just this place. He was feeling less and less comfortable being here with her. He hadn't sabotaged her. He hadn't done anything illegal. And it had happened before he'd really known her. But being surrounded by the buildings and knowing what they meant to her… It was starting to weigh on him.

If his lawsuit succeeded, he'd take all this from her. He'd take her job, and her dreams for this place, and that joy she felt with every story she told.

He could see her here, telling the story of Providence to a group of kids, drawing them in past their boredom. Bringing the place alive. Making it real. Hell, she'd even managed to make him feel a friendly sort of affection for the place, and he had every reason to hate it.

His grandfather had given Merry Providence, but it had been done out of meanness. If Shane had only done what the man had asked, if he'd only given in, Gideon Bishop would've left a pittance for this town. Enough money to buy a plaque, maybe. An easement around the property. But most of the two million dollars would have gone to Shane as a reward for learning to obey. There'd be no Providence Historical Trust. Merry would've stayed in Texas. Her joy over Providence might be temporary, but she wouldn't have had it at all if Shane had changed his name. And he would never have touched her.

Hell. He couldn't regret that, could he?

She waved as she approached, her face bright with curiosity and excitement. Shane packed up his tools and turned to meet her.

"Hey. I thought I heard a car pull away."

"Grace dropped me off so she could borrow my car. I hoped I could talk you into a ride home."

"I think I can be persuaded. How was the meeting?"

"Super great! Well, I haven't heard anything, but I

think it went well. I'm trying to convince them to get more aggressive."

"More aggressive?"

"Yes! We need to move forward and stop pussyfooting around. That's a Western term, right?"

"Sure."

"Anyway, possession is nine-tenths of the law, and all that. So if we can get more money released and start making improvements and pushing forward with plans before anyone else knows what's happening… God, maybe we could even get this place open. Get the community invested. And if the money is already spent, then what's that asshole going to do?"

"Asshole?"

"Oh, I'm sorry. I'm sure he's fine. But the promise of money doesn't exactly make for good behavior, does it? Hey, look at me! I'm power hungry."

He smiled, half in amusement and half because this conversation had become surreal. "You seem pretty nice to me."

"You'd be surprised."

"Yeah? What'd you do?"

He'd only been teasing her, but her forehead crumpled with worry. She shook her head.

"Merry?"

"I can't tell you."

Shit. She looked serious. "Hey, it's okay. Is something wrong?"

She shook her head, but her eyes glimmered with tears that hadn't been there a second ago.

"Merry," he murmured, folding her into his arms. "What's wrong?"

"Nothing. I'm stupid. I just…"

He kissed the top of her head, distracted for a moment by the scent of her. "Don't cry, sweetheart."

"Okay." She nodded and pulled back. "I'm sorry. It's just that I may have run over a mailbox."

At first he had no idea what she was talking about and shook his head blankly. "That doesn't sound so awful."

"But it is. I was meeting with the board, and I was upset when I left, and I knocked down a mailbox, and they thought it was vandalism. And then…"

Holy shit, she was talking about his *grandfather's* mailbox. "Um. If it was an accident, then you have nothing to feel bad about. Just tell Kristen, and…" Crap. "Just tell the board."

Merry groaned. "I can't. That whole sign thing? The so-called vandalism? That was me, too."

He couldn't help it. His jaw dropped open and he stared at her like she'd lost her mind. Because she obviously had. "Are you kidding me?"

"Oh, God, I knew I shouldn't have said anything!" She covered her face and shook her head. "Why did I say that?"

"Merry, why would you have made that sign?"

"I just needed them to call an emergency meeting! To take this all more seriously. They treat the Providence Historical Trust like it's an excuse to get together and rehash old arguments. I needed to give them a reason to get serious. That's all it was. I did my best not to make it scary."

Too many thoughts went through his head. Anger that he might be blamed for what she'd done. Shock that she'd even done it. But also a big helping of amusement. She looked like she was confessing a murder. Poor Merry.

"See?" she whispered. "I'm pretty terrible. And all for a little money."

"Oh, Jesus, Merry. You didn't do that for money. You did it for Providence, and you know it. You're in love with this damn place."

"I don't think that makes it better," she whispered.

Good God, this woman was fucking cute. "No? Well, maybe my surprise will make you feel better."

That wiped the worry from her face. "Oh, my God. Yes! What is it?"

"Come on. We need to take my truck for the first leg, then you'll be good with walking?"

She looked down at her tennis shoes. "I'm always in comfortable shoes. It's one of my hottest secrets."

"Ha. After last night, I don't think that's even close."

She slapped his shoulder and nearly collapsed in laughter. "You're awful."

"How was it with Grace last night? I can't help but notice I still have my balls."

"Congratulations! I think she's cool with it. I told her you were okay and I'd like to keep you around for a little while."

"Yeah? I'm okay? High praise." He opened his truck door for her and picked her up to slide her onto the seat. But first, he slid between her knees and kissed her. "You were very naughty last night," he whispered.

"I was not! That was you!"

"Naw, it was all your idea, remember?"

Her cheeks were such a pretty pink that Shane had to kiss her again.

"You're awful," she repeated, but her soft smile belied the words. And the way she sighed against his mouth wasn't bad, either.

God, he was hungry for her. So hungry to taste as much of her as he could before it ended. He wanted to devour her. To get enough of her that he wouldn't have to miss her when she was gone.

"Mmm." He tried to pull her closer, but she straight-armed him.

"What about my surprise?"

"Shh. I have another surprise for you."

She convulsed with laughter. "Are you fourteen?"

"We're all fourteen when it comes to girls. But if you're shooting me down, I guess I'll retreat graciously."

He loved the way she grinned at him when he circled around and got in the driver's seat. Like she was delighted. Then again, she was always delighted.

Her grin held as he turned onto the road and drove higher into the foothills. "Where are we going?"

"Up."

They edged higher, and Shane drove slower as the dirt road turned into something that more closely resembled a trail. Delicate aspen branches whispered over the cab of his truck. The world was green around them.

"It's so pretty. Where's the creek?"

"About twenty yards to the left of us and way downhill. This is about the spot where you found the ice house. We'll have to stop in about ten minutes and walk the rest of the way."

"The rest of the way to where?"

He winked. "You don't want to ruin the surprise, do you?"

"Actually, no. I love surprises. When I was little, my mom and I lived in pretty small places. I always knew where she hid the Christmas presents. There weren't too many choices. But I'd never have peeked. I can't even imagine it. Why would anyone do that?"

Shane had always been the kid shaking his presents and trying to tease open the ends of the wrapping paper. "I don't know. It's like a special form of torture, knowing something is there and not looking."

She shot him a look of pure disapproval. "That's insane. Half the pleasure is in the anticipation."

"Half of it? I wouldn't go that far. For example, I can enjoy thinking about what I'll do to you tonight, but I guarantee you, it won't be close to half as good as touching you."

"Okay. I'll give you that. It is pretty damn awesome to touch me." She laughed, making clear she was joking, but it was nothing but truth to Shane. He wasn't sure how it had gotten so hot so quickly, but just teasing her had him hard as steel.

She was clearly sensitive about not being the type of woman men found sexy, but he'd meant what he'd said yesterday. Maybe other people didn't see her as conventionally sexy, but somehow that made it all feel more wrong in the best kind of way.

She was the girl next door. The kid sister. The woman who might walk into a party and not draw the attention of the room. But that wasn't who she *was*. That wasn't what she meant to him. What she meant to him was laughter. And a kind of easy smile he'd never had.

And filthy fantasies he never could have suspected she might entertain.

"Here's our stop," he said, parking the truck well back from the washed out area of the road. She jumped out before he could even reach for his door handle. "Don't run ahead, all right? The road isn't stable."

Merry rolled her eyes. "They didn't invent hiking in Wyoming, you know. I'm not a bumbling idiot."

"I suppose that might be true. So just stay with me because I want you to."

She smiled at him and the light filtering past the leaves danced over her face. "Okay."

He cast a curious eye down the canyon as they edged along the narrow trail. There was no flash of light today, but he could definitely see something white down there. He didn't say anything to Merry, though. If it was something awesome, he'd save it for another surprise, just to have the chance to make her happy again.

"Do you have family here?" she asked as they walked.

"Just my mom."

"Is she great?" she asked.

Shane smiled and shook his head. "She's fine. What about your mom?"

"My mom is the best. No offense."

"None taken."

"She's just incredibly strong and kind. She taught me how to be happy and independent. She wasn't always around a lot when I was little because she worked, and sometimes she'd take on another job during the holidays, but I always understood that she was doing it for me. For us. We were a team."

"She sounds pretty amazing. Will she come visit you here?"

"At some point, I'm sure. She and Grace are pretty close. Maybe she'll come for Christmas. It must be beautiful here during Christmas."

"Well, it's snowy, anyway. And a little crowded."

"I think I'll love it."

He was sure she would love it, if only because she seemed to love everything. "You said you don't ski?"

"No, but I'm going to. Will you teach me?"

"I've only been a couple of times. That hobby's a little expensive for me, and I can't afford to break a wrist."

"Chicken."

He winked, then paused to watch her closely as she traversed another narrow section of trail. The road flattened a little here before it disappeared around a bend. They were almost there, and Merry seemed to sense that. She was walking faster, smiling wider.

"All right. Are you ready?" he asked.

She did a little dance in the dirt. When he just raised his eyebrows and didn't move, she shoved him. "What? What is it? Tell me."

"Come on." He took her hand and heard her whisper, "Oh, my God," under her breath in anticipation.

Shane laughed. "I really hope this lives up to your expectations. Now you've got me self-conscious. But…" He led her around the last curve. "Here it is."

Merry shrieked at the sight of the cabin, then covered her mouth as her scream dissolved into giggles. "Look at it! What is it? Is it part of Providence?"

"I don't know. I have no idea how old it is or who lived here, but I thought you might want to find out."

"Oh, my *God!*" she screamed, jogging a little closer to the cabin before skidding to a stop. "Can I go in? Do you think the landowner would mind? Nobody has lived here for a long time, right?"

"The last time I saw it was over twenty years ago, and it looked about the same. I'm sure it's fine to explore."

"This is insane, Shane. Look at that chinking. And the notches! I think it's really old. It could even predate Providence. Do you think it could be a trapper's cabin?"

He shrugged, but he knew she wasn't really asking him. She hadn't even looked at him since she'd spotted the cabin. She raced forward to look into one of the tiny windows cut into the logs, not that there was much of an interior. The roof had long since fallen in.

"It's totally unstable, but maybe I could poke around the edges, see if…" She fell into silence for a moment, then her head popped up, she spun around, and Shane found himself catching her as she leaped for him.

"Thank you. Thank you!" She kissed his mouth and jaw and cheek, knocking his hat to the ground. "Thank you, Shane. It's amazing. You're amazing."

"You're welcome." He tried to kiss her, but she was gone again, bouncing back to the cabin. He watched her go. Watched her forget about him completely and lose herself in exploring the old building. And Shane was pretty sure he hadn't been this happy in a long time. Maybe even decades.

He had a feeling Merry was this happy a lot. When she left she'd take that with her, but he'd hang on for as long as he could.

CHAPTER SIXTEEN

WHEN IT STARTED GETTING dark, Shane forced her back to the truck. She supposed that was only fair. After all, the poor guy had just stood around for three hours while she filled her phone with pictures and tentatively moved a few logs at the edges of the cabin. She'd been rewarded with the sight of a metal tool, maybe a log splitter, she wasn't sure. But it looked similar to one that she'd found in Providence.

Log cabins weren't her specialty, but she'd done some research about one for her last position. A tiny little cabin on the Texas plains that a local municipality had wanted help documenting. This one was a different style and had been exposed to completely different weather conditions, but she was almost sure it was older, which would make it pre-1860. Very early for Wyoming.

A tiny hum of excitement leaked from her throat. To cover it up, Merry coughed into her hand as Shane opened the truck door for her. "I'm almost sure there were mentions of a cabin somewhere in the contemporary writings from Providence. Maybe in one of the diaries." She tapped a knuckle against her chin. "Or maybe a diary from a settler in Jackson. I'm going to have to read through them all. But I need to go through and reference them, anyway."

Shane made a sound of feigned interest.

When he got into the truck, Merry turned to him and a big grin spread over her face. "Did I already say thank you?"

"Yes, ma'am."

"Thank you," she said again, just for the hell of it. "It's the nicest thing anyone's ever given me."

"Well, I don't think you're allowed to take it home."

"We'll see. Maybe one wagonload at a time. Think anyone will notice?"

"Probably not. With the road that way, we might be the first people who've seen it in years."

She leaned across to kiss his cheek. "Thank you. But I feel bad. I didn't get you anything."

"Aw, shucks," he drawled. "You gave me a hell of a surprise last night."

Collapsing into giggles, she slapped his arm hard. "Shut up."

"But if you feel bad, you can make it up to me. I've got a couple of ideas."

"Yeah?"

"Maybe we could act out one of my fantasies about you this time."

Embarrassed as she was, Merry couldn't help but perk up at that. "Did you fantasize about me?"

"Yes. Unless you find that offensive. In which case, of course not."

"I'm serious!"

"I may have jerked off to you one morning."

She felt ridiculously pleased. For all she knew, men jerked off at least once to every woman they met. But she still grinned at the thought. After all, she knew how lovely he looked doing it now. "What did you think about?"

"Uh."

Merry cocked her head. Then she sat back and looked at him. "Shane Harcourt, are you blushing?"

"No."

"You are! What did you think about? Something naughty? Look how pink you are. Come on. Spill it."

"I, um, pictured you on your knees. And your mouth…"

It may have been mean to laugh, but she couldn't help it. "Oh, God," she yelped as she slapped a hand over her mouth.

"Sorry," he said.

"Yeah? Are you sorry? Or do you want me to do that?"

He shot her an incredulous look. "I assume that's not a real question."

"What? I wouldn't want you to lose respect for me." She couldn't keep a straight face.

He growled.

When she stopped laughing, she nodded. "Okay, I'll try it if you're into that sort of thing."

"Oh, you're hilarious. Has anyone ever told you that?"

"Yes."

He shook his head. "You're kind of insufferable when you're this happy." But he reached for her knee and squeezed it.

"And sexy?" she asked pertly.

"Yes." His hand left her knee and slid behind her neck. "And sexy."

He leaned in to kiss her, and Merry was instantly aroused. Actually she'd already been aroused after talking with him about such naughty things. So aroused that she wasn't even worried about what she'd promised. She didn't have all that much experience with pleasuring a man with her mouth, but the idea suddenly seemed grand. She'd get on her knees for Shane. Hell, she'd happily get on all fours and bark like a lapdog. Probably not called for, though.

She'd never done it in a car, either. It seemed too public. Too risky. But they were more alone here than they'd be back home. No one to walk in. No one to knock.

She put one hand on his thigh and slid it higher.

"Mmm," he murmured into her mouth, then groaned more deeply when she pressed her hand to his already thickening erection. She thrilled at the way he swelled harder beneath her touch. She'd never been a sex object before. And she'd never, ever been the aggressor. It was a newfound power to make a man like Shane Harcourt shift beneath her touch as if he were restless for more. More of *her*.

She stroked him, torturing him, teasing him. God, he was so gorgeous. She'd never really thought of a naked man as gorgeous before, but now that she'd seen Shane naked and wet and stroking himself, she felt greedy for the sight of his cock.

"God, you're a tease," he moaned.

"Who says I'm teasing?" she whispered, not quite believing those seductive words had come from her.

He pressed himself harder against her hand as his head fell back against the headrest. "Stop."

"You want me to stop?"

"If you don't stop, you're going to have to finish." His laugh was tense, but Merry wasn't laughing.

She reached for his belt buckle. "Don't you want me to finish, Shane?"

His eyes popped open and he looked at her.

She slipped his belt free and tugged at the buttons of his fly.

"Oh, hell, yes, I want you to finish," he growled just as her hand closed over his thick shaft. He tilted the seat back a little, very generously giving her more room.

She smiled and told herself she wasn't nervous as she ducked her head.

"Oh, God," he breathed before her mouth even touched him. "Merry."

She could do this. It wasn't that difficult. And surprisingly, it really wasn't. Because this time, just the sight of him and the scent of his skin and Merry's mouth was watering. It wasn't awkward at all as she closed her lips around him. In fact, she sighed with pleasure and felt almost greedy as she took him in.

There was something strangely powerful about this. About making a big strong man like Shane sigh. About making the breath hiss from his throat when she sucked. She glanced over to find that he'd wrapped one big hand around the handle of his door and his knuckles stood out white against the skin.

"Oh, Jesus, Merry," he whispered. "God, that feels so good."

She would've smiled if she'd been able to, but her mouth was stretched around him. There was no chance she could take all of him, but she did her very best, and was rewarded with a panted curse as his hips jumped a little. This was actually…fun. And she was nearly squirming with excitement.

His hand slipped over her hair, then pulled it back from her face.

"Christ, you're so gorgeous," he growled.

She hesitated, her eyes darting up to find him watching.

"Don't stop. Please. Suck me, Merry. Take me."

Merry closed her eyes and pretended he wasn't watching. She concentrated on getting him off, pressing her tongue along his shaft and loving the taste of his arousal against her, loving the way his dirty words shivered along her nerves. He urged her on in a hushed rasp that gave her the confidence to take him deeper.

"God, I'm going to come," he said. "Merry… You have to…"

She'd never done that before and had never even wanted to, but today was a fantasy. Today she was someone else. Someone daring and risqué, so she moaned around him and sucked harder.

"Oh, fuck. Yes. Yes." His hips pushed up and she tasted him on her tongue as he came. She swallowed, then again and again, amazed at herself even as she did it. Amazed that she wanted it and she'd taken what she wanted.

Shane whispered her name. She felt his fingers tremble against her head as she rose up. Her cheeks were already warm with embarrassment, but he looked at her with an openness she'd never seen in his eyes. "That was…so fucking good."

She tried to bite back a grin. "As good as your fantasies?" she asked, then wished she hadn't. What if he said no? What if he—?

"Considering how damn hot and sweet your mouth was…about a thousand times better than my fantasy."

He buttoned his pants, then reached behind her seat, giving her a chance to hide her ridiculously pleased smile. Good Lord, was she really proud of herself over a blow job?

"Hey, I'm sorry about, um… Or thanks for… Ha. What I mean is, do you want a drink?" He offered her a bottle of water still cold and wet from the cooler.

"Thanks." Her cheeks burned, but that had no effect on her grin. "Aren't you a gentleman? You keep these around just for emergencies like this?"

He laughed and scrubbed his hands over his face. "No, that was a first. I can assure you the water is strictly for work, but I'll make an exception in your case."

"Hey, thanks."

He watched her until she squirmed, then winked and started the truck. "Let's get you home. Your turn."

Your turn. That was one hell of a promise. She couldn't wait.

Still grinning, she leaned her forehead against the window and watched long shadows slide by in the light of the sunset. This may have been the perfect day, the call from her cousin excepted.

Crap, she'd forgotten about that. She shot Shane a look and wondered if she should ask. But hell, why not? He'd made her day with that surprise. Maybe even her year. And he was probably in a pretty good mood at the moment. It only took her twenty minutes of silence to work up the nerve.

"Shane?"

"Yeah?"

"I have to go to a party tomorrow. My cousin's in town and I couldn't say no, but I'm supposed to bring a guest…"

His eyebrow rose.

"Would you go with me? I understand if you don't want to. We're just friends, so…"

"I'd say we're a little more than friends."

"Yes, but we're not…you know."

He nodded, and she realized she'd been half hoping he might correct that. Stupid.

"A party sounds fine," he said. "What time?"

Merry let out a quiet sigh of relief. "Nine."

"Great. I'll knock on your door around eight-thirty."

"That sounds perfect. And look super handsome, okay? Just like this." She waved a hand down his body.

He shook his head. "You want to show me off to your cousin? I'm honored."

"I do. But more than that, I want to rub her snotty little face in you. Not literally. Just in the figurative sense that I want her to know we're…um…I'm sorry."

"No, I've never been arm candy before. This'll be interesting. Am I allowed to talk, or should I only speak if spoken to?"

"Just look pretty."

"Got it."

Merry was laughing so hard by the time Shane parked the truck, she nearly fell when she stepped out. She'd closed her door before she noticed Cole standing at the top of the steps. "Hi, Cole," she called. She'd been planning on going straight to Shane's apartment, but this made things a little awkward. Cole was clearly waiting for his friend.

She walked past and tried to look casual. She didn't register how tense Cole was until he spoke to Shane. "Can I talk to you for a minute?"

Merry had the door half open, and as she turned to get another look at Cole, she realized Grace was standing in the doorway of their apartment.

"Hey, Grace. How was your day? Mine was damn awesome, I have to admit. In fact, it was kind of spectacular."

Grace didn't answer her smile. Merry stopped just inside as the door to the Stud Farm closed behind her.

"What's wrong?"

"Come inside the apartment. We need to talk about something."

Merry paused, her happiness draining down a slow, cold vortex. "Grace, what's wrong? I'm serious. Tell me."

"Come inside," Grace repeated, but Merry heard shouting from outside and turned back to the front door.

"What's going on?" she whispered as Shane's voice vibrated through the door. She reached out to turn the knob.

"Merry, don't!" She heard Grace's boots rush across the wood, but the door was already open. And Shane and Cole were squared off at the bottom of the steps.

"How the fuck could you do that?" Cole yelled. "That's despicable."

"It isn't what you think," Shane started.

Cole pushed him. "Are you kidding me? You were fucking using her!"

"I wasn't."

"Don't be such a coward. Admit it!"

Cole pushed again, and Shane threw his arms off with a violent toss of his hands. "Fine! I was using her, but it isn't how it looks. I—"

"It isn't how it looks?" Cole growled. "Funny, because it looks like you're screwing her over and screwing her at the same time." He shoved one more time, and this time Shane tripped over the edge of the lawn and went down as Cole yelled, "What kind of man are you?"

Shane surged up as if he meant to throw a punch at Cole, but his wild gaze caught on Merry and he froze. His eyes widened as his fists slowly lowered. "Merry," he rasped.

Cole spun to look at her. "Ah, shit. Grace, you were supposed to keep her inside."

"What's going on?" Merry whispered. A murmur drew her spinning attention toward the saloon, and she saw a few people on the porch watching. Listening. "What is this?" she asked.

Shane started toward her, but Cole grabbed his shirt and yanked him back.

Grace's hands closed over Merry's shoulders from behind. "Come inside. *Please*."

"I'm sorry, Merry," Shane said, holding her gaze with his dark, desperate eyes. He yanked free of Cole's grip and started up the steps. Merry backed away until they were all crowded into the front hall of the building. The door shut, cutting them off from the curious audience. Funny, this space had always seemed large before, rising two stories up to the ceiling. Now it felt so small she felt panicky.

"I'm sorry," Shane repeated, looking so hopeless that Merry's stomach turned to stone.

"What did you do?"

"Merry," Grace whispered. "Cole heard you say something about the lawsuit against Providence."

"Yes."

"Cole didn't know. He had no idea."

Merry looked from Shane's wild eyes to Cole's solemn ones. "Didn't know what?"

Cole grimaced and shook his head. "I didn't know there was a lawsuit. He only said there were probate issues."

"Who? I have no idea what you're talking about. Just tell me. Please!"

Shane's head dropped. He'd lost his hat sometime during the fight, and he looked vulnerable now, his short hair messy, as if they'd just gotten out of bed. But that was no comparison to the vulnerable pain in his eyes when he looked up. "It's me, Merry."

"*What's* you?"

"I'm the one suing Providence."

"What?" Merry pulled her chin in. Then she laughed. "No, you're not. The man who's suing is Gideon Bishop's grandson."

"That's me. I'm his grandson."

"No." She shook her head, almost relieved now. "It's not you. Look." She spun out of Grace's hold and walked into their apartment to grab a folder. "See?" She pulled the bio of Gideon Bishop free and let the folder fall to the floor. She held up the paper. "He was survived by his grandsons, Alex and Shane—" her voice broke over that syllable "—Bishop."

"Bishop is my father's name. I took my mother's name when I was nineteen. Because of my dad and..." His voice trailed off. Merry just stared at him.

"No," she said again, a little louder this time.

"I'm so sorry. At first, I admit, I helped out at Providence for the wrong reasons, but then, I swear to you—"

"You," she croaked. Her throat seemed to be closing as the truth sunk in. "You were spying on the town? That's why you made friends with me?"

"No, that's why I took the job. Not—"

"Oh, God. That's why you were so nice. That's why you... That's why you flirted with me, and..." She trailed off in shock.

"No," he ground out. "No, that's not true, Merry. Don't think that."

He moved toward her. Cole tried to grab him but wasn't quick enough to stop him. But Grace was.

She jumped forward, and the slap rang through the space, bouncing off the walls to echo up to the second floor. "Don't you fucking touch her," Grace snarled as a red handprint flamed to life on Shane's cheek. "I will kill you, do you hear me? I'll kill you if you touch her again, you sick asshole! I'll tear your eyes out and shove them up your—"

"Grace!" Merry screamed. "Stop. Just stop! I can't do this!" She rushed into the apartment, slamming the door behind her. But that didn't stop the wild orchestra of raised voices that seemed to shake the room around her.

Oh, God, this was... She couldn't think about it. She couldn't, because there were so many things. Dozens of things. All cutting into her from the inside out. All of them sharp and jagged and so completely *wrong*.

She'd hired the man who was suing the trust. She'd lied about it and covered it up. She'd told him things about board discussions. And, she'd told him what she'd *done*. The mailbox and the sign and all the lying.

Merry's legs slowly gave up their control and she sank to the floor. There was more than that, of course. There was so much more, but she couldn't think about the other things. No. She was going to be fired. She'd lose her job. She'd be disgraced and she'd never get another museum job again. And that might not be the worst of it. What if she was charged with…something? What if she'd done something illegal?

She buried her face in her hands and refused to think of the rest. Just this was bad enough. Just this was too much to bear.

Oh, God. How could it be *him?*

The door opened, but there weren't any more voices. There was no more shouting. She heard it shut.

"Merry," Grace whispered. "Are you okay?"

Merry shook her head.

"I'm so sorry. I'm so sorry, sweetie."

This time she nodded.

"Come on. Sit on the couch."

She obeyed, forcing her body to move to the couch and pulling herself into it. "I need a drink," she whispered, thinking she meant water, but when Grace handed her a shot of tequila a minute later, Merry realized that was exactly what she'd wanted. She tossed it back and didn't even shudder. She wanted even the memory of the taste of him gone from her mouth.

Grace took the shot glass and produced the bottle to pour another. "Listen. That asshole…he doesn't matter. You hear me? It was just sex."

Merry shook her head. She wasn't thinking about that now. Or ever. She tossed back the second shot. "When the board finds out I hired him, it'll be over."

"But you didn't know it was him! He lied to you! They can't blame you for that."

"Yes, they can. Because I wasn't supposed to hire anybody. They wouldn't approve anything, not even the smallest expense, so I went behind their backs, and I hired him. I was going to have to pay him out of my own pocket until I could get the board to cover it. Now… Oh, God, Grace. They'll fire me as soon as they find out. What am I going to do?"

"Maybe they won't find out."

"He'll tell them! That was the whole point of helping me. He wasn't doing it because he liked me. He even volunteered his work for free. He said he wanted to do his part, give back to the community, but what he wanted to do was ruin everything. Grace… *What am I going to do?*"

"Nothing! He won't say anything. Cole won't let him. *I* won't let him."

"Oh, Grace." The tequila was sinking in now, permeating her blood, working into her cells. Merry leaned into the couch and let her head fall back as numbness washed slowly through her. "It's two million dollars. He's not going to back down, not even for Cole. Shane can buy new friends with that kind of money."

"No, we can… We can…"

Merry was sure she'd never heard Grace so distraught. She reached out and this time, Grace wouldn't dare stiffen up or ignore the hug. This time she had to wrap her arms around Merry and squeeze tight.

Merry drew a deep breath. And then another. She'd been a fool. She'd been worse than a fool. She should've known the moment he'd come on to her that something was off. She wasn't that kind of girl. The only reason someone would want her that way was—

She gasped and shoved the thought away. She couldn't face it now. She couldn't. But thank God for tequila. The room was already spinning. This hurt, but it wouldn't hurt for very long tonight. She'd be totally numb soon. "Oh, God, Grace."

"Don't cry," Grace whispered. "Please don't cry."

But Merry wasn't crying. She couldn't summon that kind of energy. Right now, the numbness was sinking in, and she was watching the pain approach from a long way off. The tequila sank deeper, pulling her mind in. "It's okay," she told her friend. "Just get me one more shot."

Grace pulled away and had another shot in Merry's hand within three seconds. "Drink," she ordered. Merry did. "You can stay here as long as you want. Don't worry about the damned job, all right? You don't need to pay rent. You know that."

Merry thought about their nearest neighbor and laughed. "I'm not sure this is the right building for me."

"Oh, fuck him," Grace growled. "I'll terrorize him. Hell, I'll have Rayleen terrorize him. That would put the fear of God in any man. He'll move out or I'll make him wish he was dead."

Merry smiled, her head lolling against the back of the

couch. Yep, she was drunk, no question about it. And that last shot hadn't even hit her yet. "Good," she murmured. She grabbed the bottle from Grace's hand and took a swig before Grace snatched it back and set it out of reach. "Is it dark yet? I want to go to bed."

"It doesn't matter if it's dark. You can have my bed tonight, hon. I'll stay on the couch. You sleep as long as you want."

"Okay. Thank you. I just want to go to sleep. That's all."

She felt funny leaning on tiny Grace as they moved toward the bedroom, but she knew it wasn't appropriate to laugh. That would worry Grace, and she didn't want to do that.

The room swam around her as she sat on the bed and let Grace take off her shoes. "This is good," she said.

Grace shot her a worried look.

"The tequila," she clarified. "Great stuff. Really smooth. Or strong. Strong. That's what I meant. I couldn't care less about smooth."

"I know."

"Get me one more shot."

"No. You'll throw up in my bed." Grace yanked Merry's jeans down and then rolled her over onto her side before she pulled up the blankets. At least she hadn't had sex with Shane today. At least she didn't need to wash him off her skin.

"Go to sleep," Grace ordered, trying to sound stern and cool and only sounding worried.

"Okay, but I'm going to wake up in a complete panic at 4:00 a.m., you know."

"No, you won't."

"I will. This is really, really bad." She squeezed her eyes shut. "And you were right about him. He was using me. He didn't really want me. You knew he had an ulterior motive and I should've listened to you."

"Hush. I didn't suspect anything like this."

"No, but you knew it wasn't real. I wanted so much for it to be real that I couldn't see the truth."

"Oh, Merry." Grace sighed, her hand stroking over Merry's hair. "I wish I could kill him for you."

Merry smiled. "Well, you slapped him. Jeez, did you really do that? You're so damn awesome, Grace."

"No, I'm just violent and terrible."

"Good. I couldn't have done that. Then again, I'm drunk now. I've got liquid courage. Or liquid belligerence. Maybe I should go kick him in the balls."

"At this point, you'd probably miss and just tilt over."

"I guess." She sighed and settled into the pillow, totally content and thankful for her current state. It was beautiful. And quiet. So much better than what she was going to feel tomorrow. "Thanks for the tequila, Grace. I love you."

"I love you, too," Grace whispered, one of the few times she'd ever said it back.

Merry heard Cole's voice, speaking softly, and then the bedroom door closed, and she drifted happily through a haze of denial and liquor. She'd take a page from Scarlett O'Hara's book and think about this another day. Specifically, tomorrow.

Or maybe she'd just stay drunk for twenty-four hours. Or forty-eight! She had options, so maybe things weren't as hopeless as they seemed.

CHAPTER SEVENTEEN

MERRY DIDN'T WAKE up at 4:00 a.m. in a complete panic. She woke up at 5:30, heavy with hopelessness. She wasn't hungover. She wasn't even fuzzy about what had happened. Four shots of tequila in the space of fifteen minutes was enough to knock her out, but it was long gone from her system now, and she was left with nothing but reality.

Reality, and the sad, sorry news that the board had approved the press kit and wanted to schedule a time for Merry to meet with the reporter.

That was no longer an option. Merry couldn't be the face of Providence, because the entire operation would be tainted by the next story. The one where she was profiled for going rogue and spending money without approval and possibly being in cahoots with the man trying to kill the ghost town. She wondered if that could be framed as embezzlement of some kind. After all, she'd spent a couple hundred dollars without the board's approval and she'd meant to funnel another two thousand or so to Shane for a complete overhaul of the saloon. Then there was the fact that she'd been sleeping with him. That was pretty damning.

Of course, the most explosive part of the story would be the tale of how Merry Kade had vandalized a board member's property and manufactured a false threat to the trust. Oh, boy. That kind of story might even be picked up by one of the big online news sites. Local Museum Curator Vandalizes Precious Historical Site. She'd be accused of trying to pin it on her lover. She'd be painted as some kind of ghost-town black widow with a hunger for hand-forged nails and full-color glossy brochures.

She was going to have to resign. There was no question. That wouldn't be enough to offset all the damage she'd done, but it would be a good start. And she definitely couldn't spearhead this press push. She'd need to remove her name from everything. All the contact information and documents she'd put together. She'd wipe it clean, and then she'd turn it all over to the board with her apology and resignation letter.

But before any of that, before she lost any right to it at all, she wanted to spend one last day at Providence. So she dressed as quietly as she could, brushed her teeth and wrote a note for Grace so she wouldn't worry. Then she tiptoed out the door and raced to her car in the gray dawn light.

The air was icy and a little moist with dew, and it felt good. Refreshing. It made the day feel promising instead of doomed.

But that promise fell away when she got to her car and saw the envelope stuck beneath the wiper. It was sealed, the paper slightly swollen with moisture, but she knew who'd left it as soon as she saw it. She pulled it free and dropped it on the ground before she got into her car and started the engine.

She felt guilty before she'd even shut the door. She

might be a crazy ghost-town black widow, but she wasn't a litterer, so she got out and tossed it onto the passenger side floor. The door sounded horrifically loud when she shut it, so Merry pulled away quickly to avoid being stopped by Grace or caught by Shane.

She needed to be alone. She loved Providence, and she needed these last few hours with it. She wouldn't be able to return until it was open to the public as a museum. And hell, her picture might be next to the cash register even then, like a girl who'd passed too many bad checks.

Rolling down all the windows despite the cold, she drove slowly through town, passing only a few joggers and the poor folks who had to get up and make breakfast for tourists. A ragged bus rumbled through, empty and ready to pick up rafters for the all-day floats down the Snake River. Maybe she'd try that one of these days. She was about to have a lot of free time.

She knew it was stupid to feel so prematurely nostalgic as she drove north toward Providence. She wouldn't be banned from the highways. She could take this drive anytime she wanted, as long as she could afford gas. But she still felt choked with grief as she watched the familiar landmarks pass. The wetlands where she always spotted beaver dams but no beavers. The grass fields that usually sheltered a herd of deer or antelope. The little sign for Warm Springs that still made her smile. *Warm* springs. Not exactly hot, but still pleasant. Another place she could still explore, but somehow knew she never would.

By the time she got to the town, the sun was just starting to peek over distant hills. Merry got out of her car and sat on the hood to watch morning come to Providence.

It was so quiet out here, but if you really stayed still, the sounds could overwhelm you. Birds, dozens of them, sang and whistled and called. They hopped through the dry grass looking for food and making a surprisingly loud racket. Every time she watched a clump of rattling grass, expecting a raccoon or weasel to pop out, a tiny little finch would expose itself.

Then there was the wind, even the faintest hint of it swaying the long grass and shushing the seeds against each other. And the sound of the stream... It was hardly even worthy of that name now, but she could still hear it when the wind calmed. The faintest little ring of water as it jumped over stones and carved around plants. She wondered what it had been like when the town was settled. It had been almost a proper river then, before it had been forced into a half dozen different channels that probably snaked down the mountain miles apart.

She knew this place wasn't hers. Logically she knew that. She was only a curator, brought in from out of town and never even meant to be permanent. This place didn't belong to her. It wasn't even her heritage. She had no family here and no ties except a best friend from L.A. who was just as much a stranger to Wyoming as she was.

So she'd be okay. She was almost sure of it.

Merry slid off the car and moved slowly through town. She marked each building with her eyes. Her favorites she walked into or she just touched the walls if they weren't stable enough to hold her weight. She didn't even dodge away from the spiders. She was too damn heavy for that kind of fear.

She'd have to find another way to prove herself to the people who loved her, if that was possible. She was beginning to think it wasn't. She was beginning to think she had nothing to prove, not because she was too great for it, but because there was nothing there. No core. No strength. Just a futile hope that she wasn't a loser.

The wind rose then, sweeping over her skin, picking up her hair and floating it behind her. Merry closed her eyes and pictured herself as that bit of dandelion fluff she'd feared she was. Any second now she'd break away and be swept off.

But not yet. She took a deep breath and let it out on a sigh, then headed to her little makeshift office to clean it up.

Two hours later, she had everything organized for the person who'd replace her, and she'd made a tiny pile of the things that belonged to her. Everything else belonged to someone else. Or it belonged to the Providence Historical Trust. Not even a person, but a group that would never love this place as much as she did.

She meant to get up then. To leave. But her hand went to the biography notes she'd taken about Gideon Bishop. In those notes was the information about his family. His descendants. About Shane.

Before she could start reading, she heard a car door slam and she sat straight with a terrified start.

Whoever it was, she didn't want to see them. Not even Grace. An ungracious thought, considering her friend would only be worried for her. Merry hung her head for a moment, took a deep breath and then stood.

But when she stepped out onto the little porch, she froze and that breath she'd taken flew from her lungs on a choked cry. It wasn't Grace. It was Shane walking toward her, his face half-hidden by the shade of his hat.

In that moment, she hated him more than she'd ever hated anyone in her life. She shook her head, but he kept coming.

"Go away," she ordered. He ignored her. "I don't want to talk to you," she shouted.

That stopped him, at least, but he was only ten feet away now. Way too close.

"Merry, please. I'm so sorry. I should've told you. I wanted to, but by then it was too late. I didn't know how to—"

"I said I don't want to talk to you!"

He took off his hat and rubbed a hand over his hair. "I know you don't. That's fair. You can just stand there. But I need you to understand that what happened between us didn't have anything to do with Providence."

"You're a liar. And I don't care about that. It didn't mean anything to you and it didn't mean anything to me."

"Merry, that's not true—"

"Why are you here? To rub it in? To gloat about how you're going to ruin all my plans? Just do it!"

"Do what?"

"Tell the board. Tell the press. Tell the judge. Just get it over with. It doesn't matter. I'm not going to wait to be fired. I'm resigning."

He shook his head. "No. Didn't you read my letter?"

"Of course not. I threw it away."

"Merry, I don't want to get you fired. I don't care

about this damn ghost town. My grandfather was going to leave that money to me, but I wouldn't give him what he wanted. He wanted to punish me. He didn't give a shit about Providence…he only created that trust to teach me a lesson. The money belongs to me."

"That's up to the courts to decide."

"Fine. Then let the courts decide it. Don't let it affect our friendship."

She couldn't believe it. She shouldn't have skipped coffee this morning, because her brain was clearly not working correctly. "Are you suggesting that I just let it go?"

"Yes. When you asked if I'd work for you, I didn't know you. And I didn't have some big espionage planned. I just figured I'd hang around a little…see if I could find out what was going on with the trust, what the plans were. But then I got to know you better. I liked you. And it all got mixed up."

"Mixed up," she murmured.

"Yes. And the sex…that has nothing to do with this. That wasn't a lie." He offered a tentative smile. "It was damn real, Merry."

A smile. He had the nerve to *smile* at her. Like she was that gullible. That stupid. That lacking in self-esteem. She walked down the stairs and the worry in his eyes lightened as she approached. Unbelievable.

"Who do you think I am?" she asked.

He shook his head.

"You think I'm someone sweet and nice and sunny? You look at me and you see someone who wants an apology? Someone who'll forgive you?"

"That's what I hope, yes. I'm sorry, Merry. You're special. I know we don't have a permanent thing, but—"

"I'm *special?*" she snarled. "Am I cute, too? And funny and kind?"

"Um…" He finally seemed to recognize that his smile may have been premature. "Yes?"

Merry poked a finger into his chest, hard. "You don't know me. You don't know anything about me. You know *nothing,* do you understand?"

He stepped backward, hands raised.

"If I'm sweet, it's because I choose to be. If I'm ridiculously positive, it's because life is easier that way. A *hard* life is easier that way. I am not stupid, Shane." She followed his retreat, drilling her finger into his chest again. "I am not fucking *stupid.* I trust people because I choose to, because if you fuck me over, it says something terrible about you, not me. I see the good in people, because that makes me happy, not because I live in fairy-tale land where bad things don't happen. Bad things happen, Shane. I've spent my whole life well aware of that. Bad things like *you.*"

"No, I—"

"You lied to me. You used my happiness as a way to manipulate information from me. You let me trust you when you knew I shouldn't have. And then you fucked me. I told you something secret about myself and you saw that as an *in.*"

"That is not true. I swear it's not true, Merry."

"Oh, you swear?" She poked him again. "You promise? Who the *fuck* do you think I am? I have seen bad shit my whole life. People have been cruel. Life has been scary. My own father never even wanted to *meet* me. So if you think I can't recognize unforgivably shitty behavior, you are sadly mistaken. I'm awkward and nerdy and ridiculous and maybe even foolish, but I'm not an idiot. And I am not weak."

She spread her arms. "Look at me. I'm strong. I'm here, aren't I? I'm not curled up in bed. I'm not crying. I wasn't even standing around hoping you'd give me an explanation I could latch onto to feel less stupid. You lied, you lied while we were friends, and you lied when it became more than that. And now I'm going to lose my job because of you. So fuck you, Shane Harcourt. *Now* you know who I am, and I am not the kind of girl who'd put up with being used and disrespected and violated."

She gave him one good shove with both hands and then walked backward. "Go away. I don't want you here, and I'm still in charge of this place for the next few hours."

He watched her. When he didn't move, she turned her back on him and walked up the steps. She even closed the door of the house, plunging herself into a sudden darkness before her eyes could adjust.

She held her breath, waiting. He couldn't come after her. He couldn't follow her into the house, because she was frozen on the verge of tears. Just waiting. Waiting. She couldn't possibly stop them at this point, she could only hold them off, but if he made her speak again, she was lost. And if he touched her, she'd fall apart. Her big words would mean nothing then.

But she finally heard his boots crunch across the dry ground, and the sound was moving away. The solid *thunk* of his door gave her the right news. He was leaving.

Merry collapsed into her chair and took a deep breath. And then she sobbed. Her head dropped into her hands and she cried so hard her chest hurt.

He had made her feel special. He'd made her feel beautiful. And sexy. And wanted.

And it had all been a lie.

The one time in her life that she'd felt honestly sexual and desirable, and it hadn't been real.

She'd told Grace she could handle it. She'd told her it was just sex and she could enjoy it for what it was. But apparently that wasn't true, because Shane's lies didn't make the sex any worse. It didn't change the fact that she'd enjoyed his body and come harder than she ever had before. But it was all ruined now. It all felt sordid and shameful.

Had he been laughing at her? Or had it just been triumph inside him as he'd talked her into touching herself for him? Putting on a show?

She couldn't believe she'd done that. It had seemed fun and scandalously good at the time, and now it all just felt awful.

"Bastard," she choked out past her tears. She was good at trusting people, but not that way. Not with her body. She'd been shy that way her whole life, and her teen years had felt like a world populated by predators. Teenage boys who didn't want to date her, but felt like they had the right to comment on her body any time they wanted. Male friends who liked the pretty, confident girls but occasionally noticed her enough to honor her with a crude offer. As if she should feel lucky they'd bother to get a hard-on and toss it her way.

She'd finally managed to lose her virginity in her

senior year of college. Not because she'd really wanted the boy she'd slept with, but because it had felt as if she wouldn't ever want anyone that way, and she might as well get it over with.

It hadn't been bad. They'd dated for a few months. It had gotten better. Then she'd successfully avoided sex for a few years, only to stumble back into it with Kenneth. Another dud, but he'd been sweet, at least. And so pleased with her naked body that she'd tried to lose a little of her modesty. But she'd never let go of her self-consciousness. Not until Shane, when she'd managed it, if only for a few stolen, heated moments.

She wanted to think that meant there was hope for her. That she was maturing and starting to find her way through the complicated world of sex. But she was worried that it really meant she'd never be able to do it again. Because now she wouldn't just be thinking about her body and her heart and her sexual performance, she'd be thinking that it was all an out-and-out lie. A tool used for her humiliation.

God. Maybe she'd just give it up.

But maybe she couldn't. Because the worst thing he'd done was give her a taste of what was possible.

"I hate him," she groaned, scrubbing her face with her shirt, and vowing not to cry anymore. She hadn't even finished the thought when more tears fell. They'd been friends, damn him. They'd been more than that.

Tears still streaming down her face, Merry gathered up her pitiful pile of belongings and walked out of Providence. She turned around and gave it one last look, defying all the standard advice about not looking back.

This place had been important to her. It could have

been the one big triumph she'd needed to start her real life. That life that was waiting for her somewhere. A life where she wasn't just a visitor wandering through.

Providence hadn't ended up being that, but she still loved it. And the grief she felt as she got into her car and drove away was far bigger than anything she'd let herself feel for Shane. And so much easier to bear.

SHANE HAD KNOWN that sleeping with a neighbor was a bad idea, but he hadn't realized just how bad an idea it was. He hadn't imagined that just getting out of his truck and walking to his apartment would be a gauntlet of shame. A few torturous seconds of hoping he didn't see Grace or Cole or even Rayleen. And all the while, half hoping he would see the one person who made him feel the worst.

Jesus.

He made himself walk slowly up the stairs, fighting the instinct to drop his head and hide his face.

He'd known what he was doing was wrong. He'd known he was deceiving her in more ways than one. But then, after a while, it hadn't felt so bad anymore, because he hadn't *meant* it anymore. In his own head, he'd known that he would go back and change it if he could, so it had seemed almost like an innocuous mistake. He wasn't going to betray her. He wouldn't say anything to the board. Nothing at all.

But he realized now that he'd jeopardized everything for her. She'd be fired just for having hired him. If anyone else found out, it would be a scandal. At the very least, she'd look foolish.

God. The regret was a physical pain inside him. An

actual ache that burned through his gut, as if it were slowly devouring him.

What the hell had he been trying to accomplish, anyway? It had been underhanded and unnecessary, and if he'd planned it beforehand, he would have tossed the idea out. But she'd handed it to him, like a present with a bow on it, this opportunity to figure out what they were doing and why, and he'd told himself it was fine because he was doing the work she'd hired him for. Hell, he'd even done the work for free.

He wished he could take it back now. He'd give anything to take it back after he'd seen her face today. So terrible and wild as she'd cut him from her life without an ounce of regret. *Now you know who I am,* she'd raged.

And she was right. He had thought of her as harmless and sweet. Even after last night, he hadn't been that scared. She was a kind and forgiving soul and he could win her back. He could convince her he was sorry and he wouldn't do it again. She'd forgive him because... Well, she had to. What other option was there? That he'd never get to touch her again?

But that was exactly the other option, because her face had been a picture of resolve. He'd glimpsed a strength he'd never seen in her before. A bravery.

In fact, that was the only option, because what else could he want from her? Love? Commitment? He couldn't do that. Had he expected her to forgive him and then go back to no-strings-attached sex?

As if to remind him of exactly who he was and what he had to offer a woman, Shane's home phone rang. He didn't bother ignoring it. As bad as his mood was, he might as well get it over with.

"Mom," he said simply.

"Oh, Shane, you're home! I just had a feeling. I don't know why. You know I get these instincts sometimes."

Yes. She'd claimed instinct a lot in her wild-goose chases. *Honey, I just know your dad is in California. I can feel it. Something is telling me to get in the car and drive.*

"I've got to get to work, actually. What's up?"

"I found someone on Facebook who looks exactly like your dad. Now, he's way too young to be him, but he doesn't say anything on his page about his father. What he does say is that he was raised in an unconventional way in a remote area of the Cascades."

"Mom." He sighed. Facebook had become her new obsession. He only hoped no one he knew ever read her updates. If she weren't still holding down a job at the feed store, he'd be worried she was truly losing it.

"I know it would be painful for us to find out he'd started a new family somewhere, but we have to accept that possibility. Once he left, he may have just been too ashamed to come back. And this boy looks exactly like Alex did at eighteen. It's eerie."

He squeezed his eyes shut. His mother couldn't face the truth. She couldn't even consider the possibility of the truth.

"Mom, I can't do this anymore. I swear to God I can't. He didn't love us. Not enough to stay and not enough to come back. Why can't you accept that? He wasn't even a good husband to you. He was sleeping with that woman for months! He wanted *out,* don't you get it? He didn't want you! You have to let him go!"

Shane heard his own ragged breath in the phone, but his mom was silent on the other end. There'd been an unspoken agreement for a long time. No one mentioned the other woman. No one brought her into the discussion. Hell, the blank was so complete that for the first five years his mother had rarely even investigated reports that people had seen Dorothy Heyer. The woman had existed only as a shadow. She was just some random person who'd happened to leave Jackson around the same time as their father. Sure, she'd been spotted at the dealership when he'd picked up the camper. But even if she'd left with him, he wouldn't have stayed with her. He hadn't loved that floozy. No way.

Now Shane had crossed the line. He'd thrown Dorothy in his mother's face. And hell, he wasn't even sorry.

"The next time you call," he said softly, "it can't be about Dad. It can't be. Or you and I won't have a relationship anymore. We can talk about my life or your life. We can even talk about Alex. But not Dad. Understand?"

"Shane," she scolded, her voice thick with tears. "How can you even ask me to let it go? Am I supposed to just move on with my life? Just forget all that pain and, and…" She began to weep, choking her words so he couldn't understand them anymore.

"Yes," he said. "That's exactly what I expect. Bad things happen. You have to move on. Like other people do every damn day. Goodbye, Mom."

He hung up and stared down at the phone in his hand, a little stunned at what he'd just done.

He'd been edging back for years. Pushing her farther away. Keeping more distance. This year, especially, he'd tried to avoid her jabs about Gideon Bishop, about what that family owed Shane and his brother, about how Gideon should go to hell for trying to force Shane into bowing to his will. All that despite the fact that she'd despaired over Shane's name change far more than the Bishop family ever had.

He'd tried to keep her out of his head, but in that moment, staring down at the phone in his shaking hand, he realized he hadn't succeeded. He'd let her in. She'd snuck deep into his mind, beneath all his conscious thoughts, and she'd lived there. Her thoughts and obsessions and resentments pushing at his mind, shaping his ideas.

And now it was so obvious to him. Her infection was so obvious, because she was in such stark contrast to Merry's moment of beautiful strength.

Merry had seen terrible things. She'd lived with heartache and abandonment, and she still walked through life with a hopeful smile and eyes wide enough to take everything in.

"Jesus," he breathed. What the hell had he done? What the hell was he still *doing?*

Shane grabbed his cell phone and texted the contractor he was currently working for to let him know he wouldn't be in. Despite his work for Merry, Shane was ahead of schedule, so he could take a day off. Then he sent one more text. A very important one. His phone rang almost as soon as he hit Send. He answered with a humorless smile.

"Yes, I mean it," he said without waiting for a greeting. "I'll be there in a few minutes. Write up whatever you need to write up."

The way he'd been living for the past year—hell, for his whole life…this wasn't who he was. It wasn't who he wanted to be. He'd tried to change his identity by changing his name, but the truth was that he'd been resigned to it. To being his father's son. To being a Bishop and everything that meant. The name change had been his one rebellion. His big fuck you to the crippling legacy they'd left him.

A damn pitiful rebellion, he realized now. He'd given in to everything else without even a semblance of a fight.

But this moment… This was his real chance to be someone better than his father. Better than his grandfather. Better than his mom.

Shane grabbed his hat and his keys and walked out the door to change his life.

CHAPTER EIGHTEEN

"I HAVE TO RESIGN," Merry said, staring at the email she'd started.

"I'm not saying you don't. I'm just saying give it a day. You're too screwed up to do this right now." Grace looked over Merry's shoulder. "I see you've made it all the way through 'Dear Members of the Board.' You don't even know what to say. Close the window. Try again tomorrow."

Merry shook her head.

Grace reached past and hit the cancel button. "Done. Let's get drunk."

"It's not even five."

"So?"

"So, it's too early to drink. And shouldn't you be at work?"

"I'm hourly. I do what I want."

Merry rolled her eyes. "Funny, my hourly positions have never been that way."

"All right, Eve let me take the afternoon off. She's pretty awesome."

"Obviously," Merry muttered.

"Come on," Grace pressed. "Let's do something fun."

"I can't." Merry slumped and let her face fall into

the despair she was feeling. "I have to go to Crystal's tonight. She's having some stupid party."

"Fuck Crystal! Are you kidding me?"

"I'm not kidding. And the worst part is that I told her I was bringing a date. Now I have to show up alone."

"Well, don't go!"

"I have to. I already said yes. Plus, this will be my last chance to face her with a respectable job. The next time I see her, I'll probably be working at the state fair corn dog booth. I need to savor this."

"No, you don't."

But Merry just sighed. She did need to savor this. "Can I take Cole?"

"I'd be happy to lend you Cole. You know that. But he's out late tonight moving cattle from some valley to some other valley. I think. I was half asleep when he told me."

"Shit. I don't want to cancel, Grace. When she finds out I've been fired in disgrace, she'll know that's why I didn't show up. I want her to know I didn't care. That I just kept going. That I…"

Her words dried up, but Grace nodded. "Okay. I can't believe I'm saying this, but take me."

"You hate Crystal."

"I know."

"You'll hate her friends."

"I'm sure. But take me. I'll be on my best behavior. And I'll be your designated driver. You can drink as much of her expensive wine as you can pour down your throat. You're about to be unemployed with no prospects. This might be your last chance to live like those people."

"What about you?"

"Oh, I had plenty of expensive wine at parties back during my old life in L.A. Now I drink beer and clean manure off my man's boots."

Merry laughed, a little shocked that she even had the urge. "Sure. When was the last time you cleaned Cole's boots?"

Grace shrugged. "Well, I thought about it a couple of nights ago when he was really tired, but then I just stretched out on the couch and told him not to bring those things inside."

"You're a regular prairie wife."

"Yeah. It's amazing how a good blow job technique can really change a man's expectations of partnership. Hell, I'll even wear a sun bonnet and ring the dinner bell while I go down on him, if that's what it takes to be traditional."

Merry wasn't just laughing now. She was choking on it, tears running down her cheeks as she tried to catch her breath. "You're so damn sick!"

"I know. I think Cole's ranch hands are a little scared of me. They call me ma'am."

"But the real question is does Cole call you ma'am when you're on your knees?"

"Of course. He's a cowboy. He's always a gentleman. Now come on." She elbowed Merry. "Let me be your date. I'll do your makeup."

"Okay. Yes. You're officially my date tonight. You're the only person in the world who could make me laugh this hard right now, anyway."

"Perfect. And you know what else we need to do? Go shopping. You need a dress."

"I can't afford a dress."

"We'll take it out of your rent. Do it for me. Please. You'll be my pretty dress-up doll for the night."

Merry smiled. This was how Grace wanted to help. This was how she showed love. "Okay. Fine."

"Yeah! And then we can rub Crystal's pointy nose in your beauty!"

Merry exploded in laughter again. "And here I thought you were being sweet and thoughtful."

"I don't want to lose my edge."

There were no worries there. Grace was all edges and hard lines. Until you got past the surface, then she was soft in ways she didn't want anyone to see. Cole had seen it, though. And for that, Merry loved him like crazy. He almost gave her hope that she could find a good man like him someday. Almost.

"Let's go," Merry said, grabbing her phone just as it rang. Jeanine Bishop's name flashed. Merry stared at it, and even Grace seemed frozen.

She should answer it. No matter what Jeanine was calling about, she should answer it and face the music. She watched the phone until the display blurred. She told herself to answer it. Just answer it. The phone finally went silent.

All her bravery had been used up in that confrontation with Shane. She'd left it on the dusty streets of Providence to dry up and blow away.

She'd find some courage tomorrow. She had to. Or she'd fake it. But tonight, she'd buy a pretty dress, have her makeup done, drink expensive wine and pretend to fit in with her cousin's friends. She'd pretend to be the success she'd always wanted to be. Tomorrow was soon enough to be destroyed. Her disgrace would be waiting with eager arms.

Merry switched off the ringer. "I'm ready. Let's go. I want to look like a sexpot."

Grace paused and shot her a careful look.

"I'm just kidding. I'll settle for looking like an actual adult for once."

"Deal. Just relax, darlin'. I'll make you a woman tonight."

Thank God. Finally somebody would.

CHAPTER NINETEEN

IT WAS LATE. TOO LATE for a trail ride, but Shane needed it. He'd spent an hour at his lawyer's office then headed back to his apartment to take the longest, hottest shower of his life before knocking on Merry's door.

She hadn't answered, which had hardly surprised him, but she actually seemed to have been gone. He'd tried Cole then, and gotten voice mail. Not much of a surprise, either. He wasn't sure if his best friend would ever speak to him again. He wasn't sure he even deserved his best friend anymore. Cole understood that life could be a series of difficult choices, but he'd always made the right ones. Shane, on the other hand...

"Shit." Shane had to get outside. He had to think. Or better yet, not think at all. And he knew just where to lose himself.

An hour later, the sun was low over the mountains, but Shane was on his horse and headed for the trail beyond Providence. He felt better once he reached the trees, less like a furious female curator might have a sight on his back from her ghost town hidey hole. Ridiculous, of course. Merry's car wasn't there, and she didn't own a gun. As far as he knew. But he breathed a little easier when he was lost in the trees. She might just be mad enough to want to kill him. Or maybe she was so disgusted she didn't even care.

He took a deep breath, and then another, as he let the horse follow the trail. But instead of riding up toward the cabin, this time he followed the canyon. It was quiet in the deep shadows, the only noise the water dancing over rocks. You couldn't even hear birds down here, and the wind was still and silent. He kept breathing, taking it in.

This was his land. His. And somehow, he'd never let that wash over him. It meant something, damn it. It meant something to own this land, and not just because it was his, but because it was a place that had belonged to his father's father, and all the people who'd come before him.

Merry had been right. Those people hadn't given up or run. They'd lived here, and died here. They'd married and had children and lost loved ones. But this land was still in the family. It was still being passed down, generation after generation. Minus one or two.

They hadn't given up. He didn't have to give up, either.

He glanced toward the north, trying to place himself in relation to the road above, but at this time of year, it was hard to find a landmark. He pressed on, passing the ice house and the memories of Merry when she'd still been happy with him.

Screw this. He wasn't giving up on her.

He liked her. As a friend and a lover and maybe something far more. He wasn't giving up. But he owed her something. Something big. Something bigger than

Providence, which he'd had no right to take from her, anyway.

The canyon narrowed here. The aspens above him began to thin and the far bank grew darker with pine. When he spotted a manageable incline on the other side, he turned his mount through the stream and urged her up the bank. She scrambled a little, but once she got her hold on the ground, she had no problem working her way up the other side to a higher plain above.

He was almost sure he was near the washed out area of the road. More importantly, he was close to that place he'd spotted something pale below the trees.

Whatever it was, if it was out here, it was old. And if it was old, then Merry would like it. She was funny that way. And perfect. And his chest hurt when he thought of her.

Damn. How was it he'd managed to screw up so badly with the only girl he'd ever fallen for? How had he managed to ruin everything before he'd even touched her for the first time? He'd been so worried about screwing up a relationship in the long-term that he hadn't realized how bad he was at dealing with women in the short-term.

He wound his way through the trees, the muffled *thump* of his mare's hooves against the pine floor pulsing through the forest like rings of water. She snorted and frightened a flock of blackbirds from a tree. Shane looked up to watch them scatter, and when his gaze fell again, he spotted white.

He pulled the horse to a stop and puzzled over the vivid white filtering through the branches of a low pine. What could be that starkly white out here, aside from ice or snow? Stone? Was it a stone building? Some kind of fort, maybe?

He turned off the path, ducking as he rode beneath a low branch, then cursing as his mare slid on grit as she picked her way over a flat boulder. When her hooves thumped on pine-needle ground again, Shane peered ahead, and he finally registered what he was seeing.

Not bright stone, but white vinyl. Straight edges, aside from where the vinyl had crumpled in on itself. He dismounted and tied off his horse before ducking beneath another low branch and moving forward. Slowly. He held his breath, alarmed by the strangeness of the sight before him.

This thing didn't belong here, whatever it was. It was out of place and not right, and he still couldn't quite process what his eyes were telling him.

But then he saw the words on the side of it. He saw the taillights. The door, popped open and bent down on one hinge. It was a camping trailer. It had crashed long ago, if the ten-foot-tall aspens growing out of one crumpled window were any indication.

And then he saw the truck.

It was twisted around a pine a few yards beyond the trailer, the deep blue paint fading and cracking in the sun. The truck lay at an angle, the driver's side still held slightly aloft by the pine trunks it had run into. Grass grew tall around its bumper, obscuring the license plate he'd memorized from photocopying thousands of missing posters for his mom. But Shane didn't need to see the license plate. He knew.

All those years of searching, all that heartbreak and abandonment, and his dad had been right here the whole time. Goose bumps broke out over his whole body, but Shane shook them off and forced his feet to move.

His brain scrambled to try to urge him back, but he didn't stop. He moved on, slowly yes, but he didn't hesitate once.

The cab was elevated on this side, and he was eye-level with the steering wheel. He braced himself, somehow expecting to see his father there, his face blackened and bloated like a horrifying scene from a scary movie. But of course, it had been too many years for that. He didn't see anything but a bowed dashboard and the jagged edges of glass that used to be a windshield.

Strangely, that was the moment he wanted to turn and run. He'd been brave. He'd looked inside. And he'd seen nothing. It was time to go. He'd done his part for his father, and now he felt like a ten-year-old boy, desperate to turn the duty over to someone else.

Shane closed his eyes for a moment. He took a deep breath and watched the shadows of the pine boughs against his eyelids. The last rays of the sun would be gone soon. He needed to hurry.

Opening his eyes, he let the air fall from his lungs and took one more breath. Then he retraced his steps to the bumper and cut across to the other side of the truck.

He'd thought the door might be wedged into the ground on this side, but it had been wrenched open and pressed to the side of the hood as the truck had tumbled down.

Just as on the other side, he saw nothing when he peered into the cab. No bodies. No horror. Just a broken truck left exposed to the elements too long.

Maybe it was all another dead end. His dad had

crashed the truck and then he'd walked away and kept on going. Left the truck behind along with his kids and wife.

Shane squatted down next to the door. The goose bumps broke out again. The door looked obscene, bent so far forward, the hinges bulging outward. It looked like a broken limb.

Even as he wished he hadn't noticed, Shane saw the way the bench seat of the old pickup slanted toward the open door. He closed his eyes again, telling himself no, but then he let his head drop. He opened his eyes. He reached toward the long grass under the lip of the truck and parted it. Nothing. He tried again, his hands arching the grass open, like parting the seas. On the third try, he spotted something near the ground. Something white and dull and definitely not vinyl.

"Oh, no," he breathed, falling to his knees at the sight of the long bone that looked so pale against the brown dirt. "Damn it. No."

It wasn't until that moment that Shane realized he'd still hoped his dad was alive. Despite all his big, belligerent words to his mom, he'd still wanted it. More than anything. To look up and see his dad standing in the doorway, older and haggard and so goddamn sorry about what he'd done.

That wasn't going to happen now. It wouldn't ever happen. His dad was dead.

He felt tears try to start in his eyes and blinked them away. He'd cried enough tears for his father, surely.

He was dead. Really, irrevocably dead.

When his throat tried to close, Shane pushed to his feet and focused on walking back to his horse.

Just to be sure, he pulled his cell phone from his pocket and checked the signal. Nothing. He kept the phone in his hand and swung up into the saddle. As soon as the first bar showed, he'd call the sheriff, but what the hell would he say?

Would he report an accident? It wasn't exactly urgent. It could wait until morning. Hell, it would be full dusk by the time he made it down to Providence. The sheriff's department wouldn't endanger its people for corpses that were over two decades old. He wouldn't even want them to. But he had to report it tonight. He had to.

Once he'd ridden down the bank and into the stream itself, Shane checked his phone again, then urged his horse a little faster.

He knew it wouldn't make a difference, but he suddenly needed to call. He needed it to be over. Over.

He reached for an itch on his cheek and his fingers came away wet. "Shit," he gasped. He wiped his cheeks and kept riding.

When he finally reached the mouth of the canyon, he drew a deep breath, nearly panicked for reasons he couldn't comprehend. It made no sense. His dad had been dead a long time.

His eyes caught on Providence as the last rays of the sun caught the roofs of the houses. He dialed 911 and raised the phone to his ear. "This is Shane Harcourt. My father went missing twenty-five years ago, and I've just found his truck. I think there are…remains. I'm out at the Providence ghost town, a couple miles off the highway. What should I do?"

What should I do?

Way too big a question to answer, even for the cops. But he listened patiently, nodding before he hung up.

What should I do? He had no idea.

Shane walked to the porch of the saloon and sat down. Fifteen minutes later, the moon rose over the old church and he was still lost and alone. Then the first hint of headlights broke the dark.

He'd started something here, and this was the place he'd finish it, once and for all.

CHAPTER TWENTY

A SMALL PARTY for Crystal apparently meant forty of her closest acquaintances milling about looking beautiful and removed. How she could possibly know more people in Jackson than Merry did was a complete mystery. Though maybe an unrestored ghost town in the middle of nowhere didn't make for the most extensive social life.

Or maybe beautiful people were naturally attracted to places like this. The house that Crystal had borrowed from a friend had a multitiered stone patio that overlooked the valley of Jackson Hole from a comfortably superior height. Maybe packs of rich, elegant people wandered neighborhoods like this one, idly slipping in and out of parties thrown by their kind, sleeping wherever they ended up at 2:00 a.m. like a big pack of viciously polite dogs.

Or possibly Merry's mind wandered when she was bored.

"Ugh," she groaned to Grace. "How long do we have to stay? Would it be rude to finish this glass of wine and then leave?"

"Probably. But there's rarely a good reason not to be rude, I always say."

"Liar. Now that you're working for Eve you've turned into a well-behaved pussycat."

Grace shrugged one shoulder. She'd finally been civilized, and she tried to pretend she didn't like it, but she was clearly more comfortable in her own skin than she'd ever been. Even though she was working in the same industry she'd left behind, moving away from L.A. had freed her somehow.

"You haven't punched anyone in months," Merry pointed out.

"Ah, but I did slap Shane."

Merry winced a little. Now that she'd gotten some of the rage out of her system, she almost felt bad about that. But not so bad that she turned down the miniature crab cake a waiter offered. Or a second glass of wine.

"This expensive wine really is good."

"It almost makes up for the company."

"I'm sure they're all lovely," Merry said. She wouldn't know because she'd huddled at the edge of a patio with Grace from the moment they arrived. "I'm glad you talked me into the dress, though. These people aren't really a summer-party flip-flop crowd."

"You look beautiful. Maybe you should pick out a guy and make your move. Get Shane out of your system with a quickie."

Merry looked doubtfully around at the men wearing expensive sport coats over shirts unbuttoned at the collar to signify they were at a party and not a business meeting. "I've never had sex with a rich guy. What's it like?"

Grace shrugged. "Same as anyone else except for

the Perry Ellis underwear. Maybe a little more man-scaping, if you're into that sort of thing."

Merry grimaced. She had no idea if she was, but it hardly mattered. Grace would be the one to rebound from a betrayal with a hostile one-night stand. Merry would rather curl up in her bed for six months to a year. Alone.

"Look at that guy," Grace suggested, pointing her chin toward the next patio up. "He's pretty damn hot."

He was. In a sculpted blond kind of way. He'd ditched his sport coat at some point and rolled up the sleeves of his shirt, which also added to his appeal, but only until Merry got a look at his forearms. They were perfectly tanned and nearly hairless. Oh, they looked strong enough, but in a Bikram yoga kind of way, not in the I-haul-lumber-every-day kind of way.

Not that it mattered. Carpenters were off the menu.

She gave up her study of the blond guy and swept the crowd. Maybe there was a big, rich rancher here. But, no. Rich or not, Merry didn't think a man like that would be Crystal's type of friend. A little too salt of the earth.

"There she is," she breathed when she finally spotted Crystal working her way through the crowd. She drank the rest of her lovely, expensive wine without even tasting it and braced herself for the assault of Crystal's family love.

"Merry," Crystal purred as she approached. "Why, you look lovely tonight."

"Thank you." Merry ran a nervous hand down the fitted black dress Grace had forced her to try on. Merry's favorite part about it was the color. A ridiculously boring thought, but black was flattering and it had allowed her a little freedom in searching the clearance rack for shoes. The magenta pumps wouldn't have gone with much else. Of course, she'd never have a need for them again. Maybe she could just wear this outfit to the Crooked R every Friday night. After all, there'd be new people there every weekend who hadn't seen it yet.

"You look great, too," she said, a compliment that Crystal accepted with ease. After all, her pale gray sheath had probably cost five hundred dollars. Merry had a feeling that estimate was a little naive.

"So you brought Grace." She didn't even bother with one of her patently fake smiles; she just narrowed her eyes in Grace's direction. Grace returned the favor.

"I did."

"What happened to that gentleman friend you were so eager to bring?"

"It fell through."

"Hah." She followed her tiny, evil cough of a laugh with a knowing grin.

"It fell through," Merry insisted, her voice rising.

"That happens sometimes. The trials of being single." A nice, subtle reminder that she'd been married for eight years and a mother for five.

Merry tried to sink her own jibe. "Well, you know how these cowboys are, rugged and free-spirited. Big and…hard to tame. It's amazing a girl can even hold on for one night. Then again, there's always another one coming down the trail. So to speak."

Grace choked behind her.

Crystal smiled tightly. "Maybe you and your friend here should just settle down together. She's always around, after all. I noticed some of her clothes at your place and only one bed."

Merry sighed. "Really? You think that insults me? Have you ever noticed how hot Grace is? She'd probably rock my world."

"Oh, I would, darlin'," Grace growled with a promising trill of her tongue.

Dropping her elegant face for a moment, Crystal rolled her eyes in disgust. "I guess you're even more like your mom than I thought you were."

"What does that even mean?"

"Figure it out. Look, I was doing my mom a favor inviting you here. You could at least be polite. Maybe even appreciative."

"Appreciative? What the hell do I care what your mom wants?"

"Because my mom was doing it for *your* mom, who called with some sob story about how we're all the family we have. But you know what? That's not true. Not for me and not for my mom. We both have husbands, and they have families, and now my brother and I have kids. So no, you're not the only family I have, Merry Slacker, and I wish you'd stop trying to push your way in."

Merry gasped in utter, dumbfounded shock. Where the hell had this come from? "Are you insane? I've never tried to push my way into anything!"

"No? How about the trips to Disneyland your family took with mine? Or the weekends at our lake cabin? And what about all those summers you came to 'visit'? All those weeks you spent at our house? You think those were about bonding?"

"Yes! Our moms wanted us to—"

"Oh, please. Those visits were a way of getting you out of your shitty neighborhood for a while because your mom couldn't afford to send you to summer camp like a normal kid!"

Merry was so shocked she just stood there blinking and trying to close her jaw. Now she understood all the years of bitchiness. All the meanness and cruelty. Merry had never been anything but a pitiful, poor relation hanging around and ruining Crystal's fun. Following her like a clingy little bird. "Take Merry with you," her aunt had called out a hundred times. A thousand. Merry had been three years younger and a million times less cool.

"Merry," Grace said from her side, "let's get out of this bitch's sight before I break my streak and end up in jail again."

"Again!" Crystal sneered.

"Yes, *again,* you stupid cow. So don't think I don't know how to make you sorry for being the shittiest person I've ever met. And I'll do it in front of all your new friends. God, can you imagine how long they'd tell that tale? It would go down in history, you everloving *bitch.*"

"Get out," Crystal growled. "And take your slacker girlfriend with you."

Merry looked at the last of her wine. She looked back at Crystal and her gorgeous silk dress. She wanted to do it. She really did. But she took the high road and set the glass on a table…just in case the low road suddenly looked too good to resist.

"You're cruel," she said softly.

"Whatever," Crystal snapped.

"I mean it. You're mean and awful. I was just a little girl. I'm sorry if I ruined your summers and one of the four family vacations you took every year."

"Oh, here we go. *I'm* sorry my mom was so much more successful than yours!"

"That's not what you need to be sorry for," Merry growled. "It was scary for me, you know. Spending weeks in a big house with people who didn't accept me. It was lonely, watching you and your friends play without me while you whispered and laughed and shot me angry looks. And the thing is… You were just a kid, too. I can forgive you for that. You were dumb and I was interfering with your life and your plans. But you're a fucking adult now, Crystal, or so you remind me every time I see you. You're all grown up and you're still no better than that nasty selfish little girl you were."

Crystal snarled, her lips thinning into a cruel twist. "You were nothing but a—"

"Fuck off," Merry said quietly. "I'd rather have no family at all than have you."

Amazingly Crystal shut her mouth. Merry turned and walked away. She tried to act cool and removed, but she was still reeling. "What the hell was that?" she whispered to Grace.

"You told her off!" Grace crowed. "You owned her!"

"But… Why would she say things like that?"

"It doesn't matter. Nothing she said was true."

"But it was true, Grace. How did I not see it? I was a charity case! I still am a charity case."

"You are not."

"Are you kidding me?" She avoided the wide wall of glass doors that led into the beautiful three-story mountain lodge with all its expensive wood and stone architectural details and skirted around to the side.

"Merry—"

"I'm pitiful, Grace. Look at me!" Her heel sunk into the grass and she leaned to the side, waving her arms in wide circles, trying desperately to grasp at balance. "Oh, God, look at me! I'm living in your apartment, on a *couch,* sleeping with a guy who was gracious enough to charity fuck me while he was screwing me over and still hanging out with my rich cousin who wished she didn't have to invite me along. You just bought me the first dress and heels I've worn in years, I'm about to lose the only respectable position I've ever had and my own mom doesn't want me anymore!"

Grace had been poised to pounce, her mouth parted to speak, hands already midgesture, but she paused at that. Tucking her chin in, she shook her head. "What?"

"I've always known I wasn't like other people. I couldn't find that thing. That one thing. Whatever else happened in your life, Grace, you always had your gift with makeup. You knew you were good at *something.* Really good at it. I'm not good at anything. Hell, I'm not even geeky enough to be good at being a sci-fi geek. But I always thought my mom was proud of me."

"She is proud of you!"

"She bought a new condo and made clear I wasn't welcome there. I wasn't even staying with her anymore! She just said, 'I won't have room for you to stay with me, Merry.' What the hell?" Merry swiped a tear off her cheek and kicked off her shoes to make her escape. But halfway past the house, she was stopped by a high stone terrace. "Goddamn it, how do you get out of this stupid place?"

"Merry!" Grace grabbed her shoulders and turned her around. "Merry, your mom isn't tired of you or ashamed of you or whatever you think is going on."

"I see how she keeps pushing me on my cousins. Hoping they'll rub off. How she keeps encouraging me to find my gift and be something better. She wants to be sure I don't fly back to the nest again like some undeveloped adolescent bird."

"Your mom believes in family. That's it. That's her deal with your cousins, and as for pushing you out of the nest, it's only because—" Grace cut off her impassioned speech with a snap of her teeth that even Merry heard.

"What?"

"She's…"

"Oh, my God, don't try to come up with a made-up reason!"

"It's not made up! Your mom is dating someone and she doesn't want to tell you!"

Going by Grace's expression of solemn horror at the secret she'd revealed, Merry felt like she should have experienced a moment of shock, but she could only shake her head and laugh. "And that's supposed to weird me out? Seriously, Grace. I'd be happy for her!"

"I know, but…"

"She wouldn't tell me to get out and stay gone just because some man occasionally spends the night."

"Um. I don't think it's a man."

Now Merry felt the shock. She blinked. She opened her mouth. Then closed it. "What?" she finally managed.

"Look, she called one day for you when you weren't

here and I heard a woman's voice. Someone walking in like she was free to come and go as she pleased. I wouldn't have thought anything of it, but your mom acted so flustered I noticed it. And then the other day when she was on video, I saw a pair of heels next to her couch. She never wears heels. She chastises me for wearing them. And these were red spike heels, and I just...I called her the next day. Just to see if she wanted to talk. To see if anything was going on. And..."

"And?" Merry demanded.

"And she said she was freaked out about telling you. I'm sorry, Merry. She was trying to figure out a way to tell you herself, but I couldn't keep my mouth shut any longer."

"Oh." Merry edged backward until her heels touched rock, and then she sat down on the first narrow ledge of the wall. "But... Why wouldn't she tell me?"

"She just..."

"Why would she think that would matter to me? She's a hippie for God's sake! She raised me to love everyone! And she couldn't even be honest about that?"

"Merry, she's your mom. Sex is weird for her to talk about. And it's complicated, because... Just call her, okay? When you get home, call her and let her tell you."

She groaned and laid her head back. "Ow," she said when it hit the edge of the next step up.

"Let's get out of here. Please? You're not a loser and this place is depressing you. Actually it's depressing me. And your mom loves you. She thinks you're perfect. So fuck Crystal."

"Oh, Jesus. Crystal even knows!"

"Her mom must have said something. What a disloyal witch. Come on." Grace grabbed her hands and pulled. "Stop groaning and feeling sorry for yourself."

"My life sucks," Merry said.

"Maybe, but groaning won't change that, and I'm cold."

When she got back to the car, Merry slouched down in the passenger seat and turned on her phone. When she saw there were four messages, her poor upset heart gave a violent twist of alarm. Four messages. That couldn't be good. Not at all. The press, maybe, calling to confirm all the sordid details of her scandalous behavior. In that moment, she was relieved she had a more urgent matter to see to.

Ignoring all the messages, Merry called her mom instead. "Mom?"

"Oh, hi, baby!"

For a moment, Merry couldn't speak. Was her mom with someone right now? Was she on a date and waving at the woman to be quiet so Merry wouldn't hear? How could she have thought it would matter to Merry? How could she have kept it secret?

Merry took a breath and told herself it would be fine. "Mom?

"Yes, sweetie?"

"Mom, Grace told me you were dating a woman, so is there anything you want to get off your chest?"

"Oh," her mom said. A heartbeat passed. Then another. And then her mom burst into loud sobs.

Tears immediately sprang to Merry's eyes. "Don't cry. I love you so much. Just…why didn't you tell me?"

"I don't know!" her mom wailed. "I was afraid."

"Afraid of what?"

"Just…failing you."

"Because you like women? Mom, come on."

"It's not that simple. I…I wasn't sure at first. When your dad left, I was *relieved*. God, I've never said that out loud. But it's true. I was happy to be alone and I felt terrible about that, because I knew it wasn't good for you. You wanted a daddy. You wanted more than just me."

"I didn't! Not really. I was a little girl. I wanted to be like everyone else."

"I know. I know. And I couldn't give you that, Merry. I wanted to. I tried. I went on a few dates when you were small, but I wasn't even interested. I assumed I was meant to be alone. And that was fine. I tried to make our home happy for you."

"You did, Mom. You always did."

"I'm glad. But when I realized maybe it was more than wanting to be alone—" She broke off into silence.

Merry wiped the tears from her face and waited.

"I couldn't give you a mom and a dad and a picket fence. I wanted to so much and I couldn't. But I couldn't give myself what I really wanted, either. I was afraid to make life harder for you than it already was. I didn't want to make you a target for bullies and zealots and…I was afraid for myself, too."

"So you were alone? That's just awful."

"It was fine. I didn't mean for it to be forever. I really didn't. But then I looked around and all those years had passed."

"So why didn't you tell me later? Why didn't you tell me *now*? You're dating someone, right? I want to know that, Mom. I want to know who you love."

"Oh, Merry. It's just… It's complicated, baby."

"Why?"

Her mom sighed, and Merry could almost hear her deflating. "Do you remember Louisa Tolliver?"

Merry shook her head, drawing a blank, but then the name sunk in. "Miss Tolliver?" she yelped.

"Yes."

Miss Tolliver had been her fifth-grade teacher, pretty and fresh out of college and brimming with excitement and hope. Merry had loved her utterly and completely.

"Miss Tolliver?"

"We had an, um, flirtation. When you were in her class. But of course, I wasn't comfortable with that, and she was worried about her job. And she was so young."

"Mom! Miss Tolliver?" Merry pressed a hand to her mouth to try to stifle a laugh that was half horror and half scandalized delight. She met Grace's eyes. Grace raised her eyebrows in question, and Merry just shook her head in disbelief before looking back out at the lights of passing cars.

"Well, I ran into her again a few months ago, and of course, she's almost forty-five, and she's out now and living happily and I just thought…I thought maybe I was ready to take that chance."

Merry just wanted to scream *Miss Tolliver* again, but that probably wouldn't be helpful. "You're dating Miss Tolliver," she said as calmly as she could.

"Yes," her mother answered. "I am."

"Wow." This was too much to take in. Like a strange, random dream you laughed about with friends. She took a deep breath. "And you were afraid to tell me?"

"I just let the lie go on for too long. I didn't know

how to say it, and I didn't know how you'd feel about Louisa. She meant so much to you."

"Yes. Well, if you're asking if I'd like it if Miss Tolliver was my second mom, I'd say it's a dream come true!"

"Oh, my word, Merry. We've only been dating a few months!"

"Do I get to call her Mom, too? Or Mama? Or something like that?"

Her mom's laughter was filled with relief and tears.

"Is she as pretty as I remember?"

"Even prettier," her mom whispered.

"Oh, Mom. Look at you with a hot younger girlfriend."

"Merry!" She laughed again, but then she said softly, "I'm so sorry."

"Don't be sorry. Just don't do this again, okay? You were pushing me away, Mom. I didn't know what to do. I didn't know why."

"I'm so sorry, baby. I should've told you. I just… God, it feels good to have it out. I've felt sick for months. The longer I kept it to myself, the harder it seemed to tell you. I've always taught you to be brave, and I couldn't tell you my biggest truth. What kind of woman am I?"

"The screwed up kind, just like the rest of us."

Her mom laughed and Merry smiled into the phone. "And the best kind. The very best. I love you, Mom. Just keep me in the loop on your super-hot dates from now on, okay?"

"I will. I promise I will. No more lying. I love you too much for that."

"And maybe you could bring her with you when you come visit. I'd like that."

"Oh, it's too soon for that, but… Hell, if it works out then maybe I'd like that, too, baby."

By the time she got off the call, Merry was limp with weariness. The day had been more than an emotional roller coaster. It had been a giant pinball machine, and she almost ignored the message icon that popped back up with new insistence. Whatever the urgent news was, she couldn't deal with it. She couldn't.

But she hit the play button anyway, and as soon as the words unfolded in her ear, she realized her insane day had only been a prelude to this moment. "Oh, my God," she whispered. Then she let out a scream that shook her own eardrums. "Oh, my God, Grace!"

Grace stopped dead on the road and turned to her with terrified eyes.

"I can't believe it," Merry said. "He did it."

"Did what? Who?"

But Merry was sobbing too hard to say another word.

CHAPTER TWENTY-ONE

MERRY PACED ACROSS their apartment for the fiftieth time. "I don't understand. It's almost eleven o'clock. Why can't anyone find him?"

"Listen, Cole just got back in cell range. He'll find Shane, all right? Just stop pacing! You're making me dizzy."

"I have to pace or I can't think. Why would he do that, Grace?"

Grace looked troubled. More than that, she looked confused. "I don't know."

"I just need to talk to him. Ask him. If he—"

Her phone cut her off and Merry answered it before the first ring had even finished. "Yes?"

"Merry!" Levi Cannon's voice boomed. "How's the savior of Providence doing?"

"Levi." She wilted a little at the sound of his voice. He'd always seemed to like her. He felt like a kind father figure, and tears sprang to her eyes at the happiness in his voice.

"Ms. Kade, you have truly pulled out a victory for this team. A complete victory. I am stunned. As is the rest of the board."

"I'm honestly not even sure I know what's going on."

"Didn't you talk to Jeanine? She said she called."

"I got her message, but…I'm still not sure I understand. He just dropped the suit?"

"He not only dropped the suit, but he cited you as
the principal reason he dropped it. He said… Just a
moment, let me get this right. 'Ms. Kade's love for the
town of Providence and her enthusiasm for the goals
of the Providence Historical Trust have persuaded me
that the restoration of the town is a worthwhile project
that should be pursued. Her unique perspective on the
project combined with professionalism and unmatched
energy are resources that will be invaluable to the development of this historical landmark.'"

Professionalism.

Tears welled from her eyes and coursed down her
face. She tried to swallow the lump in her throat.

Levi cleared his own throat. "I'm sure I don't have
to tell you there'll be no more discussion of this being
a temporary position. I won't hear of it."

For a moment, she felt such fierce pride and joy
that she couldn't breathe. She'd done it. She'd found
her place. And she'd succeeded at it. But in the next
moment, fear and regret rent that joy with a painful
slash. She didn't deserve this. She'd done everything
all wrong.

"Mr. Cannon, I…I don't think I deserve this. I can't
imagine what I said or did or…" Visions of what she'd
done with Shane suddenly cascaded through her mind,
but she shook it off. She wasn't some femme fatale so
skilled at sex that she could persuade men to give up
millions of dollars. "I need to confess something. Something important. I'm the one who destroyed that mailbox. Or, rather, I bumped into it with my car and it fell

over. I'm sorry. And then that sign. That stupid sign! I just wanted the board to call a meeting. I'm so sorry. And ashamed. And—"

She stopped talking when she realized Levi was laughing. Frowning at Grace's pointed look of question, Merry shook her head in confusion.

"Oh, my God!" Levi howled.

"Mr. Cannon?"

"Those old biddies and their hand-wringing! And it was you the whole time!"

"I can't apologize enough. When I hit the mailbox, I'd just found out that you hadn't hired me for the reasons I'd thought. I was just a temporary placeholder and I thought if I owned up to hitting the mailbox, you'd fire me on the spot. I picked it back up. I thought it was fine, but… My deception was inexcusable. And then I made it worse."

"Well, I suppose if you were my daughter, I'd make you go over and apologize and pay for the repairs. But you're not my daughter, so I'm free to just laugh."

"If you want me to resign, I understand. And there's more, I'm afraid."

"More?"

"Yes. I hired…I mean I *accidentally* hired Shane Harcourt to work on the saloon. I had no idea who he was. His name wasn't Bishop!" She choked on tears again. "It's obviously unforgivable."

There was silence for a moment as Levi took in her words. "Darlin', whatever you did was obviously the best thing that could've happened to Providence. If he intended to work for you and take advantage, I guess it got all turned around on him in the end, didn't it? You beat him at his own game. That's darn impressive."

She could hardly believe what she was hearing. "So you don't want me to resign?"

"Your techniques may be unorthodox, but they obviously work. I won't hear of you leaving now, so I hope you enjoy working out there in the dust and dirt."

"Thank you," she whispered. "I love it so much, I can't even express it. Have you talked to Shane, by chance?"

"Nope, but I'll shake his hand when I do. His grandfather was a hard man, and I didn't expect him to be any different, but I guess he's got a bit of a soft side after all."

He did. She knew he did. She'd seen it, but after everything, she'd no longer trusted herself. And if he had a soft side, and if he'd meant it that he'd changed his mind about what he was doing... Maybe he'd meant everything else, too.

She had to find him.

Merry got off the phone and resumed her pacing. "What does Cole say?"

"Nothing yet."

"They're not going to fire me."

Grace smiled. "I gathered that. Does that mean I bought you a hot dress and threatened your cousin for nothing?"

"I'm sorry. I'll pay you back."

"Girl." Grace gave her a quick hug, but for once, Merry was the one to break away, too restless and distraught to stay in one place.

She crossed the hall to knock on Shane's door one

more time. Maybe he'd somehow slipped past them. But he wasn't there. She even tried the doorknob, more than desperate enough to violate his privacy, but it was locked.

When Grace's phone rang, Merry bounded back into the apartment in three huge strides. "What? What is it?"

Grace shook her head, said a few words to Cole and hung up. "Shane still isn't answering. He hasn't responded to texts, either."

"Damn it." She didn't know why she felt such urgency. What he'd done was done, after all. Seeing him wouldn't change that. And what explanation did she want, exactly?

But somehow she felt she'd feel better if she could just hear why. *Why.*

Her head popped up. She stared at the window. "The letter."

"What?"

"He wrote me a letter this morning and I just tossed it on the floor of my car."

"Good girl," Grace said, then winced. "I mean... Sorry. I guess he wasn't as big of an asshole as I thought. So maybe you should go ahead and read it."

Merry was already out the door, running toward her car. If she'd had any light at all to see by, Merry would've stood next to the car and read it, but it was too dark. She sprinted back into the apartment and started reading.

"What does it say?" Grace asked.

Merry shook her head and sank slowly down to the couch as her eyes flew over his words. His apology. His explanation about a father who'd disappeared and a grandfather whose only tie to Shane and his brother had been a need to control. The last, final demand he'd made of Shane, and the last, final humiliation he'd dealt.

Gideon Bishop had funded the trust out of spite, and Merry could understand perfectly why Shane would fight that. The money should have gone to him. She'd give it to him if she could. In fact, the letter made it more shocking that he'd dropped the lawsuit. He had an emotional justification for wanting that money, so why had he changed his mind? There was nothing here about that.

The letter was just an apology, and a halfhearted explanation, and a promise that he'd never say a word to anyone about what she'd confessed to him.

I didn't know you when I decided to deceive you, Merry. I didn't know your heart and soul and body. What I did was wrong, and I can't excuse it, but I never meant it to be a betrayal of all the beautiful things I know in you now. I didn't mean that, and I wish I could take it back.

My God, had he given up two million dollars because of her? That was…awful. Amazing and humbling, but still awful. She couldn't let him do that, not even for the sake of Providence.

Handing Grace the letter, she replayed the brief conversation they'd had that afternoon. He hadn't said anything about dropping the lawsuit. Then again, she'd cut off any conversation he'd wanted to have.

"Did Cole tell you about his family?" she asked Grace. "About his dad abandoning them? About his grandfather?"

Grace shook her head and glanced up from the letter. "No. Nothing."

Merry stood and walked to the window to stare up into the dark sky. She couldn't even be angry with him now. She couldn't be relieved. She couldn't be anything but torn and confused and tormented. She'd gotten everything she'd wanted tonight. The truth from her mom. Security at her dream job. Even triumph in the face of Crystal's bile.

But all of that felt uncertain. In fact, it felt almost unimportant. Because Shane hadn't just given up millions of dollars. He'd given up so much more than that, and Merry needed to know why. But the phone didn't ring, and Shane never came home.

CHAPTER TWENTY-TWO

SHE HADN'T SLEPT AT ALL. She'd meant to. She'd pulled out the sofa bed and lain down and forced herself to close her eyes. But at five-thirty, she'd given up and taken a shower. After fifteen minutes standing with her head under hot water, the only ideas she'd come up with were to break into Shane's apartment, search out his mom's phone number and stalk a man who may or may not want to see her.

Or she could just be patient.

"Fuck that," she muttered as she got out and toweled off. She couldn't be patient. She couldn't do *nothing*. She also couldn't break into Shane's apartment, if only because she had no idea how to. Although... She shot a look toward the closed bedroom door. Grace would probably know.

She considered it for a good thirty seconds, then shook her head. He probably hadn't left a note detailing his plans on the off chance that a crazy chick would break in to track him down. So instead of waking Grace up, Merry tiptoed into her room and checked her phone for texts from Cole. There were none. She was back at square one. So she got in her car and drove in slow circles around town.

There was no point hurrying. She wouldn't find him.

But she couldn't sit around anymore. Her brain was a tumbling mess of confusion and betrayal and hope, and she had to move or she'd go mad.

The hope was the worst part. It wanted to fill her up. It wanted to overtake everything else. Hope that everything was going to be okay for her, but the worse, more insidious hope that she could have better than okay. She needed to find him and cut that off at the knees. Lay it to rest. Or maybe, just maybe, let it grow.

Trying to stamp down her own ridiculous thoughts, she stopped for a latte and then drove out of town, automatically heading toward Providence. It seemed as good a destination as any. Maybe it would bring her some peace, or maybe she'd find some clarity about what Shane had done. At the very least, she could do a little busywork and move back into her office.

She tried to breathe deeply. Tried to relax. And the drive helped. The rising sun turned the sky to a beautiful silver-blue that took her breath away. The last of the snow on the far peaks of the Tetons glowed white and pink and pale gold, and she felt a moment of such sharp relief that tears sprang to her eyes. This place didn't just *feel* like home. It was home, now. She wouldn't have to leave. There'd be no moving on.

Her mind started turning through the possibilities, and by the time she turned onto the dirt road, she'd given in to the excitement of the big news. This was no longer going to be a piecemeal effort. With the release of funds, the first thing she'd do was hire a restoration consultant to be sure she was on the right track. Then she'd finish the saloon, start on the church and start writing up content for the placards that would need to be ordered for every building. Of course, there were still the historical documents to be organized and cited and…but that could wait for winter, which would not only stop work, but also make the town inaccessible for long periods of time.

She was so completely drawn into the excitement of planning that she didn't notice the vehicle ahead of her until she was almost at the pullout for Providence.

Frowning, she took her foot off the gas and let the car slow. Why was there a big white SUV parked just at the edge of the trees ahead? Was it someone from the trust? Or should she be worried for her safety? Then the logo on the side of the truck became visible. And the low light rack across the top of the cab.

A sheriff's truck.

"Oh, no," she breathed, worried even before she drew even with the place where she always parked and saw that Shane's truck was there. *"Oh, no."*

She parked her car in the middle of the road and jumped out, eyes flying between Shane's truck and the sheriff's SUV a hundred yards farther away.

Shane's door opened, and Merry lurched toward him. "Shane!"

Her relief at seeing him was immediately quelled by the exhaustion on his face. His gaze met hers with weary sadness as he rubbed a hand over his stubbled jaw. "Hey, Merry."

"What are you doing here? What's going on? There's a cop car and…the lawsuit…"

"I found my dad," he said quietly.

She froze in the act of reaching out to touch his arm. "What?"

"I came out here to think, and I wanted to… I'd spotted something that day I took you up to the cabin, and I wanted to check it out."

"I don't understand. What does that have to do with your dad?"

"He bought a camping trailer the day he disappeared. He was with his girlfriend, so everyone assumed they hit the road. But I think maybe…I think he was taking the trailer up to the cabin."

She shook her head, still completely lost.

"I found his truck and the trailer below one of those washed out areas of the road. Either the road collapsed beneath him or he didn't see the gap until it was too late. I don't know. But…he's been here the whole time, Merry. He never left."

She didn't know much of the story, just what he'd revealed in his letter, but she could see enough of it on his face. The stunned sorrow, the years of pain and so much regret. "Shane, I'm so sorry." She let her hand reach toward him again and touched his arm. "Have you been here all night? Is the sheriff's office…" She didn't know how to say it. How did you speak to someone about his father's body?

He shook his head, his eyes on the arm she was touching. "Last night they couldn't do much more than cordon off the scene. They found two partial skeletons in the grass, but it was too dark to start the recovery. They told me to come back at dawn, but I couldn't leave. I just thought…Jesus, it's stupid. It's been twenty-five years, but I didn't want to leave him alone for the night. Knowing he's been here this whole time, and…"

"That's not stupid. It's not. You should have called me. I would've stayed with you."

A bitter smile flashed over his face. "Yeah, somehow I didn't think you'd be sympathetic."

"Shane Harcourt!" She shoved him hard enough to make him step back. "You're an idiot!"

"I know."

Guilt shot through her like a bullet. "I'm sorry. I didn't mean to yell."

"You have a right to."

"I don't, but I've been looking for you all night, and I'm so confused. Shane…*what did you do?*"

He watched her for a long moment without answering, his dark, weary eyes getting sadder as the seconds passed. "I did the right thing," he finally said. "I'm sorry it took so long."

"No! It's your land and your family! I understand now why you fought it. Providence shouldn't be built out of spite. It shouldn't be brought back to life as a way of hurting you. That's so wrong, Shane! Gideon Bishop did something terrible to you, and I don't want to be a part of that."

"You're not, Merry. You're the opposite of that. I've spent the past year so damn angry. Hell, more than the last year. When my dad left, it broke us. My whole family. My brother was angry from the age of nine on, and I was sucked into denial and delusion by my mom. She always believed he was out there somewhere. Always believed he was coming back. She made me believe it for a long time, too. When I finally woke up, I think I was angrier than my brother ever was."

"Of course you were. You had every reason to be."

"Apparently not." He glanced up toward the hills.

"Did you decide to drop the lawsuit when you found him?" She was relieved at that. It'd had nothing to do with her.

But Shane shook his head. "No. I did that for you, Merry."

"Shane, I—"

He cut off her alarmed words by taking her hand and tugging her a little closer. "You showed me what life could be like if I was willing to let go of the anger. To accept the past and live like I at least *wanted* to be happy."

"I don't understand."

"You haven't had a perfect life, but you don't walk around angry and scared."

"Oh, I wouldn't say that," she murmured, remembering the way she'd lashed out at Crystal. She'd also thrown a few choice words at Shane.

He smiled. "I know you get angry. You're a woman, not a saint. But you see the possibility in things, Merry. You see it in every day. You see it in this pile of run-down buildings and spiderwebs. You even see it in me. And all I could see was a challenge to try to get back a little of what was taken from me. As if that would change anything."

"But the money. It should be yours."

"Why? Because I had the good grace to be born? I didn't give my grandfather the time of day for over a decade. I didn't even want his name. I told myself I wanted nothing from him then I happily took his land and demanded his money, too. Like a selfish damn child."

"He was the one who was selfish!"

"And I was so much better?" he asked, raising an eyebrow. "Come on. Look what I did to you."

She couldn't argue with that. He'd used her and betrayed her. No matter what he was going through or how he'd tried to make it up to her, she couldn't deny that.

His gaze fell. He turned her hand over in his and traced the lines of her palm with his thumb. "I'm so sorry, Merry. You made my life sweeter. You let me see things I needed to see. And all I did was hurt you."

"That's not true," she whispered.

"Everything else I tainted with a lie."

She curled her fingers and captured his. "That's true. But you've taken that back now with an awfully grand gesture. I think we might be able to find a way to be friends again."

"Friends," he repeated.

Despite the way the word ached inside her, she nodded. "I don't want you to be alone out here like this. It's not right."

He nodded, but then his forehead creased in a tortured frown. "I don't want to be friends."

"Oh." She tried to tug her hand back. Right. Just because he'd given up the money didn't mean he was happy about it.

But he didn't let her go. "I've spent my whole life telling myself I'd never be good at this. That the men in my family were nothing but philanderers and escape artists and people who could never be counted on. Hell, all the way back to Providence, even. But I don't have to be that. I can't use that as an excuse just because love scares the hell out of me."

Merry blinked. "Love?" she croaked.

"Yeah, I know. You might not even like me right now. You certainly don't trust me. But that's fine. That won't stop me from loving who you are, Merry Kade. That won't stop me from loving your smile and your laugh and the stupid jokes you crack when you're nervous."

"Oh." She shook her head in shock.

"Or the way you can't stop talking about this damn town that shouldn't mean anything to you. Or how you get shy and turned on all at the same time in a way that makes me crazy to touch you even as I tell myself I should go slow."

Her heart thumped faster in her chest. Her cheeks burned. She couldn't believe what he was saying. She refused to believe it, because it scared the shit out of her.

"Shane, I don't know. I hardly know you, and what you did... That hurt. What if I can't get past it?"

"I understand. We haven't known each other long and I've been holding back, not just from you, but from myself. I'm not asking you to love me. Heck, I'm not even saying we should be together. I'm just asking if you can forgive me. Maybe not today, but sometime. And if you can, I'd like a chance. Just a chance. I love who you are, Merry, and I think it could be way more than that, but all I need right now is to know if you'll consider it. If you'll just...consider me."

She didn't let herself answer right away. This was a serious question and she couldn't take it lightly. Could she forgive him? Could she ever trust him? Could she give it a chance? He'd hurt her, badly. He'd lied. He'd embarrassed her. And he'd tried to take something from her that meant so much.

But could she hold on to that forever in the face of what he'd given up? Of what he'd realized?

He'd been hurt, too, after all. Badly, and by so many.

Despite her hesitation, she knew in her heart she could at least try. But before she could answer, another truck approached down the dirt road and pulled up next to them. She recognized Nate Hendricks in the passenger seat. The driver tipped his hat. "Shane," the deputy said. "The sheriff wants to set up base just up the road… We'll cut over to the creek just past Providence."

"Sure," Shane said.

"Forensics should be here within the hour."

He nodded and the truck drove on. As they watched it go, Merry reached for Shane's hand and squeezed it. "I'll stay here with you," she said softly.

He looked down at their entwined fingers, then back up with a question in his eyes.

"You're worth the chance, Shane. We're both worth the chance."

He moved forward, just slightly. Just a fraction of an inch, his gaze falling to her mouth as if he meant to kiss her. But he stopped then, and cleared his throat as he squeezed her hand. "Thank you."

"You're welcome." She smiled at him and closed the space he'd meant to, to press a slow, sweet kiss to his mouth. Some of the tiredness was gone from his eyes when she pulled back. "That was for Providence."

"Yeah?" He finally managed a genuine smile. "I give you a ghost town and I get one kiss? You drive a hard bargain, lady."

"Don't ever forget it."

"I won't. And I'd say it was a fair trade. I'd do it again for you, if I could."

"Aw, what kind of girl would need two ghost towns?"

"A very, very odd one," he said, then muttered, "Aw, screw it," and pulled her into his arms. "Almost as odd as you, Merry. But not nearly as beautiful."

When he kissed her, an honest kiss with none of those lies between them, Merry knew she'd lied. He wasn't worth just a chance. He was worth every terrifying feeling welling up inside her heart, everything she was afraid to give. She'd give him that. She would.

EPILOGUE

SHANE LEANED AGAINST the post of the saloon porch, watching as that big pain-in-the-ass Walker pulled Merry out into the center of Providence's road to dance. Fiddle music wound through the buildings as strings of tiny white lights swayed in the breeze. There hadn't been this many people in the old town in almost a century, he'd wager.

The members of the board huddled in a loose circle at the edge of the porch, talking up every city or county official who got near. This party was a bit of an open house for important members of the community. The saloon was nearly fully restored and they'd started work on the church, but it was mid-September already, and things would shut down soon. Merry was already fretting about it, but Shane would be happy to see her again. The twelve-hour days she'd been working were leaving him lonely.

Open house or not, Shane felt like this party was more of a celebration of Merry's work than anything, and her face glowed with happiness. He couldn't even resent the wide smile she aimed up at Walker as the man spun her around. She was coming home with Shane tonight, and that was all that mattered to him. She could dance Walker into the ground for all he cared.

"Hey there, handsome," Rayleen said, walking over to offer him a beer. "If Christmas is neglecting you, I've got a few tricks up my sleeve."

He clinked his bottle against hers. "Oh, yeah?"

"Yep." She took a swig and looked him up and down. "You ever heard of the prostate gland?"

The beer he'd just tipped into his mouth nearly sprayed out on his choked gasp. Instead he managed to swallow half of it. The other half nearly drowned him. He coughed like a madman, causing heads to turn, but at least he hadn't sprayed the backs of Jeanine and Kristen Bishop.

"Good Christ," Rayleen said, slamming a palm against his back. "You young men really need to get out more often. You're sheltered as schoolgirls."

Refusing to let his mind consider the picture she'd tried to paint, Shane shook his head. "Everything's great with Christmas. I mean, Merry."

"Good. She seems like a good girl. A little flighty."

He quickly changed the subject. "You look nice tonight."

Rayleen shifted and patted a hand to her hair. Then she shrugged and looked out over the dispersing crowd. She did look nice. In fact, she'd worn a pretty blue calico dress, though she still wore old shit-kickers on her feet. "Look at these two," she muttered, tilting her chin toward his two stepgrandmothers.

The women had squared off in furious conversation just a few feet away.

Kristen pointed a finger at Jeanine. "You're the one who never supported his interest in history and culture. All you cared about were those horses!"

"Me?" Jeanine screeched. "Are you kidding? Gideon told me you demanded a heater in the stables because you just had to have that Arabian."

Kristen gasped and Shane watched the color fall from her cheeks.

"Oh, yes," Jeanine pushed. "He called to complain about you all the time. Said he needed a trusted ear, someone to talk to. That was me, *Kristen*."

Rayleen let out a long sigh. "Oh, boy. Women."

"You may have been younger," Jeanine snarled. "Maybe even more beautiful, but he never had any use for prissy little—"

"Jesus Christ and cheese and crackers!" Rayleen barked.

Both women jumped and spun around. Shane held up his hands and stepped a few inches back. There was no way he was getting involved in this.

"Rayleen Kisler," Jeanine gasped. "Are you eavesdropping?"

"Eavesdropping?" she scoffed. "The goddamn mountain lions are eavesdropping. We can't help but hear you."

"Well, I never," Kristen said.

"I never, either," Rayleen agreed. "Because it seems to me that you two are arguing over a dead man. A dead man! Hell, if one of you really wants him, I'd hope I was the other, because there's no point hanging on to a corpse."

"He was a special man!" Kristen Bishop insisted.

"Well, he's dead now, woman!" Rayleen yelled.

Both of the Bishop women looked around to be sure

no one had heard. When they found themselves alone, they aimed eerily similar looks of disgust at Rayleen.

She laughed. "Well, look at that. Go on, then. Hang on to your self-righteousness. Hope it keeps you warm at night. But in case you hadn't noticed, there are a whole lot of ancient cowboys around these parts, and whatever their flaws, they're a hell of a lot warmer than a dead man, ladies."

They both glared.

"Suit yourself," Rayleen said. "More cowboys for me."

The Bishop widows looked at each other. Then back at Rayleen. "Why?" Jeanine ventured. "Where do you meet these men?"

"Sweetheart, I work in a bar. I'm tripping over them." She laughed, but the women just stared at her.

Rayleen glanced at Shane. He looked away as if he weren't listening. "Fine!" she barked. "There's a bridge club over at the recreation center, and they have singles parties the first Saturday of every month at the senior center. If you want some old man pickins, those are your best bet."

As if on cue, Easy appeared in his worn-out jeans and bolo tie with a crisply ironed shirt.

Jeanine gave Rayleen one last glare, but then Kristen nudged her and tipped her head toward Easy. They both cast gentle smiles in his direction as he crossed the road toward them.

Rayleen growled. "And if I catch you making eyes at Easy, I'll snatch them out of your head and feed them to the crows."

The women gasped, looking both outraged and defiant, but Shane noticed that they moved away and didn't look in Easy's direction again.

"Rayleen," Shane murmured under his breath, "you finally staking a claim on that old cowboy?"

"I'm considering it," she snapped. "If he don't piss me off first."

He decided to drop the subject. She didn't seem to have much patience or good humor when it came to Easy, not even with the man himself. Shane edged away, but not before he noticed the way she scowled when Easy asked her to dance. Still, she said yes. Good Lord, that woman and her niece weren't very different.

And neither was anything like Merry who was laughing as Walker swung her out of the group of dancers and over to the refreshment table. That was Shane's cue to cut in.

"Hey, sweetheart," he murmured in her ear then watched her shiver a little at the feel of his breath on her skin.

"Hey," she said, her voice noticeably husky.

He smiled even as Walker turned around and offered her a glass of champagne. "Beat it, Walker," he said.

Walker smirked and offered his own glass to Shane. "Enjoy," he said, tipping his hat in farewell.

Shane forgot about him and leaned close to Merry. "You look like you're having a good time."

"I am. It's all so exciting. Everyone seems excited, right?"

He glanced around. Everyone seemed happy, but the majority of the excitement was all Merry. But he didn't tell her that. Instead he snuck a quick kiss then tugged her out into the street when he heard the band slide into a slow song.

An hour later, the party was winding down. Shane said goodbye to Cole and Grace as Merry walked the board members to their cars. "Are you sure we shouldn't stay and help?" Grace asked.

"No, we're going to get it shut down, and then the party folks will come clean up the lights and chairs and generator tomorrow. I'll have Merry home in a few."

"Don't forget her curfew," Grace said, flashing a grin. He'd finally started to win her over, but it was slow going. She wasn't quite as quick to forgive as Merry was. But Cole tugged her away.

"Come on, darlin'. Let's leave the kids to their fun."

Fun, indeed. By the time Merry came back, the band had packed and left and the last few guests were heading out. He finally had her alone. As if she'd read his mind, she jumped into his arms and he spun her until she squealed. "Are you a little drunk?" he asked.

"No. Just happy. The new parking area looks great. And the road!"

He shook his head at the way she went dreamy-eyed over the road grading of a wide dirt lane that connected one end of a ghost town to the other. But he had to admit it had transformed the place. With the sagebrush and weeds gone from the center of town, Providence looked poised to spring back to life. As if it had just been sleeping for the past century and Merry was going to wake it up.

"I wish you'd invited your mom," she said quietly as he kissed her nose and set her on her feet.

"No, she's getting better, but we're still just as likely to argue as not. I didn't want to fight at your party."

"She's trying," Merry insisted.

"Yeah, she's trying to make him into a saint. I won't have it. He was a man, and he's dead, and she has to move on. Or at least keep her thoughts to herself."

Merry took his hand and squeezed. "Come on. I already tied up all the trash bags. I just need you to turn off the generator for me. I noticed a few spiderwebs near it earlier."

"If that's all it takes to be your hero, I'll save you any day of the week, Merry Kade."

He found the generator controls while Merry watched from a safe distance away. When he hit the switch, they were plunged into darkness and a silence he hadn't realized had been missing.

"Oh," Merry whispered. "I should've brought a flashlight."

"There's a half-moon tonight. Just give your eyes a minute to adjust."

But it only took a few seconds for her to look up and gasp. "My God, Shane. Look at the stars."

He'd seen the stars out here a thousand times. He didn't need to look up. He'd rather stare at the pale wonder of her smiling in the dark. "Yeah. It's beautiful."

"I think I can see the Milky Way!"

"You're going to get a crick in your neck. I've got a better idea."

They walked through the center of town and Shane led her to his truck, then pulled a blanket from the back and spread it over the bed. "Come on," he whispered, scooting her up onto the tailgate before he joined her.

"Look," she whispered, eyes sparkling and wide in the moonlight.

"I know." He brushed a strand of hair from her cheek. "It's amazing." He wanted to keep watching her, but he lay beside her and looked up at the sky. Crickets chirped a chorus around them and distant aspen leaves rustled in the breeze, the dry sound of them a hint that winter was coming. He could almost smell the snow on the air. He breathed deep and let himself relax.

"This is everything I want, Shane."

He smiled at her words. "Yeah?"

"It's so beautiful here. The night and the stars and the mountains. It feels right. And…you feel right."

His smile faded.

"It feels like home. Like I've always been here and yet everything feels possible, still. Everything."

Everything did feel possible. All those things he never thought he'd have. Shane propped himself up on his elbow and looked down at her. He touched her cheek and watched her eyes close.

"I think I love you, Shane."

His heart skipped a beat and then another. He had to part his lips to draw a careful breath. They hadn't discussed love again. Not since that day. They'd wanted to take it slow, but now the force of it hit him like a train at full speed.

He slid a thumb over her full bottom lip then pressed his mouth to the same spot. "I know I love you, Merry," he murmured against her skin.

"Yeah?" she asked, and he heard the tears in her voice before he saw them slip down her temples.

"Yeah." He kissed her mouth again. Then her chin. Her jaw.

"Thanks for bringing me here," she whispered. "To Providence. To Jackson."

"I didn't bring you here." He tasted her throat.

"You did. If not for you, they never would've hired me. I never would've had all this beauty."

"Well, then." He slid a hand along her thigh, bringing her skirt along with it. "I should thank you for bringing me yourself. For bringing me…everything."

When he touched her, she gasped, her back arching.

"Shh. Look up at the stars. I want to see them in your eyes when you come."

"But what if someone comes back? What if…?" Her protest ended on a sigh as he stroked her.

"There's no one here but us, Merry." He eased her panties down and freed himself, then moved between her thighs and slid into her slowly. So slowly that they both sighed when he was finally as deep as he could get. "It's just you and me and everything we never thought we'd have."

"I love you," she breathed, and he came with those words in his ears and her quiet cry of release still echoing to the sky. This was the man he wanted to be. Forever.

* * * * *

Return to *USA TODAY* bestselling author

CHRISTIE RIDGWAY'S

Crescent Cove, California, where the magic of summer can last forever...

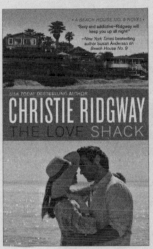

Globe-trotting photojournalist Gage Lowell spent carefree childhood summers in Crescent Cove. Now that he desperately needs some R & R, he books a vacation at Beach House No. 9 —ready to soak up some sun and surprise old friend and property manager Skye Alexander. Their long-distance letters got him through a dangerous time he can't otherwise talk about. But when he arrives, the tightly wound beauty isn't exactly happy to see him.

Skye knows any red-blooded woman would be thrilled to spend time with gorgeous, sexy Gage. But she harbors secrets of her own, including that she might just be a little bit in love with him. And she's convinced the restless wanderer won't stay long enough for her to dare share her past—or dream of a future together. Luckily for them both, summer at Crescent Cove has a way of making the impossible happen....

Available wherever books are sold!

Be sure to connect with us at:

Harlequin.com/Newsletters
Facebook.com/HarlequinBooks
Twitter.com/HarlequinBooks

HARLEQUIN® HQN™
™ www.Harlequin.com

PHCR715

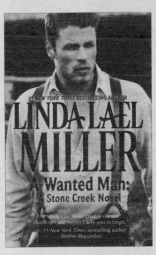

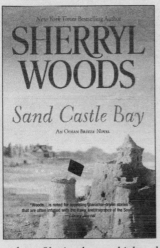

REQUEST YOUR FREE BOOKS!

2 FREE NOVELS
FROM THE ROMANCE COLLECTION
PLUS 2 FREE GIFTS!

YES! Please send me 2 FREE novels from the Romance Collection and my 2 FREE gifts (gifts are worth about $10). After receiving them, if I don't wish to receive any more books, I can return the shipping statement marked "cancel." If I don't cancel, I will receive 4 brand-new novels every month and be billed just $5.99 per book in the U.S. or $6.49 per book in Canada. That's a savings of at least 25% off the cover price. It's quite a bargain! Shipping and handling is just 50¢ per book in the U.S. and 75¢ per book in Canada.* I understand that accepting the 2 free books and gifts places me under no obligation to buy anything. I can always return a shipment and cancel at any time. Even if I never buy another book, the two free books and gifts are mine to keep forever.

194/394 MDN FVU7

Name _____ (PLEASE PRINT)

Address _____ Apt. #

City _____ State/Prov. _____ Zip/Postal Code

Signature (if under 18, a parent or guardian must sign)

Mail to the **Harlequin® Reader Service:**
IN U.S.A.: P.O. Box 1867, Buffalo, NY 14240-1867
IN CANADA: P.O. Box 609, Fort Erie, Ontario L2A 5X3

Want to try two free books from another line?
Call 1-800-873-8635 or visit www.ReaderService.com.

* Terms and prices subject to change without notice. Prices do not include applicable taxes. Sales tax applicable in N.Y. Canadian residents will be charged applicable taxes. Offer not valid in Quebec. This offer is limited to one order per household. Not valid for current subscribers to the Romance Collection or the Romance/Suspense Collection. All orders subject to credit approval. Credit or debit balances in a customer's account(s) may be offset by any other outstanding balance owed by or to the customer. Please allow 4 to 6 weeks for delivery. Offer available while quantities last.

Your Privacy—The Harlequin® Reader Service is committed to protecting your privacy. Our Privacy Policy is available online at www.ReaderService.com or upon request from the Harlequin Reader Service.

We make a portion of our mailing list available to reputable third parties that offer products we believe may interest you. If you prefer that we not exchange your name with third parties, or if you wish to clarify or modify your communication preferences, please visit us at www.ReaderService.com/consumerschoice or write to us at Harlequin Reader Service Preference Service, P.O. Box 9062, Buffalo, NY 14269. Include your complete name and address.

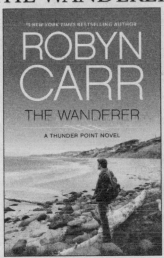

VICTORIA DAHL

77609 REAL MEN WILL	___ $7.99 U.S.	___ $9.99 CAN.
77602 BAD BOYS DO	___ $7.99 U.S.	___ $9.99 CAN.
77595 GOOD GIRLS DON'T	___ $7.99 U.S.	___ $9.99 CAN.
77462 CRAZY FOR LOVE	___ $7.99 U.S.	___ $9.99 CAN.
77434 LEAD ME ON	___ $7.99 U.S.	___ $9.99 CAN.
77390 START ME UP	___ $7.99 U.S.	___ $8.99 CAN.
77356 TALK ME DOWN	___ $6.99 U.S.	___ $6.99 CAN.
77688 CLOSE ENOUGH TO TOUCH	___ $7.99 U.S.	___ $9.99 CAN.

(limited quantities available)

TOTAL AMOUNT	$ _____
POSTAGE & HANDLING	$ _____
($1.00 FOR 1 BOOK, 50¢ for each additional)	
APPLICABLE TAXES*	$ _____
TOTAL PAYABLE	$ _____

(check or money order—please do not send cash)

To order, complete this form and send it, along with a check or money order for the total above, payable to Harlequin HQN, to: **In the U.S.:** 3010 Walden Avenue, P.O. Box 9077, Buffalo, NY 14269-9077; **In Canada:** P.O. Box 636, Fort Erie, Ontario, L2A 5X3.

Name: _____

Address: _____ City: _____

State/Prov.: _____ Zip/Postal Code: _____

Account Number (if applicable): _____

075 CSAS

*New York residents remit applicable sales taxes.
*Canadian residents remit applicable GST and provincial taxes.

HARLEQUIN® HQN™
™ www.Harlequin.com

PHVD0413BL